Alfred the Great;
Edward the King

(#10 in the entire historical set)

(#1 in the King Edward Sagas)

By Bruce Corbett

ISBN: 978-1-7380048-4-3

Dedication

Son, you outgrew my lap, but never my heart
.....Author Unknown

To Andrew, with love.

AUTHOR'S NOTE

This is the tenth book in the Ambrose historical adventure series and the first in the Edward series. In this novel, Alfred dies and his son Edward struggles against his cousin Ethelwold for the throne. When the council of advisors, the *Witan*, chooses Edward, Ethelwold rebels, seizing two royal estates and kidnapping and marrying a nun. When Edward marches on him, however, Ethelwold flees north, to the Vikings of Jorvik, (Northumbria) who make him king! Within a year, he brings an invasion army of Danes south, to Essex. The Danes of Essex submit, and the following year they combine forces with King Eohric of East Anglia, raid deep into Mercia, and cross the Thames into Wessex. Edward calls up his army and goes after the retreating Danes, pushing north far into East Anglia.

Edward orders his *fyrdmen* home before the Danes can assemble an overwhelming force, but the Kentish *fyrd,* off raiding on its own, is slow to follow orders. The Danish army manages to surround it, and a fierce battle ensues, called the **Battle of the Holme**. Though the Danes keep the field, losses are high on both sides, and the Kentish *fyrdmen* are able to break free of the trap. Both Eohric, the Viking king of East Anglia, and Ethelwold, are killed in the vicious battle. Finally, Edward is secure on the Wessex throne, though Wessex is exhausted and Edward is eventually forced to sign a peace accord with both East Anglia and Jorvik.

I have absolutely no evidence of an attempted poisoning of King Alfred or of a band of Danes arriving in Dorset before Alfred's death, but Ethelwold was very likely in communication with the Northumbrian Vikings. Although I did find mention in my research of an alliance between Wessex and Scotland, I have no details. It is at least plausible, however, that Edward would want the Scots and Picts (recently united into one nation) to cross their borders into Viking Northumbria and tie down large numbers of Danish warriors that could otherwise be sent south to attack Wessex.

Alfred's funeral is purely a figment of my imagination, but by using the wonders of the internet, I was able to track down several documents describing a little about the coronation ceremony of Anglo-Saxon kings. The quoted material of Edward's coronation is actually copied from a public domain document describing the coronation of the West Saxon king, King Ethelred II, AD. 978. I decided to leave it in the quaint language I found it in, as it reads sonorously and seemed appropriate for the solemnity of the occasion. Since it was my understanding that most West Saxon royal wives, at least in Alfred's time, were not crowned as queens, I left out that portion of the 978 ceremony. When Ethelwulf, father of Alfred, brought back a young princess from the Frankish court and insisted that she be crowned as queen, it seemed to cause a great deal of trouble, which his eldest son used to his advantage when he decided to keep the throne even after his father had returned from the Continent.

My greatest problem with this story was the dates. I used several translations of the Anglo-Saxon Chronicles, and each one used different dates for everything from Alfred's death to the Battle of the Holme. In the end, I picked a version that made sense to me and stuck with it, adjusting the dates from other versions to conform.

Ethelwold's dream was interesting. One historian I read pointed out that if the *Witan* had chosen him instead of Edward, England might have been united much sooner than it was, and generations of strife might have been avoided. I suspect that it is more likely that the Danes would have quickly achieved dominion over the entire island. Anglo-Saxon puppet kings generally had a short and unhappy reign under Viking masters.

I know that I did not do justice to the history of the north. I was fascinated by the ever-changing fortunes of the northern Britons, the Picts, the Scots, Strathclyde, the kingdom of Dál Riata that straddled the Irish Sea, and the Norse settlers in England. The intricate historical details of the northern kingdoms are not particularly relevant to the story of Wessex as I am telling it, however, so I glossed over the more intricate details concerning Alba. I picked on Blackpool more or less indiscriminately. The maps were very vague about where the southern border of Alba was in 900, so I made an educated guess and picked a town that would be just a little south of that point.

As I am writing this, I am looking at a picture of the ancient coins indicating that the Vikings of Northumbria had chosen Ethelwold as king. They are real, although they do not actually have 'Ethelwold Rex' written on them. I cheated just a little and simplified the quote to avoid a long and distracting explanation.

The Varangian Guard was actually constituted under Basil II, not Basil the 'Bulgarian'. I just moved the process forward by some years.

The ending is as accurate as I can make it, even explaining the approach that Edward would use in later years to conquer what became known as the Danelaw. I did speed things up a little, however. It was not until 906 that Edward was able to arrange a truce with the Danish kingdoms, and the conquest took many more years.

This is really the story of Edward the Elder, how he came to the throne and fought the invading Danes after his father died. Ambrose, Polonius and Phillip, however, will continue to play a major part in the struggles against the Danes of Northumbria and East Anglia.

Some years before this story begins, in 876 A.D., King Guthrum of the Danes invaded the Anglo-Saxon country of Wessex. Trapped at the town of Wareham by Alfred the Great and his West Saxon army, the Viking leader agreed to a truce, but, instead, slipped out and retreated to Exeter. After a Viking rescue fleet was destroyed in a storm, Guthrum was forced to sue for peace and retreated to East Anglia, a country that he and his ravaging Vikings had already conquered.

Just after Christmas 877, Alfred, whose army was disbanded for the winter, was caught by surprise by a second invasion of Guthrum's army. The Saxon king was forced into hiding in the forest of Selwood. Eventually he found his way to Athelney, an island surrounded by marshes. From there, he organized a secret gathering of his fighting men. Meantime, to the west, one of his *ealdormen*, Odda, destroyed a second Viking army newly arrived from Wales and led by Ubbi Ragnarsson.

A single major defeat could mean the end of Saxon Wessex. All of the Angle, Saxon and Jute kingdoms north of the Thames were reeling or had already crumbled under the Viking onslaught. Alfred's army managed to gather in May, however, and they confronted the Vikings at Edington. Alfred won a great victory and the broken Vikings fled to Chippenham. After a two week siege there, the Danish king, Guthrum, agreed to be baptized and signed a peace treaty with Alfred. Wessex was saved. This story is told in **Alfred the Great; Viking Invasion**.

In 885, Wessex was threatened by a new enemy. Another Viking army, fresh from France, landed in Kent and besieged the town of Rochester. This is where **Alfred the Great; King's Revenge**, begins. Guthrum and his powerful army were bound by treaty to stay out of the fight, but his men were ever hungry for more land and adventure. Much of the territory north of the Thames River belonged to Guthrum. If the Viking king joined his forces with the Danes from France, Wessex may have been finally overwhelmed. Alfred arrived with his army before the city fell, and the combined Saxon forces routed the Vikings, who fled precipitously, even leaving behind their entire horse herd.

In the story, **Alfred the Great; Young Edward**, a Viking alliance brought an unprecedented number of Viking warriors into Wessex. Again and again, Haesten, a Viking pirate leader, invaded Wessex. Again and again, he pillaged, was eventually cornered and besieged, and then managed to break free and retreat to safe territory.

After six years of peace, Alfred is dying. Ethelwold, son of a previous king and passed over in favor of Alfred, raises the standard of revolt. Quickly driven out of Wessex, he is accepted as king in Northumbria (Jorvik) and **Alfred the Great; Edward the King**, begins.

Individual words in italics generally have special meaning and the details may be found in Appendix I. I hope you enjoy the story.

The author,
Bruce Corbett

TABLE OF CONTENTS

CHAPTER 1

Vikings!

The lookout was perched on the crossbar of the great square sail, clinging tightly to the mast while he scanned the horizon for the first signs of the cliffs that would indicate they had reached the Isle of Wight. From there, their home port of Portsmouth was but a short trip away. The winds had blown contrary for hours, and his companion *thanes* were exhausted from manning the massive oars. They all looked forward to tying up their long-ships in Portsmouth harbor and spending a little time with their families. Suddenly, he caught a glimpse of three sails peeking above the horizon.

He called out excitedly. **"Three sails to the east!"**

The fleet commander picked up a speaking trumpet and yelled up to him. **"Who are they?"**

"Don't know, Commander! The hulls are still below the horizon and I can't make out the crests on their sails!"

The fleet commander cursed volubly, and then lifted his speaking trumpet again. **"Steersman, come about to the east! Captain Osred, signal the other ships to follow. King Alfred will have our balls if we do not check out a fleet of ships sailing our coast. Row, you lazy bastards! Your wives and mistresses will have to find solace in somebody else's arms for just a little while longer!"**

The little fleet came about, and, when the winds cooperated, the crews, in turn, pulled in their oars, hauled up the great square sail and then collapsed on their rowing benches. The change-of-course and approach of the eight vessels were eventually noted by the strangers, because the three vessels at first grew rapidly larger, but suddenly reversed direction and fled eastward.

The fleet commander recognized the crest of one of the more

powerful *jarls* of *Jorvik* on the sails of the retreating ships, but could not further close the distance. At last, as dusk neared, he ordered the fleet to turn back toward the Isle of Wight and the shelter of the majestic bay by the little settlement of St. Helens.

CHAPTER 2

Alfred Lies Dying

The king was propped up on his sick bed, and he had had his crown placed on his head. Each member of the *Witan* bowed as they entered his *bower*, and then made room for the members following.

The king's voice was weak and hoarse. The important men of the kingdom, both lay and ecclesiastical, stood silently so they could hear the faint words of their dying king.

"Members of the *Witan*! Loyal friends! I know I am soon going to meet my Maker, but I yet worry about Wessex. We are the last free *Angelisc* country on the island of Britain, and the Danes are yet panting after our riches and our women. In my earlier years, I was forced to hide in a forest and then a swamp, praying that the Viking invaders did not find the location of my immediate family and the few faithful companions who had escaped Guthrum's sneak attack. I offer my thanks to all of you who wrought a miracle that spring. Against all odds, we managed to raise an army and defeat the heathen devils. Thanks to you, and to countless others, too many who have succumbed to grievous battle wounds, our kingdom has managed to survive, and even prosper. Our *burhs*, with their permanent garrisons, not only control the rivers, fords and roads of our land, but now give our people protection and us the freedom to move Wessex's *fyrdmen* wherever needed. Our summer and winter armies mean that no longer do the Danes find us unprepared for their treachery or aggression. Our innovations have managed to keep the ungodly heathen at bay. I am recognized as *bretwalda* of Wales and *Anglish* Mercia, and the Scots and Picts, while they don't love us, are yet our allies. Victory after victory, and much Saxon blood, has driven the Viking invaders out of our country. In my son's, or perhaps my grandson's time, I hope and expect that all of Britain will once again be one country, but under West Saxon rule!

I thank you for all for the blood you have shed, your lifelong support, and the courage so many of you have shown. My dream, however, and, indeed, the very existence of this country, is very much in jeopardy. Mighty Northumbria fell to Viking adventurers. *Frankland*, less than a hundred years ago the ruler of most of Europe, is now not even capable of chasing out the Viking bands who have been rampaging through its territories for over a generation.

Why have these mighty empires fallen so low? The answer is simple. Divided leadership. Both suffered from civil war. The constituent parts have found, to their sorrow, that they have nowhere near the strength of the whole. Lord Polonius taught me this lesson a long time ago with a handful of straw. The lesson has stuck with me all my life. We must face the heathen host with a united front, or like a single straw, we all snap easily and fall into the dustbin of history."

Alfred broke into a coughing fit and brought up a little blood. Polonius moved forward to help him, but he waved the Byzantine aside. "No, good friend, there are few tasks left for me to do before I leave this world, but this is the most important one remaining! If you would prepare a good draught of your elixir, I would be pleased to drink it in but a few minutes.'

Finally, looking exhausted, the king struggled to continue. 'All our good work, all our sacrifices, can yet be undone by discord amongst you when I die. I have made it clear to all of you that I have named Edward, my eldest son, as my heir. He was thrust into battle at an early age, and his record speaks for itself. This young man has led our *fyrdmen* to victory after victory, without a single defeat. It is a record I wish I could claim . . . Yes, yes, Ethelwold. I am aware that the right of *primogeniture* is not always followed in this land. It generally is, but was, in fact, not followed when my brothers and I were chosen. That was, however, only because there were no sons of suitable age when each of my brothers died in turn, and the country was in the midst of a series of Viking invasions. Given the situation, this august body picked the man who was most ready to deal with the challenge.

I am aware, Ethelwold, that some here have championed your case, and I am told that you will be considered a candidate for the throne when it comes time to replace me. You will do me the courtesy of letting me finish my statement before you attempt to teach your king the rules of succession . . . As *Ealdorman* Ethelwold no doubt wishes to remind me, a king may state his preference, but it is the *Witan* that has the final say in choosing the successor.

That is your task, members of the *Witan*! I implore you on this. Whoever you choose, the choice must not split the empire into two separate camps. To do so will be to destroy the last free *Angelisc* kingdom in all Britain. Divided, Wessex will inevitably fall to the Viking hosts to the east and north, who watch and wait patiently for any sign of weakness . . . Edward, on your knees, my son!"

The handsome young *atheling* slipped quickly to his knees in obedience to his father's sudden command. He looked up questioningly into his father's face.

"My son, I want you to swear, in the presence of these august men of the *Witan*, and in the sight of Almighty God, that you will accept the decision of the *Witan* on the matter of who will rule in my place after I die."

Edward's voice rang out. "Beloved father and king, I swear on my honor that I will bow to the will of the *Witan*."

Alfred struggled to speak loudly enough that all in the room could hear. "Members of the *Witan*, guardians of my kingdom, I charge you now to do the same. When I am gone and you meet in council, you may disagree with each other. You may raise your voice in discord, but once you have made the choice and the votes have been counted, I charge you all to accept the decision of the majority! Only in this way will the kingdom not be torn asunder in the way of Northumbria and *Francia*. On your knees! I want to hear each of you repeat the oath."

Each man dropped to his knees and spoke the requisite

words. Ambrose watched Ethelwold carefully. At last he reluctantly slipped to his knees and mouthed the words.

Alfred raised his right hand, and the room quieted again. "Thank you, councilors. I think that I need to rest again, but I want you to remember the importance . . . no, the necessity of unity. If you cannot work as one, then Wessex will surely fall. Choose with your head and your heart when the time comes, and may God bless you all!"

CHAPTER 3

The Poison

As Polonius entered the kitchen, he saw a young woman pouring a vial of powder into a horn of mead. The Byzantine scholar and royal spymaster spoke sharply as he rushed to her side.

"Girl, what are you doing?"

The girl was startled and almost dropped the vial. "Why, Lord, I am preparing King Alfred's mead, as I do every night."

Polonius seized the girl's wrist with one hand, and, with the other, he pried the vial loose. "What was in the vial, girl?"

"It is medicine for the king, good sir!"

"And who told you to put it in the king's mead?"

The girl looked silently at Polonius and bit her lip.

Polonius called to the nearest kitchen helper. "You! Go find Thane Phillip and tell him I need him immediately!"

The giant thane entered the room within seconds, looking worried and with his massive broadsword slung on his back. "What is it, Polonius? This lad here said that it was urgent!"

"I caught this girl putting something into King Alfred's mead!"

"Do you know what it was?"

"Not yet. Hold her while I look more closely."

Handing the girl's wrist to Phillip, Polonius sniffed the vial, then slapped the open end of the vial against the palm of his hand. A few fine grains fell out of the container, and Polonius rolled the grains of the substance between his fingers. "I am not sure, but it reminds me of Monkshood."

Phillip looked puzzled. "What is Monkshood?"

"It is a plant from which is made a rather potent poison called Aconite. You might know it as Wolf's Bane. It has a long history.

It is said that the wife of Emperor Claudius gave her sweet husband a fatal dose of the poison in his mushrooms."

"Then you are saying that this serving wench was trying to poison King Alfred?"

"I pray not, but I will do a little test, and we shall soon find out."

"What about the wench?"

"I fear the worst. For now, take her to the interrogation shed, turn her over to Ramm, and tell him to put her in chains. We will know the truth soon enough, and then we will see if we need his persuasive skills."

As the terrified girl was dragged away by Phillip, Polonius poured the mead into a wide bowl and called over an old hound that was attempting to scavenge food in the royal kitchen.

🏴

Ambrose, prince of Wessex and older bastard brother of the king, stepped through the doorway into the dark interior of the interrogation shed. With him came the Byzantine scholar, Phillip, and Edward, eldest surviving son of King Alfred. The serving wench, naked, was manacled, and the chain, that stretched up into the rafters of the shed, forced her to stand on the tips of her toes.

She recognized the royal prince, and called out to him. "Oh, Prince Ambrose, thank God you have come! You know me! I am Cate of Bridport, a *burh* in Dorset. There is some kind of terrible mistake! These rough men cut me best clothing from me and hung me like this for all to see! May I at least have a covering?"

Prince Ambrose spoke. "Cate, you hang there because you have been accused of the most heinous crime a subject of this land can possibly commit. Your lack of clothing is the least of your worries right now. If you are innocent of any crimes, I will personally buy you the nicest clothes we can find. If you are guilty - you are not going to need any more clothes - ever. Girl, did you put a powder in King Alfred's mead?"

"Aye, Prince, but it was just to make him better!"

Ambrose sighed and turned toward the Byzantine scholar.

"Polonius, will you explain to this girl just what is going to happen to her this day?"

"Of course, Prince. Cate, I caught you putting a strange powder into the king's mead."

"Yes, Lord. I told you - it were medicine."

"Girl, the powder you put in King Alfred's drink is a deadly poison that would have killed him in minutes, just as surely as I am talking to you now."

Cate looked at Polonius with horror. "No, Lord! I am a good and loving subject of King Alfred! It were him, who, after me Garr fell at the siege of Chester, took me in and gave me a job as a serving wench. I owe the king everything and would never harm good King Alfred!"

In answer, Polonius turned to Phillip. "Weapons-master, would you please bring in the body that lies just outside the door?"

Phillip returned a moment later with the limp body of an aged hound. He lay the dead dog gently on the floor, and Polonius continued. "Girl, this hound has done one last service for her royal master. She drank the mead you planned to give the king. After drinking the mead you prepared for the king, the hound threw up and then lost control of her bowels. Shortly after that, the poor beast's heart started to beat erratically, and then she died. That, girl, is what you intended for your king!"

"Oh, no, Lord. I told you, I could never harm King Alfred!"

Polonius' smoldering anger burst free. "Look at that hound, girl! Before you leave this shed, you are going to wish it was you who drank that poison, and not that poor dead dog! Prince Ambrose has asked me to explain to you what is going to happen here to you. The interrogators over in the corner have started a fire in order to heat their implements. Their job today is to extract every bit of information from you that they can. You have no idea how much pain they are going to inflict on you! They will start by taking birch switches to you, and then a whip. They will beat you, systematically, as you have never been beaten before. When their arms get tired from that, they will use the hot irons to burn you in private and tender places. When you wake up tomorrow, in screaming agony, they will start all over again, and then the day after that. Eventually, when you stop responding to the whips and the hot irons, they will remove your fingernails. After that, they will shatter your fingers and toes, one at a time."

"But Sir, how will I be able to work if me fingers and toes are broken?"

"Cate, you still have not grasped the enormity of what you tried to do, If you are found guilty, you are going to be condemned to a terrible death. For the sin you have committed against your lawful king, the bishop himself will come to excommunicate you from Holy Mother Church. After he speaks the words, your body can never be buried in consecrated soil and your soul will be condemned to eternal damnation.

When you are a torn and battered wreck, and we are finally satisfied that we have wrung from you every bit of information that you know, you will be put in that iron cage over there, and what remains of you will hang in the square, naked, so that boys can throw rotten fruit at you. There you will stay until you starve to death. Then the birds will pick at your dead flesh. That is your fate girl! You will suffer hell on earth, and then God will send you to a place of endless torments!"

The girl went ash white. "Oh, no, Lord! You don't understand! I but tried to help the king!"

Polonius pointed at the ground. "Look at that poor hound again, Cate, and tell me just how you were trying to help the king!"

The girl looked from one to the other in panic. "I am sworn to secrecy, Lord."

"Soon you will be begging us to listen to your most intimate secrets.' Polonius turned to the chief interrogator. 'Ramm, you may begin. See if a dose of the switch will loosen her tongue."

Cate looked at the supple switch the burly man picked up, and the tears started to flow. "Oh, sirs, you do not need to hurt me with that! I will tell you anything you want to know!"

Polonius held up a hand to stop the interrogator from striking with the switch he held in his hand. "Hold a moment, Ramm. Let's hear what she has to say."

"Sirs, it were last week. Seger, *thane* of Ethelwold, *ealdorman* of Dorset, arrived at the king's court. He called me aside and told me that King Alfred was terribly ill and needed a special medicine if he were to survive. He told me that me *ealdorman*, Ethelwold, wanted me to give the king the special medicine personal like. He told me that I were to say nothing to no one - it were to be a happy surprise when the king suddenly got better."

Polonius frowned. "Did that not seem curious to you?"

"Aye, it did, Lord, but when I said that I could not do that without your permission, he told me that *Ealdorman* Ethelwold held me ma and da captive, along with me two sisters. You sees, Lord, I am Dorset born, but came here to marry me Garr . . . until he fell in battle at Chester. Anyways, he told me that me family back in Bridport would die a very slow and painful death if I told anyone about our conversation or if I refused to obey the command of me lawful *ealdorman*."

"So you admit you tried to poison your king!"

"So I tried to help me king and protect me family, and if that were wrong then kill me now! You have to believe me - I never meant to hurt King Alfred!"

Polonius turned to Prince Edward and Ambrose. "Well, princes . . . What do we do now?"

Ambrose thought for a few moments before he spoke. "Cate, you can help show us your innocence by agreeing to tell your story to the members of the *Witan*."

"The Royal Council? Prince, me *ealdorman* is part of the council and would be there. He would hear me story and make me family suffer terribly . . . "

"And if I can protect your family from Ethelwold and his thugs?"

"Then yes, Prince! It is only the thought of me family that makes me hesitate. I only pray that God will forgive what I almost did!"

Ambrose turned to face Polonius. "Scholar, how long would it take for a ship and crew to get to Bridport in Dorset?"

"We have horses saddled and messengers standing by. A

messenger could be on his way within minutes. I will write the arrest warrant and you or Prince Edward can affix the king's seal to the document. There is currently a squadron of the fleet based at Portsmouth, so, by road and sea . . . perhaps three days in all, Prince."

"And could a messenger who rides all the way do it faster?"

Polonius thought a moment. "Not if the ship sails right away, Prince."

Cate spoke up in alarm. "Sirs, you cannot arrest my family! They have done nothing wrong!"

Ambrose turned to the girl. "You misunderstand, Cate. We will seize them with a strong force so Ethelwold's officers will not dare to interfere. Once we have them safe aboard ship, we will bring them here and protect them from your *ealdorman*. They will not be under arrest."

"Prince, you would do that?"

"Only if you keep your promise to tell the truth of what happened before all of the *Witan*."

"Yes, Prince. If me family is safe, I swear I will tell the truth of what happened - even if the devil himself tries to stop me."

Ambrose smiled. "Then that is settled. Oh, and Polonius, add an arrest warrant for *Thane* Seger. I want him brought back, as well, to answer to these charges."

Polonius nodded. "Consider it as good as done, Prince. I will go and draft the document right away."

Edward stepped from the shadows. His father, the king, was gravely ill, and the young man was the most likely successor to the throne. He looked at the beautiful girl hanging naked in front of him, and spoke. "And Cate?"

Ambrose replied. "I would suggest she stay here under close guard. I think we should keep her shackled so that she cannot run or kill herself, and we want to be very sure that Ethelwold's minions can not get to her. The odds are better than even that *Thane* Seger left someone to cut her throat after she had done the deed. Dead serving wenches cannot tell embarrassing stories."

Phillip turned to the Saxon interrogators. "Ramm, you heard Prince Ambrose. The girl is to come to no more harm, at least for the moment. Give her a blanket to sleep under and a bucket for her personal needs, then loosen the chain enough that she can lie on the ground. I do not, however, want her ever to be left alone - not for even one minute. You can take shifts, but one of you must be awake and watching her at all times. If you so much as need a piss, you will wake up your partner to take over your shift. I want no unwelcome visitors tonight, and I want a suicide watch on her. Is all that clear?"

The burly *churl* bobbed his head. "It will be as you command, Weapons-master. One guard outside and two within. Two always awake."

CHAPTER 4

Why Poison?

As the sun dipped below the horizon, Ambrose met Edward, Polonius and Phillip in the king's planning room. Edward turned to his uncle. "Uncle Ambrose, what are we going to do about the murder attempt?"

"I think that we must speak with your father."

"But Uncle, he is very weak."

"He is still king, and he needs to know what is going on. Scholar, is the king lucid?"

"Aye, Prince, but probably in considerable pain. It is almost time for his next dose of poppy juice."

"Then would you see if he is up to talking with us before you give him your elixir?"

Polonius nodded. "Of course, Master."

The scholar returned minutes later and signaled the little group to follow him up the stairs to the king's *bower*. Alfred was propped up on his bed. His face was wan, and when he spoke, he spoke in a hoarse whisper.

"Polonius tells me we have important business to discuss today. How can a dying king help his family and best friends?"

Ambrose spoke. "Brother, Polonius caught one of your serving wenches trying to poison you earlier today."

Alfred instantly grew more alert. "And do we know who is behind this foolishness?"

Ambrose replied. "Foolishness? That is a strange word to use when your mead was poisoned this very morning!"

Alfred attempted to laugh, but only succeeded in starting a coughing fit. At last he was able to speak.

"Look at me, brother! I am not long for this world."

"Brother, I pray that you will yet recover and live a long and healthy life."

"Thank you, big brother, but at this point, I just pray for release. I may have hours, days, or even weeks left, but I am not going to recover from this. I have fought this illness for years, but, in His infinite wisdom, God has decided that my time on earth is nearly done. This does not make me sad. The pain will finally stop and I look forward to finally seeing the face of God. What puzzles me the most, however, is who would be so foolish as to take the risk of trying to kill an already dying man."

"The tool used was one of your serving wenches, name of Cate."

"Cate? But I gave her a job when her husband fell at Chester. Surely she can not hate me so much!"

"Brother, she doesn't hate you at all. She was manipulated by your nephew, Ethelwold. I believe her to have been duped into it. She thought, or at least hoped, that she was giving you a special medicine. To encourage her to obey, Seger, Ethelwold's lieutenant, spoke to her and told her that her sisters and parents would be tortured to death if she either spoke up or refused Ethelwold's instructions."

Alfred spoke, but Ambrose had to lean forward to hear his words. "That sounds like my good nephew Ethelwold. What has happened to Cate?"

"Brother, as we speak, she hangs in chains in the interrogation shed."

"And what do you intend to do with her?"

Ambrose replied. "She has already confessed and given us the details we need to know. I have sent, in your name, a ship and a hundred *thanes*, with arrest warrants so we may get her family out of Ethelwold's clutches. I also ordered the *thanes* to arrest Seger, the *thane* Ethelwold sent to pressure Cate. To no great surprise, he seems to have left Winchester shortly after talking with her. In return for the safeguarding of her family, Cate has agreed to sing publicly like a songbird in spring. With your permission, brother, I will take all the members of the *Witan* currently here to the interrogation shed tomorrow, to hear her story. I suggest we have an arrest warrant drawn up for when Cate spins her tale. It should be interesting. Ethelwold will likely be in the room, as a member of the *Witan*."

"It seems, brother, that you have everything well in hand. Ethelwold has been a thorn in my side for most of my life, and I sometimes wonder if I should have just let Polonius have his way with the man years ago. A lot of innocent people would be alive today if we had killed him then. What are you planning to do with the girl after she sings?"

Ambrose smiled. "If she cooperates fully, I thought I might ask the king to banish her to a convent for the rest of her life. What she did was wrong, but I believe her to be an innocent dupe."

Alfred whispered. "You are a merciful man, brother. Come to me when you are satisfied with her cooperation, and I will confirm the order. I do not want the torture and death of a young and foolish girl to be on my conscience when I go to meet my Maker . . . And now, brother, the most important question."

Ambrose leaned forward. "And what is that, Alfred?"

The king broke into another coughing fit, and it took him almost a minute before he was able to speak. "Why . . . why would Ethelwold attempt such a thing when I am soon to die naturally?"

"Brother, that is what we are all struggling with, and why I wanted to speak with you. To risk using poison is to risk being caught, when Ethelwold would get the same results sitting back and just waiting."

Polonius absently rubbed the brand that had been burned on his forehead many years before, when he had been a slave. "Ethelwold is no fool. I cannot see him taking such a risk unless . . . unless Ethelwold had to synchronize your death, Sire, with something planned in advance."

Ambrose grew more excited. "Such as an uprising or the arrival of a Viking invasion force?"

Polonius pondered. "I doubt that he is going to lead a revolt when the *Witan* has yet to cast its vote and he is sitting in Winchester surrounded by your loyal supporters. Why take such a risk when he might win through a simple vote? He has certainly invested a lot of time and gold trying to sway the members of the Witan to his point of view."

Alfred whispered. "Can he win the vote, Polonius?"

"Nothing is assured in this world, Sire. But I have bribed one or two of the more venal and reminded the others of your dying wish. Prince Edward is popular and respected militarily. Perhaps most interestingly, several of the members of the *Witan* asked what Prince Ambrose, Phillip, and I would do if Ethelwold is crowned."

King Alfred wheezed. "And what did you tell them?"

"That the prince and our families would be departing immediately for the land of the *Rus* to pursue the trade that we have shamefully neglected for so long."

Alfred tried to smile. "And just how did they take that news?"

"They did not seem happy."

"I should think not! This kingdom owes the three of you a debt that can never be properly repaid. Your strong right arms, your brains and knowledge, and your loyalty, have been instrumental in what we have achieved. Even your worst enemies will acknowledge that much!"

Ambrose looked very thoughtful. "Thank you for your kind words, brother. By Polonius' impeccable logic, he is saying that Ethelwold must have arranged for a mercenary force to arrive and it would be inconvenient to have you alive when they arrive."

Polonius grinned. "Well done, Master! Exactly my thought. A courier arrived just this day from Portsmouth."

The king coughed again and again, but eventually he was able to be understood. "And just what news did the courier bring?"

"Three ships were spotted off the Isle of Wight, but they fled when a squadron of our southern fleet tried to approach," said Polonius.

Ambrose spoke. "Were they able to identify the ships?"

"The men exhausted themselves trying to catch up, but were unable to close the distance. The sails of all three ships, however, bore the crest of one of the *jarls* of *Jorvik*."

Ambrose mused. "Northumbrian Vikings openly flying their colors. Polonius, that explanation even makes sense to this poor benighted barbarian. As long as King Alfred is alive, the arrival of Viking warriors in Dorset is an act of war. On the day of his death, however, Ethelwold could land foreign soldiers and call them faithful supporters, mercenary recruits, or whatever else he pleases. Until the *Witan* convenes and then makes its choice, there would be no new king to forbid the arrival of armed Danes in our midst."

Edward looked puzzled and spoke out. "But what is the point of landing a force of Viking warriors on the shores of Dorset?"

Ambrose looked at Edward. "If Alfred is dead, there is no supreme authority, and a strong force of Dorset *fyrdmen* and northern barbarians, probably Danes, along with a good dose of bribery, just might overawe the members of the *Witan* into supporting Ethelwold's cause. If that didn't work, he would have the men necessary to rise in open revolt."

Edward stood silently for long moments before he spoke. "Then you are telling me that Ethelwold may plan to raise his banners in rebellion if the *Witan* chooses me, and may have even arranged for a Viking force to land and support him?"

Ambrose stroked his face. "It is only guesswork, but it seems to be the only explanation that fully answers the question."

The young prince was angry. "Then what are we going to do about it?"

Alfred raised his hand, and all waited for the king to speak. It was a great effort for Alfred, and his voice barely carried.

"We fight, my son! Tomorrow, you are going to discredit Ethelwold in the eyes of the *Witan*. After Cate tells her story, he will stand condemned and be out of contention for the throne. He will have outsmarted himself!

There are more conspirators than just Ethelwold, I suspect.' Alfred struggled to catch his breath before he continued. 'We share the island with two powerful Viking kingdoms, both of which have tried to steal our land more than once. I want messengers sent immediately to Eohric of East Anglia and Knutr of *Jorvik*."

Polonius spoke. "What are we to tell them, Sire?"

"I want to warn them against any interference in our succession process, Polonius. Further, I want you to exercise a couple of our secret feathered messengers."

Polonius nodded. "What are the orders they carry, King?"

The king whispered hoarsely. "Keep two ships each at Rochester, London, and Dover, but order all the rest to sail immediately for Portsmouth. I want every ship we can spare patrolling the coast of Dorset, ready to take on any more Vikings who stray into our waters. I am damned if I am going to allow my nephew to land a Viking army in our midst!

On a separate matter, I want all of the members of the *Witan* who are not here to be sent for. Nephew Ethelwold has made sure that all of his supporters are present and ready to vote. Let us do the same with our own friends and supporters. Let the couriers ride with the dawn."

Polonius looked puzzled. "Even if we manage to prove that Ethelwold is a traitor tomorrow morning?"

"The Danes just might decide to invade without Ethelwold's cooperation. I think we must move the ships and warn the kings off, whatever transpires tomorrow."

"And the members of the Council?"

"Send for them. I feel the release of all my earthly cares approaching soon, and a vacant throne is a potential disaster for Wessex. And now, I want nothing more than for you to let a sick man rest and for Polonius to give me my dose of poppy juice. The pain is becoming unbearable!"

↾

As they exited the king's chamber, Ambrose put his hand on Polonius' shoulder. "Where are you off to, Scholar?"

"First I am going to put a bevy of Bishop Asser's priests to work with pen and ink, writing urgent summonses to the *Witan* members who have yet to make it here, and then I am going to write some very small instructions that I hope will be winging their way toward Dover, Rochester and London right after sunrise."

"I need a small favor, Wizard."

"You know, Master, I always worry when you call me that. It generally preceedes a request for some impossible task."

Ambrose smiled. "If the tasks were easy, I would not need to ask a brilliant wizard to perform one of his miracles, would I?"

Polonius smiled in return. "Now I am really worried. Ask, Master. You know that you have but to command and this poor servant will obey. If it is seriously difficult, however, it might cost you a bottle of fine Italian wine."

"Done, scholar! When you have completed this miracle, I will buy you the finest bottle in all of Winchester."

"Aha! That means I will never see it. There are few civilized men in Winchester who understand the lure of a fine wine. You barbarians just like to guzzle your ale and mead!"

Ambrose laughed. "For you, my friend, I will either personally steal it from Alfred's personal stock, or I will have it bought in London and shipped directly to your table. Would that be satisfactory?"

"Only if you would do me the honor of helping me drink it, Prince. I will yet train your palate to appreciate a fine vintage. Before you go steal it, however, you might tell me what impossible task I am expected to perform tonight, in order to earn my prize."

"My friend, you are going to feel guilty drinking that wine, knowing that you barely earned it. I just need you to conjure up three Viking long-ships, complete with Danish-speaking crews wearing Viking attire."

"That's it, Master? I expected more of a challenge for my unique skills. Surely you want more than just that?"

Ambrose nodded. "Now that you mention it, I need the sails to carry the crest of one or more East Anglian *jarls*. And I need the ships docked at Rochester within a couple of days."

Polonius stared at his friend. "And may a humble servant dare ask just why you need three Viking long-ships, oh great master?"

Ambrose smiled again. "Humble? That will be the day! I

think, my friend, that you need to pack for a sea voyage, but first you better find some liniment. That and a thick sheepskin for your saddle."

"Does this sudden request have anything to do with your brother's instructions to send emissaries north to the Viking kings?"

"For an over-educated Greek scholar, you show surprising flashes of insight, my friend."

"And may I humbly remind you just what happened the last time we rode north as emissaries? You are going to attempt to milk that cow one time too many, and both of us are going to receive one almighty kick!"

"Polonius, I am sure that I don't know what you are talking about! I remember being treated as an honored guest. Eohric even gave us the hostages we demanded, without too much fuss."

"Only because he intended to take them back before we could leave his territory, and then use our bodies to help fill in some nameless bog!"

"But I seem to remember that we sailed directly across the Thames and saved him any embarrassment," replied Ambrose.

"Only because, my prince, I conjured up a captured long-ship that managed to slip past the Viking fleets."

"Exactly. And now I need that ship and crew back, plus two more."

Polonius sighed. "The things I do for a sip of decent wine! Very well, Master. Your command will join the other orders I am drafting this very night."

CHAPTER 5

Cate Is Killed

Cate lay on the hay that the interrogators had brought her and tried desperately to fall asleep. The hay pricked her tender skin, the night was cold and the single blanket was not enough to keep her naked body warm. Worst of all were the cold steel manacles and the heavy chain that clanked forlornly any time she tried to shift position. She thought the greatest indignity of all, however, was when she had to use her bucket, and one or the other of the interrogators would watch and grin. She was at least grateful that she was not still hanging from the shortened chain. Her toes still ached from the effort of supporting the entire weight of her body. Shudders ran through her when she thought about what the rough men had been about to do to her. She was glad that the darkness hid their terrible implements from her view. She trembled as she thought of the torments that had been planned for her.

Cate heard a muffled cry, quickly cut off. Moments later, the door to the shed swung open, and three shapes slipped into the chamber. The guard on duty rose to his feet, but whatever protests he was going to make were interrupted by the spear that was thrust into his throat. He sagged and then fell to the ground. The fire was low, but the coals cast off enough light that Cate could see a second stranger step over to the sleeping guard, the one who had fondled her breasts as she had hung helpless and naked from the chain. The stranger slashed the sleeping man's throat with a long *sax*. A large pool of blackness spread out on the ground, and Cate knew that her last guard was dead.

She was about to scream, when the third stranger spoke quietly to her. "Hush, now, Cate. *Ealdorman* Ethelwold sent us to rescue you!"

She tried to point to the man who lay closest on the floor, then realized that it was impossible while wearing manacles. "That one there, he has the key to my chains."

The stranger faced her, with the light bouncing off his face from the feeble fire. Cate could see a smile on his face as his teeth flashed in the light. "You know, I don't think that I am going to need a key, my sweet."

"But sir!"

The last thing Cate saw was the flash of light off the man's *sax*. She tried to breathe but found that she could not. She put her hands to her throat, but they were instantly covered in a warm liquid, and she was completely unable to stem the rhythmic flow of blood. Within seconds she was unconscious.

The third stranger looked down at the dead girl, and the first spoke. "Thane Seger said he would exchange her head for the gold! Get on with it! If we are not a long way away from here by sunrise, it will be our heads that young Edward will be collecting!"

ᚠ

Polonius rose before first light. Kuralla, his beloved wife, groaned at the early hour. "Come back to bed and keep me warm, Husband. I will make it worth your while!"

"There are few things I would rather do, now that you are awake, my beloved, but I am restless. I left a young woman hanging in chains last night, and, if she does not cooperate today, we will have to start cutting her into little pieces."

"You mean Cate? Husband, you told me she tried to poison the king! What else could you have done?"

"I don't know, Beloved. I can only pray that she keeps her promise to cooperate. Otherwise I shudder to think what those great oafs will do to her. I think I will walk over to the interrogation shed to make sure that all is well. In just a few hours, I must arrange for her to meet with the members of the *Witan* so she can tell her story."

Kuralla yawned. "Well, that should at least solve the problem of Ethelwold being given the throne by the *Witan*."

"You are right there, my love. If we can prove this charge, it is likely that we will be removing his head within the week. Now that is something that will give me great satisfaction to see!"

Polonius had the first inkling that something was not right when he saw that there was no guard at the door to the interrogation shed. While he looked in puzzlement, the door swung idly in the gentle early morning breeze. The Byzantine scholar filled each hand with a throwing dagger, and then peeked cautiously into the shed. In the faint pre-dawn light, he saw that Ramm and both of his assistants lay dead in pools of their own blood, and Cate's head was missing. Polonius almost threw up, but he took several deep breaths, stepped forward to briefly put his hand on her body, and then he ran for Ambrose's quarters.

Polonius was panting from his exertion as he pounded on Ambrose's door. He called out.

"Wake up, Prince! I need to see you now!"

Gretchen, clutching a blanket around her, opened the door. "What is it, Polonius? Ambrose is dressing and will be here shortly."

"Thank you, my lady. King Alfred's would-be assassin is lying dead in the interrogation shed."

"Dead? You mean Cate?"

"Aye, my lady."

Gretchen put her hand to her mouth. "You are sure that she is dead?"

"There is little doubt, my lady. Someone removed her head!"

Ambrose strode into view. "I heard that, Scholar. What in the name of sweet Jesus happened!"

"This was not the work of sweet Jesus, Prince! Maybe Lucifer. The guards are all lying in pools of their own blood, and

Cate is lying there minus her head!"

Ambrose's face turned red. "This is the work of bloody Ethelwold! He has removed the only evidence we had linking him to the attempted murder."

Polonius paused, and then replied. "Unless we can catch the minions who killed Cate! Hot irons will encourage them to tell us who gave the original orders."

"Aye, you are right, Polonius. Is there any way to know when Cate died?"

"I checked. Her body was not yet cold, Ambrose."

"Then they can't be too far away yet!' The prince turned to the roving sentry who guarded the king's Great Hall and had been attracted by the disturbance Polonius had made.

'Sentry! Rouse King Alfred's Personal Guard immediately! I need forty mounted men, along with two officers and a spare horse for each man, and I need them here, in front of me, as soon as possible. Now repeat your instructions!"

The sentry hesitated for just a moment. "Ah . . . Rouse the commander of the Personal Guard and tell him you want forty men here, as soon as possible, with two horses apiece, the detail commanded by two officers."

Ambrose smiled. "Good man! Run now . . . and tell them I need some expert trackers. Also, I want the *tun's* gates closed until further notice."

"Aye, Prince Ambrose!" With that, the man ran toward the barracks.

Polonius spoke to Ambrose. "Do you think there is a chance of catching the killers?"

"Maybe. I don't know. If the killers are smart, they will go back to wherever they are living, and go back to bed. I am actually hoping, however, that they were foolish enough to ride away in the night."

"Why do you think that, Prince?"

"I had a very wise teacher from Byzantium, an exceptional scholar, I am told, who taught me the logical thinking of famous Greek philosophers."

"And what did this wise man's brilliant thinking process

allow you to deduce?"

"If they were going to stay in hiding nearby, they would have left her head on the body."

"And why would you think that?"

Ambrose shrugged. "I am guessing that they were told to bring the head as proof of the success of their task. Now that they have it, it would be essential to get away with it. It is hard to hide a head within the Winchester *tun* walls from the search teams we are about to send out. Ergo, the people who took it have departed from Winchester."

"And how will you know if they left?"

"Ah, that is simple to a man trained by a world-famous Greek thinker. First we don't find the head within the city walls. Second, we ask the guards at the gates who rode out during the night."

"The killers could have just slipped over the walls, Prince."

"Not with their horses. Would you slip over the wall and try to walk away with someone's head in your possession?"

Polonius smiled. "I might if I left my horses outside the gate earlier in the day. Still, your logic has almost reached the level of a middling Greek student, Prince. For a simple barbarian, it is actually pretty good."

"Praise from the scholar! This is a memory I will cherish for a long time!"

"Don't let it go to your head, my prince! I just believe that one should give credit when credit is due. Let us wake Phillip and get some officers to question the night guards before they end their shift. It would help a lot if we could tell our pursuit column who they are looking for!"

Ambrose replied. "Speaking of which, my scholarly friend, just what direction are we sending the riders in?"

"One group to try and follow any tracks, and another doing a *Long Ride* down the main road to Dorset?" Polonius said.

Ambrose answered. "It is almost as if you believe that my beloved nephew is behind all this. I will lay odds that he is still within Winchester's walls, and probably sleeping like a baby."

A ghost of a smile flitted across Polonius' face. "I won't take that bet!"

The prince nodded. "I believe that the only safe place for the killers would be in Dorset, under Ethelwold's protection. You do realize that Cate's death is going to put nephew Ethelwold back in the running for king when Alfred finally dies?"

"I know it, my prince. He finally gave us the evidence we needed to get rid of him, and now he has managed to snatch it away! Our best hope now is to catch the killers."

"Polonius, we can still make the accusation. We heard the truth from Cate's lips."

"We can, Prince, but you can be sure he will have been somewhere very public all night, and it will be his word against that of a servant girl - and one that cannot even tell her own tale. Do you remember when he had his men fill the ditch in front of his palisades at Wareham and let King Guthrum escape after we had him trapped?"

"How could I forget?"

"And where was he while his men did the deed?"

"If I remember correctly, he went off with Bishop Asser on some 'important' business."

"Exactly. He made very sure that he had witnesses and an iron-clad alibi."

"And he hung the officer who had obeyed his orders, before we had a chance to interrogate the man. I would not be surprised if we found that friend Seger has very recently left for a long pilgrimage."

"Prince, Cate was our proof, and she is now dead. We can try for Seger, but we had better get the Personal Guard after the killers as soon as we can. I am going to predict that the assassins are fated to live a very short life."

"You mean, Polonius, that Ethelwold will arrange to have their bodies dumped into a bog somewhere?"

"Their lives are likely to be measured in hours or days, Prince; not weeks."

As Polonius spoke, Phillip came around the corner. He was both armed and armored. Ambrose smiled and spoke to the old warrior.

"Then we had better hurry up and catch the damned

assassins! Phillip, what say you to a ride?"

"Only if we head toward Dorset, Prince. I have heard the news and am eager to catch up to some murderers."

Ambrose smiled again. "You read my mind, old friend!"

Polonius looked indecisive. "I am not sure it is a good time for me to leave, Master."

Ambrose nodded. "I agree, Scholar. I think that you should stay close to Prince Edward."

"Do you think that Ethelwold would try an attempt on his life, Master?"

"Unlikely, but your magic knives close to him do give me comfort. I was really thinking about you advising him and coordinating the manhunt from here."

"You are right, Master. I will go find him and see if I can give him a shoulder to lean on. I probably also have some messages waiting for me that arrived during the night."

Ambrose nodded. "I was actually thinking of letting the thanes of the Personal Guard do the hard riding, but Phillip and I can at least ride to the nearest royal estates and check to see if any suspicious riders have been spotted. After that, we will return to Winchester. I suspect that we will be back within a day or so."

ᚱ

The thanes of the Personal Guard spurred their mounts forward. Each leading a spare mount, they headed down the road to Dorset. As they galloped away, Ambrose prayed that they managed to catch up with the three nondescript riders who had demanded that the gates be opened some two hours before the dawn and had paid in good silver for the privilege. Twenty other men, expert trackers all, had exited earlier, and they were scouting the edges of the old Roman road, looking for traces of the three killers leaving the road.

Ambrose and Phillip swung into their own saddles once the dust had settled. Phillip spoke. "How far do we go, Prince?"

"I do not want to leave Alfred's side for too long, but I want to do something! How about we ride as far as the first royal estate? I am hoping that by then our keen young *drengs* will be dragging our quarry back with them."

Even as Ambrose and Phillip followed the young *drengs* of Alfred's Personal Guard out the gate and onto the Dorset road, Polonius launched his pigeons. As the birds spiraled upward, the scholar cursed himself for not arranging for bird stations along the Dorset road. His message to apprehend three riders could only travel as fast as the fastest riders, and those were already on their way. In the time it took the riders to just reach the Dorset border, his swift birds will have delivered messages to London, Rochester and Portsmouth.

℞

Ambrose spotted the dust first. He spoke to Phillip. "Some riders come, old friend! I see a dust cloud ahead."

"It could be a cart of hay, Prince, or a company of traders."

Ambrose smiled. "Or our young drengs, returning from a successful mission. Let's get off the road and take a break, and we will soon find out!"

Phillip first stretched his arms out and then pulled gently on his left rein. "With pleasure, Prince."

The dust cloud eventually evolved into a body of fyrdmen riding toward Winchester.

Phillip stepped onto the road, and the cavalcade stopped in front of the big man. The weapons-master spoke. "Godric, why are you returning to Winchester? Have you been successful?"

"Yes and no, Weapons-master!"

Ambrose stepped onto the road. "It is normally one or the other, Godric. Enlighten me as to which it is."

The *duguo*, commander of the group sent out a few hours before, turned his head to face Prince Ambrose. "We retrieved three strangers who seem to match the description we were given, Prince."

"Excellent, but where are they?"

"They are mounted on three of the spare mounts at the back, Prince."

"Then the answer to Phillip's answer is 'yes!'"

"But we found the three of them hanging from tree boughs beside the road, Prince. They will not be answering any questions today, or ever. We brought the bodies back for identification."

Ambrose turned to the big man at his side. Tutor, mentor and companion, Phillip had traveled the world with Ambrose, and they had saved each other's lives more than either could count.

"By the beard of sweet Jesus! Ethelwold has done it yet again, Weapons-master! He has managed to remove the proof we needed one more time!"

"He is playing with us, Prince. He sits at Winchester, waiting for your brother to die, and orders his men to deliberately leave these dead men visible, hanging close to the road. It would not have taken long to bury them somewhere in the woods. He wanted us to find them!"

"But it would probably take at least six men to overwhelm and hang Cate's killers, so, somewhere, between here and Dorset, is a band of fighting men . . . Godric, Phillip and I will take the three bodies back to Winchester. I want you to turn around and ride hard for the Dorset border."

"What am I looking for, Prince?"

"Here is my ring. I am giving you full authority to arrest anyone you suspect. Collect any suspicious-looking men you find, and bring them back to Winchester. Somewhere out there are the men who hung these three, and I pray to Almighty God that you will manage to find them!"

"Prince, there are forks in the main road. They could easily decide to take a more circuitous route back."

"You are right, Godric. The odds are against you, but there is no hope of catching them if we do not try! Use the ring to get some fresh mounts at any royal estate if you need them, stop at each *vill* on the way, and ask if they have seen any strange riders. They are out there somewhere."

The officer, who had ridden in the king`s Personal Guard for years before he was granted several *hides* of land, stood at attention in front of Ambrose. "I will do my best, Prince!"

Ambrose smiled. "I know you will! I am counting on it. Go

with God, Godric!"

CHAPTER 6

Ambrose Plans a Trip to King Eohric

Ambrose spoke to Edward and Polonius. "Nephew, I have asked King Ethelred of Mercia to call up a strong force of his *fyrdmen*. They will be gathering within days."

Edward looked puzzled. "But Uncle, why do you want Ethelred to raise his host now? If he calls his *fyrdmen* away from the fields before the crops are planted, then his people could face hardship and even starvation toward the end of winter."

"Prince, you need a loyal and powerful army north of the Thames - one you can count on. It is unlikely that anyone in Mercia supports Ethelwold in the power struggle. It will also, not incidentally, cause great anxiety to Eohric of East Anglia, especially when Ethelbert completes his mobilization and moves his *fyrd* to the East Anglian border. As to the cost of taking the men and perhaps even have the rest abandoning their fields to move to the defensive *burhs* - I think that the cost of that action should be borne by the treasury of Wessex."

Edward looked concerned. "Uncle Ambrose, I suspect that buying food for the large number of people affected will cost a very great sum."

Ambrose nodded. "True, Prince, but we are paying with Viking treasure that we seized in battle, and, whatever the cost in gold and silver, it is a small price if it buys you a loyal army that allows you to stop Eohric from invading."

Edward sighed. "You make a good point, Uncle. Aside from Ethelwold, what else are we facing?"

Ambrose turned to Polonius. "Scholar?"

"Ethelwold's *fyrd* is not so large that we need fear it too greatly, though he could make it very expensive if he can keep his *fyrdmen* loyal to his cause and we have to dig his forces out of all of his strongholds."

Prince Edward frowned. "And how would we handle such an uprising?"

Polonius smiled. "With your agreement, Prince, we will bribe the most venal thanes to surrender. They will be more than a little nervous when thousands of the king's *fyrdmen* cross the borders into Dorset. The thanes have sworn an oath to follow their *ealdorman*. Our first order of business, therefore, must be to appoint a new *ealdorman*, have the church absolve the *fyrdmen* of their oath to Ethelwold so they can swear loyalty to our new man, and spread the word throughout the *shire*."

Ambrose spoke. "It is not the Dorset *fyrd* that we need to fret about, Edward. As Polonius says, we will bribe them, appeal to their loyalty, besiege them, or kill them, as is necessary. The men that will remain loyal to him when faced with a royal army are not a large enough force to be of great concern."

Edward nodded. "So what do you think Ethelwold is counting on?"

Polonius hesitated before he replied. "Viking intervention? It could explain the mysterious ships that fled when our fleet approached them."

Ambrose nodded. "Could some have made it past our fleet?"

The scholar answered the question. "Viking ships sail our southern coast almost daily. Yes, one or more ships could have landed without our knowledge."

Edward looked puzzled. "What could he offer the Danes?"

Polonius turned toward the young prince. "If I were Ethelwold, I might offer all or part of Ethelred's Mercia to Eohric or Knutr in return for his support in putting me on the throne."

"Polonius, such a move could destroy the very Wessex he inherits!"

"Prince Edward, the Thames was our northern border not so long ago. In fact, it officially still is. For all that Ethelred is our good friend and ally, he is still a king in his own right. I suspect that Ethelwold would consider the loss of Ethelred's Mercia to be a small price to pay for the throne. It is much more than he has now and, at the same time, he gets rid of a stubborn and hard-fighting foe."

Edward sighed. "My father has ordered the fleet to the Dorset coast. You think we might also face Viking armies again. What else?"

Ambrose answered. "Polonius, do you have the lists?"

"Aye, Master. Sire, Ethelwold has spread a lot of gold in order to buy influence and friendship amongst the kingdom's thanes and *ealdormen*. I have a list here of any noblemen who might be sympathetic to his cause. If they rose as one, the kingdom would truly be facing civil war."

Edward's eyes blazed as he stared at the lean Byzantine. "Such as who?"

Polonius replied. "Anwell of Cornwall is one I would not trust. The Cornishmen tried an alliance with Vikings in the past, and there are others, too."

"Then how do we deal with Anwell and his ilk?"

Ambrose answered the question. "We try to make sure the country does not split between you and Ethelwold. That is why your father required you to set the example and for all of the *Witan* to swear that oath to accept the council's final decision.

The Danes are another matter. That is why I have asked Ethelred's Mercians to gather near the border."

"Uncle, you know that Eohric will not take that well."

"I am counting on it. Let us remind him that we can take the war to him, with devastating results. With your permission, I plan to travel north to assure him that we would not be the first to breach the frontier."

"Uncle, your journey into Viking territory worries me a lot. It is not for nothing that the Danes have taken to calling you 'Daneslayer'.' A ghost of a smile flitted across his face. 'I fear that you are not universally popular amongst our Viking neighbors."

"But I am an adopted Dane, Nephew, who speaks their language, has lived amongst their eastern cousins, the *Rus*, and earned their respect. The Danes have little sense of honor toward any foreigners, but their code of conduct for their own people is impeccable. And if that is not enough, I will have Ethelred and his Mercian wolves hovering near the border, eager for the chance to reclaim some of their lost territories. Eohric would know that my blood would be savagely avenged. Besides, Polonius is helping me arrange a little surprise for our Danish neighbor."

꫞

Ambrose leaned against the railing of his vessel while the Viking horns brayed the alarm. Dozens of warriors who had been in the fields ran for the fort, while the sheep baaed and the cows mooed. Within scant minutes, a force of over a hundred armed warriors, led by King Eohric himself, marched down to the *tun's* dock. The burly king suddenly grinned. "I see four Danish ships floating on my river, and one carries a white shield. By the beard of *Odin*! Is it really Prince Ambrose come to see me again?'

The king scanned the four vessels that floated lazily just off-shore. 'This time you brought a lot of friends with you, Ambrose of Wessex! Are we at war?"

Ambrose smiled in return. "That will be up to you, King Eohric. If I had wanted you dead today, I would have landed quietly a little downriver, put my warriors ashore, and let the Saxon swords harvest you and your men. We both know that you are heavily outnumbered, Eohric."

"How did you get past my ships and the fort on the lower reaches of the river without raising an alarm, Prince Ambrose?"

Ambrose replied. "Your sentries were most co-operative. They even confirmed that you were in residence here."

"They are not likely to do that, or say anything to a Saxon, let alone such confidential information!"

Ambrose shrugged. "Then be glad we are not yet enemies. Look about you, King. My ships were all built by Danish craftsmen. My crews wear Danish clothes. Would you like to hear them speak in Danish?"

The king looked angry. "So you once again tricked your way into a Viking kingdom. Some fools on duty today will suffer the *blood-eagle* before this day ends, thanks to you. Beware, Prince. You are going to play that game once too often, and it will cost you your head!"

Ambrose smiled. "Oddly, Lord Polonius warned of the same thing, so this time I brought enough sea thanes with me that it is your head that is in greater peril, King Eohric. That is not why I am here, however. You may keep your head for now. I am on a peaceful diplomatic mission, hence the white shield."

"Emissaries do not normally travel with four hundred warriors at their back, Prince-of-Wessex."

"Five hundred. Emissaries do not normally have to fear for their lives, King-of-East Anglia. The last time I visited I trusted who I thought was an honorable Danish king."

"And I greeted you as a welcome guest, Ambrose of Wessex!"

"Eohric, do not insult my intelligence! If I had not changed my route home through your lands, I may have found myself in a bog with water between me and the sky!"

"Prince, you have lived amongst us. You know that the white shield is sacred to the Danes. There was no trickery. I say again - we treated you as an official emissary and even gave you the hostages you requested!"

"Do you really think me such a fool, Eohric! You had every intention of rescuing the hostages before I could get them back to West Saxon territory. Do you think I do not know about the ambush that you arranged on the road to London? Did your warriors plan to fly the banners of Haesten when they attacked us? Perhaps one or two of my escort may have managed to escape, thus reporting the vicious attack by Haesten and his dastardly warriors - a hundred Roman miles from their real location! Do I really look that naive, Eohric?

You proved yourself to be a man with little honor, king, and we hung your hostages. This time I brought enough men that you are not able to try anything so foolish again. Just so there is no misunderstanding - my standing orders are that my crews are to burn everything and kill every Dane within a day's march of here if there is even a hint of any trickery."

King Eohric sighed and then suddenly laughed. "You are welcome, Prince-of-Wessex. I think I would prefer to call you Canuteson the Daneslayer. The name suits you. It is at least always interesting when you come to visit."

"I think I will remain Ambrose of Wessex today, since you did not choose to respect an adopted son of a great Danish warrior the last time I was here, Eohric."

"You are wrong there. I did, Ambrose, in every way that I could. The warrior called Daneslayer just asked for too much."

"You mean that you did not want to give me hostages, since you had already arranged to break our treaty and you knew we would hang your hostages when we discovered what you had done."

"I told you then that I was not bound by Guthrum's treaty, but you are guessing correctly, son-of-Canute. Sometimes a king must weigh one oath against another and decide which one takes precedence. Still, it would have made me very sad if Haesten's pirates had killed you that day."

"It was not your fault that your men did not manage to successfully ambush us that day, King, but that is not why I have returned to see you."

"Come ashore, Prince, and I will offer you food and drink. My hospitality is legendary."

"So, we have decided, is your lack of honor, King Eohric."

"A king does not betray an oath lightly, Ambrose. I did what I had to do.' King Eohric sighed. 'What is it that I can do for you, Prince?"

"Alfred is dying. Soon Wessex will have a new king."

"I know that, Ambrose.' The king smiled. 'My spies are almost as good as yours."

"My king wanted me to tell you that we will not countenance interference in the succession."

King Eohric smiled again. "Sometimes a king must do what he can to help a friendly neighbor."

Ambrose nodded. "Then you feel you must support the legitimate claimant to the throne of Wessex?"

"It is not interference if I have been asked by a Saxon friend to assist him, Ambrose. It is what good neighbors do. You have put it well, Prince! You have summed up what I need to do very succinctly."

"I am relieved to hear you say that, King Eohric, but only the *Witan* can decide who is going to be the next king of Wessex."

"Ambrose, you foolishly support a young lad over a seasoned veteran whose father was also king. You know as well as I that Ethelwold is the one who has the better claim. His father was king, and his mother a queen. Your precious Edward cannot make that claim."

"The young lad you refer to, defeated the largest Viking army ever to invade Wessex. You should know, Eohric. In fact, there were five separate invasions, and each time we killed more of your East Anglian warriors."

"Come now, Ambrose, we both know that young Edward's victories were due to you, Polonius and Phillip. Now you I would lend two thousand warriors to at any time, if you would just declare yourself in the running, *Atheling*."

"I have refused the nomination before, King, and I will do so again. And to answer your unstated question, Polonius, Phillip and I will serve Edward as faithfully as we did Alfred. If we are the power behind Edward, well, we are not going anywhere."

Eohric grinned. "You give me yet another reason to support Ethelwold, Ambrose. I suspect that he would have little desire for your services. I think you now know that I believe Ethelwold to be the legitimate claimant."

Ambrose replied. "Just remember, Eohric, that the rightful ruler of Essex is King Alfred, and the heir to East Anglia presently lives at Alfred's court. It may be that we should support these just claims with West Saxon fighting men. Beware, King; two can play that very dangerous game."

Eohric grew suddenly angry. "Why have you come to my land, Ambrose of Wessex? It is never a wise thing to insult a king of Danes."

"*Victory-Maker* stands ready to prove the truth of my words if you wish to declare a *holmgang*, King. I have not come this time to extract meaningless oaths. I have come to speak blunt truths."

"Then speak your truths, Ambrose of Wessex. I will listen."

"I came to bring you a message, Eohric. Several Viking ships have been seen off the coast of Dorset, and I want you to know that Wessex considers that the first acts of war. We believe them to have been Northumbrian. Our fleet on the southern coast is now being strengthened, and we will sink, without hesitation, any Viking ship we catch.

Even as we speak, you have couriers killing horses to bring you news that a strong army has appeared on your western border. Edward asked me to tell you that they will not cross the border unless you provoke us. As I told you before, we will not tolerate your interference in our succession process. Do not send your warriors south. If you do, this time we will bring the war to your territory.'

Ambrose stood straighter, and his voice cut across the narrow strip of water. 'Remember my words, King Eohric! You have been warned. You provoke Wessex at your peril!"

Eohric put up his hand for silence. "Today, prince of the Saxons, as you say, we speak only in truths. I owe you that much. Tell your young pup who would be king that Eohric does not at present plan to send his host into West Saxon territory - nor did I the last time Vikings fought Saxons."

"We killed hundreds of your warriors, King!"

"You killed hundreds of young men who ignored their king's advice and flocked to Haesten's banners. Ambrose, you lived among the *Rus* Vikings for years. A young Viking warrior listens to his heart, and has the right to abandon a king if he does not agree with the king's commands. It is the way of the Vikings, Ambrose. You lived among the Rus Vikings, so you should know that."

"I am glad that you are not coming south, Eohric. I would have hated to have had to take your head."

"Remember, Ambrose. The king will not bring his army south. Some of my young warriors may have other ideas."

"I will tell the king your exact words, Eohric."

"Then go in peace, Saxon."

Without another word, Ambrose signaled the captain. The crewmen slipped the oars into the water and smoothly aimed the vessel down-river. The other vessels turned and slipped into line one at a time. King Eohric watched impassively from shore as the four ships raised their sails, proudly displaying the Viking king's royal crest on each!

CHAPTER 7

A.D. 899. "This year died ALFRED, the son of Ethelwulf, six nights before the mass of All Saints. He was king over all the English nation, except that part that was under the power of the Danes. He held the government one year and a half less than thirty winters; and then Edward his son took to the government...."
.... The Anglo-Saxon Chronicles

The great bell of Winchester Cathedral began a steady tolling. Everyone within hearing of the deep pulsating sound knew what it meant - a great king had finally lost his battle with illness and gone to meet his Maker. Alfred, the youngest son of a West Saxon king had, against all odds, succeeded to the throne. Against all odds, and alone of all the Angle, Saxon and Jutish kings in Britain, he had kept his country free of the Viking plague. Thousands of brave warriors had died in the struggle, and more than once Alfred had been forced to pay treasure to get the stubborn Danes to leave, but the treasure had bought him precious time, and now his country, with its new fleet, its summer and winter armies, and the many defensive *burhs* scattered throughout the land, was able to hold off anything that the Danes could throw at Wessex. That king, soon to be called the Great, had finally died, and the land was going into mourning.

Ambrose had spent the entire previous day at his brother's side. He had held his hand as Alfred slipped into a deep coma. Ealhswith had finally sent him home long past midnight, telling him to get some sleep. Ambrose had resisted, noticing his brother's labored breathing, but eventually he had gone. Now he lay in bed as he listened to the tolling. He spoke to Gretchen, his wife.

"He seemed near death when I left him. I pray that God takes him to His bosom. Alfred was a true Christian and a great king."

Gretchen lay against him. "He was also a great brother, husband and father."

"Aye. Aside from his determination to develop our defenses against the Danes, he set up the palace schools and attracted scholars from many lands. Never again will there be ealdormen and athelings who are unable to read or write. After Polonius taught the king the skills, my brother even became a scholar. It is amazing to think that a man who could not read until Polonius taught him how, could eventually translate into Saxon such major works as Gregory the Great's Pastoral Care, Boethius's Consolation of Philosophy, St. Augustine's Soliloquies, and the first fifty psalms of the Psalter!"

Gretchen put her arm on her husband's shoulder. "What happens next, husband-of-mine?"

Ambrose shrugged. "We bury a king, and appoint another."

Gretchen looked skeptical. "Is it really that easy?"

Ambrose grimaced. "Not on your life! The Archbishop of Canterbury is here and will make arrangements for a state funeral. That part should be simple enough."

"And Ethelwold?"

"That, my love, is the rub! That, and our Danish neighbors. If ever Ethelwold wanted to try for the throne, now would be the time."

"But surely you, Polonius and Edward are ready for more treachery?"

Ambrose nodded. "Ethelred still has his Mercian *fyrdmen* assembled north of the Thames to counter any move from Northumbria or East Anglia. There is, however, no king. Ethelwold can now bring in as many mercenaries as he can afford, and there is no one with the authority to deny him the right. Until the Witan sits and chooses a successor, the country is effectively leaderless."

"But he could just wait and see if the Witan makes him the legitimate king."

"I have no doubt that he will do just that. The question is, what will he do if he is not chosen?"

Ambrose could feel a shudder run through his wife. "Husband, does he have a chance of winning?"

"It is possible, my love, but Polonius has been active with the members of the Council. As things stand, Ethelwold will not win."

"And if the odds change and Ethelwold does?"

"Then we ride south to Portchester. There you will find two dragon ships ready to sail. If Ethelwold is chosen, I want you to gather our family and go to the horse farm directly south of Winchester. There you will find Thane Osgar with some of the fastest horses in all Britain. He will give you his best mounts. Take the horses, our family, and ride south as fast as you can. Tell no one where you are going."

"Husband, you are telling me to run!"

"My love, listen to me very carefully. Our family would not outlast Ethelwold's coronation by more than a week! If he wins, you take the family and ride for your lives!"

"Husband, I do not like the way you keep saying 'you'. If I ride south, I ride with my husband! I want you to be very clear on that. I am too selfish to let you stay behind and make some sort of noble but ultimately futile sacrifice. And what about Phillip's, Polonius' and Edward's families?"

"Polonius and Phillip are well aware of this contingency plan. They helped organize it. We will tell Edward if and when he needs to know."

"Why would you not tell him now?"

"Because a secret only remains secret when as few as possible know it. If word got to Ethelwold, our families would die - to the last man, woman, and child. Ethelwold is utterly ruthless and he carries a great hate. There is room for Edward and all his family, and we will tell him if and when he needs to know."

"I am almost afraid to ask what happens if Ethelwold loses."

Ambrose sighed. "It is a question I have asked myself a thousand times. Will he go back to Dorset and sulk, or will he lead his Danes in a sneak attack? For that matter, how many Danes has he got hidden in Dorset?"

"Husband, surely Polonius' spies have discovered some clues about what he would do."

"They have, my love, but they are not what you want to hear."

"Husband, I always want to know the truth. Please don't hide it from me because I am a mere woman."

Ambrose laughed. "You are never a mere anything, but I will speak only truth to you, my love. The reports are that he has a force of Danes, and they have moved up to a camp in the forest just north of his capital. Ethelwold has not sent out a general call-up to his *fyrdmen*, but small groups have been spotted and also seem to be gathering in the forest. We also know that there have been a series of 'accidents' to his thanes who have shown 'excessive zeal' for Wessex.

"In the name of Sweet Jesus! Is Ethelwold preparing for an attack on Edward?"

"He has not moved men to the border yet, but it is clear that he is quietly building a strike force for something."

Gretchen sighed. "Husband, I pray that God will grant Wessex peace."

"Amen, my love!"

CHAPTER 8

Urgent News

Gretchen shook her husband awake. He looked up and reached for her. "Come here, my love! I want to feel you in my arms."

She slapped his hand away even as it slipped over her left breast. "It seems you want to do more than hold me, husband-of-mine, but we have no time for such things right now. Polonius wants to see you immediately! He is waiting for you in the king's planning room."

Ambrose shook his head to clear it. "Then your needs will just have to wait, my beloved. Matters of state must come before personal desires."

Gretchen smiled. "You are confused, dear husband. It is **your** needs that will have to wait. Hurry now!"

Ambrose slipped on some clothes and was ready within a minute or two. He kissed his wife as he passed. "Farewell, beloved! I will be back just as soon as I save the kingdom."

She laughed. "Then, with your cousin around, I may have to remain chaste for a very long time."

⚐

Ambrose found his friend pacing the floor of the planning room while Edward stood across the room staring at a map hanging on the wall. Polonius seemed very upset.

Ambrose spoke. "What is the problem, Polonius? Gretchen said it was urgent."

Polonius held up a tiny slip of paper. "It is, Master."

"Then out with it, my scholarly friend! Don't make a poor

ignorant barbarian try to guess the thoughts of an illustrious Byzantine scholar."

Edward joined the two and sat down. He smiled and spoke. "Don't look at me, Uncle! I just arrived and am as confused as you."

Polonius smiled a little smile that was almost a grimace. "As you both know, Princes, I have sent several dozen spies to infiltrate Dorset. I sent several of my best men to hide in the forest near Ethelwold's capital, and I provided them with several pigeons from the roost here to speed up communication."

Ambrose nodded. "And, my friend?"

"And I just got my first intelligence."

"And for this you tore me from my wife's loving arms?"

"More likely I saved her from your snoring . . . Before you interrupted me, Master, I was going to tell you that Ethelwold's tame Vikings were seen to be on the move."

Ambrose sighed. "That is interesting, and could potentially be a serious problem. The next questions are . . . how many, and where are they moving to?"

"The exact location remains unknown, Master, but there were over a hundred of them, and they were seen moving east by smaller tracks toward the border of Hampshire."

"That is cause for great concern, my friend!"

"And there is more, Master."

"Say on, Scholar."

"Several hundred of his Dorset *fyrdmen* were seen on the main road heading from Dorset to Winchester."

Ambrose mused. "Then there are at least two separate forces moving up to near the border, and possibly eventually converging on Winchester . . . Edward, you have perhaps two hundred of Alfred's Personal Guard here, and perhaps another hundred thanes and *ealdormen* at court. Added to that, we have the permanent garrison of Winchester, and each *ealdorman* has a small Personal Guard with him. That means we have defenses, but would likely be vulnerable to a force of anything over a thousand."

"And now you know why I woke, you, barbarian prince. We

do not know the numbers of the approaching Dorset *fyrdmen*. If Ethelwold is smart, and he is no fool, he will have his men converge from several different directions, so it will be hard for us to accurately guess the total numbers. If he has managed to gather sufficient men, then Ethelwold could have the throne with one well-co-ordinated attack, without worrying about any election . . . Princes, what do we do?"

Edward spoke. "I think we should summon the *fyrd* of Hampshire - immediately!"

Polonius looked concerned. "And what do we tell them, Prince Edward . . . that we are going to war with Dorset?"

"No, Scholar. How about we tell them that the Hampshire *fyrd* is being given the honor of escorting their king during his funeral? It is going to be a great spectacle. A thousand thanes in full armor shall march in the parade commemorating Alfred's death, and they will then remain in Winchester so that they can be used for crowd control and ceremonial purposes."

Polonius replied. "Ethelwold will never buy it, Prince Edward."

Ambrose smiled. "Actually, he doesn't have to. He cannot match the numbers without putting his whole *shire* on a war fitting. I am betting that he will get the message."

Polonius nodded. "It is a clever counter-move, Prince Edward. If we are all agreed, I will write the letters immediately. We must send to the nearest garrisons for a start, and then I will ask each *ealdorman* for a token force from their followers, plus a request for more from their home *shire* to send for a representative force 'for the ceremony'. All members of the royal families must be brought into Winchester immediately and provided with guards. I would estimate that we need at least another thousand warriors here, and we need them sooner rather than later!"

Edward asked a question. "Polonius, how long to raise such a force?"

"If we strip the local garrisons and borrow from the *ealdormen* who are already here, we could have several hundred within a day or two to add to the permanent force. Even with my bird friends, it could take up to a week to raise the rest."

Ambrose replied. "The Hampshire men and a loan of loyal *fyrdmen* from the *ealdormen* must be our first priority. Write the letters, Polonius, and Edward or I will place the king's royal seal on them. Oh, and Polonius, do you have a spare sheet with Alfred's signature on it?"

"Of course, Master. He left a box of sheets pre-signed for when he wanted me to write something in a hurry."

"Then Polonius, I seem to remember that on his deathbed he made you regent until you can turn over the royal seal to the duly elected king."

"But Master, I don't remember . . . Oh, wait. It begins to come back to me . . . it was just before he died."

Ambrose turned to Edward. "Or just after. Nephew?"

"Yes, I am sure that is what I heard, and if he didn't say it, it was only because he died before he could put that thought into words."

Ambrose nodded. "Excellent, then we are agreed. Polonius was duly appointed as regent!"

Ambrose walked over to Edward, and then he slipped to his knees. "Edward, this *seven-night* a great king has died. I declare that I now recognize you as king. I am your man, now and always."

"Rise, Uncle! I am not king yet, whatever we may want."

Polonius knelt beside his friend. "You are my king, Sire! I will accept no other."

Edward replied. "But the election has not yet been held."

Ambrose spoke. "Edward, if you are not elected, then Polonius, Phillip and I, along with all of our families, have agreed to go into exile. Ethelwold will never be my king. I would also suggest that you consider joining us. You know that Ethelwold will exact a terrible revenge on our loved ones if he is ever given royal power."

Edward looked at Ambrose. "You have a plan, don't you?"

Ambrose replied. "There are ships and horses waiting as we

speak, but the walls have ears, and I would prefer to give you the details if and when you need to know."

🏴

Ethelwold was furious. The thane was polite, but insistent. "The regent has requested your presence, *Ealdorman*."

"Regent? There is no bloody regent. At the death of the king, the Witan chooses a new king, and I am next in succession."

Thane Godric was patient. "That may be as you say, *Ealdorman*, but Lord Polonius has a royal document that gives him authority, and he has requested your presence."

"Damn the man, Leng! I want fifty bodyguards! I will go see this trumped up former slave and tell him what I think of his bloody authority!"

🏴

As Ethelwold stalked into the main chamber of the king's Great Hall, he noticed Ambrose, Polonius, Edward and Archbishop Plegmund sitting at a table. The angry *ealdorman* stormed over to stand in front of them. He focused his eyes on Polonius as he spoke. "What kind of damned trick are you playing this time? Alfred appointed no regent before he died!"

Polonius smiled and held out a document stamped with the king's seal. "Nevertheless, here is the very document, with King Alfred's signature and the royal seal intact. Archbishop Plegmund himself has been kind enough to attest to both the signature's and the seal's authenticity. Would you like to examine it more closely?"

"It is in your writing, you Greek knave!"

"Of course it is. I wrote out most of King Alfred's proclamations."

Ethelwold threw up his hands in frustration. "Fine, Alfred left you caretaker until the *Witan* selects the next king. Your job then is to turn over the royal seal to the next king. What of it?"

Polonius spoke. "As regent, it has come to my attention that possibly hostile warriors are even now making their way toward Winchester. I am asking each *ealdorman* to volunteer a group from their Personal Guard in order that we can mount an adequate defense against any unpleasant surprises. How many can you volunteer? I notice that you brought a fine contingent along with you."

"I am the future king and I need them all to protect me from knaves and scoundrels who would steal my throne!"

Polonius continued. "I also wanted to inform you that there has been a call-up of a portion of the Hampshire *fyrd* and they are marching to join the brave defenders of this *burh* even as we speak. As of this moment, Winchester is under a state of emergency. The gates will be kept barred and the walls will be manned twenty four hours a day. The regent, or an officer appointed by me, will personally screen any fyrdmen before they are allowed to enter. No exceptions."

Ethelwold pointed at Edward, Polonius, and Ambrose. "You! You three are in this together! Greek, you are a popinjay, a fraud, and a pederast!"

Polonius stared for several moments at the angry *atheling* before replying. "Those are fighting words, and you, sir, are a bully, a murderer, and a craven coward."

All heard the sharp intake of breath by Archbishop Plegmund. Ethelwold instinctively reached for his sword. "You simpering Greek! How dare you malign a royal *atheling*! I should have you horse-whipped!"

Polonius spoke quietly. "Go ahead, coward! Draw your sword, or, better yet, declare a *holmgang* between us. Your Viking friends will explain the rules to you. They are actually getting quite close to the Hampshire border. The rules are really quite simple, however. Even you should be able to comprehend them. Two men go to a little island, and generally only one returns. Are you ready to show the world that you are not an arrant coward?"

Ethelwold suddenly slammed his sword back in its scabbard.

"Oh, no! I know what you are up to! You are attempting to make me angry enough that I will go up against your magical throwing daggers!"

Polonius grinned. "Then you are going to ignore a mortal insult and prove the validity of my statement?"

"I am not going to die with one of your damned blades stuck in my eye!"

"Then obey your regent, *Ealdorman*! You are to send your tame Vikings back to the hell where you found them, and order your *fyrdmen* to turn around immediately. If either group crosses the Hampshire border, I will declare you to be an outlaw and you will not be eligible to be considered for king."

"Justice is coming, Greek!"

"Say the words, *Ealdorman*, and God will give you justice this very day! Is that not right, Archbishop?"

"It is true, my son. Things that have been said here today cannot be unsaid, and a man's honor dictates that he deals with it. My children, God will guide the righteous man's sword to victory!"

Polonius smiled. "Surely, *Ealdorman*, you are not afraid of a man who is barely capable of lifting your big clumsy sword?"

"There will be justice for you when I am king, Greek! You can count on it!"

"Then if you are not man enough to face me in fair combat, you have permission to leave the presence of your regent!"

꙰

Archbishop Plegmund stared in shock at Ethelwold's back as the *ealdorman* strode angrily out of the Great Hall. The prelate turned to Polonius and spoke.

"May God be merciful! Good King Alfred's body is barely cold and Wessex is close to civil war! Gather what defensive forces you can, Regent. I think that I will schedule an official meeting of the Witan two days hence. We clearly cannot go too long without a king on the throne. Prince Edward, do you agree?"

"The sooner we have a new king the better, Archbishop."

"Then I will go arrange it now!"

CHAPTER 9

The Witan Convenes to Choose a New King

Two days after King Alfred's death, and a few days before his funeral, Archbishop Plegmund convinced the Witan, after considerable rancor, that the realm could not long be without a king. They were finally ready to vote to choose the next king. The Archbishop of Canterbury convened the meeting early in the morning, and when Edward and Ethelwold moved toward their normal seats, the archbishop called out to them.

"*Athelings* Edward and Ethelwold, both of you carry the blood of Cerdic, and are thus eligible for the title of king. Both of you have supporters on this Council who have proposed your name. We thus have two candidates, and the Council must now make the difficult decision between the two of you. I must therefore ask you both to leave the king's Great Hall until we can make the choice. Guards! When the two *athelings* have exited, I want you to seal the doors. No man will enter or leave this hall until God has seen us choose a new king!"

Edward and Ethelwold exited together, and the door slammed shut behind them. Ethelwold looked around him to see who was near and, seeing no one, he spoke quietly to Edward.

"When I am finally chosen king, Cousin, I suggest you take your bastard uncle, your Greek spy, and the old man who still thinks he is the greatest warrior in Christendom. Travel far and fast! If you think that Byzantine admiral, what's-his-name, Demetrious - harassed your uncle along their two thousand mile journey home from the east, just wait and see what I do to you!"

Edward looked confused. "Ethelwold, you bear a grudge for not being chosen king the last time, but the kingdom was in jeopardy and the *Witan* chose a proven warrior over a young boy."

"Your father stole the throne that was rightfully mine! Why should I not be angry?"

"My father did not steal it, Cousin. The Witan voted - just as they are doing now. My father would have preferred the life of a scholar to that of king. To be king was a duty to him, not a pleasure."

"If he felt that way, then he should have stood as regent and honorably turned over the crown when I came of age! I will never forgive or forget what Alfred did to me!"

"Ethelwold, you are a hothead and a fool! My father gave you Dorset to rule and saved your miserable life several times over."

"Saved my life? You have been listening to that Byzantine pederast of yours too much for your own good!"

"Ethelwold, do you really think that my father did not know about your secret negotiations with King Guthrum? You let the Viking army seize Wareham when Guthrum was hard-pressed, and then you ordered the ditch filled in so he could escape with all his horses."

"Your crazy uncle arrived with Devon *fyrdmen* and seized my *burh*! He kidnapped my sons and left guards to watch over me and my family! I was threatened with death if I called out my *fyrdmen* in defense of the realm!"

"All that is true, Ethelwold, but you are missing the point."

"What point have I missed?"

"My father showed Christian mercy and let you live! He had far more evidence than he needed to have had you dismembered as a traitor."

"There was no proof, and the rumors were just heinous lies told to discredit me! Besides, that was long ago."

"Ethelwold, Cate told the whole story of the attempted poisoning before your hirelings managed to remove her head."

Edward could see the sweat appear on the *atheling's* face, but he blustered. "The word of a serving wench against that of an *ealdorman* holds little weight!"

"Ethelwold, Ambrose, me, and Lord Polonius all heard her

words. We know the truth of what happened."

Ethelwold started to turn away from Edward. He snarled the next few words. "Flee while you can, boy, or you will face my wrath, and you will not like it!"

A young *thane* breathlessly caught up with Edward. He spoke. "*Atheling* Edward, the *Witan* sent me to find you and bring you back to the Great Hall. Wessex has a new king!"

Edward looked at the young man. "And is his name Edward?"

"You will know soon, *Atheling*. I was told that only the Archbishop of Canterbury can make the pronouncement."

Edward entered the Great Hall, and Ethelwold was not far behind him. The tables were set up in a large square, around which sat the bishops, the archbishop, *ealdormen*, and the more important *thanes* who made up the council. Both Polonius and Ambrose sat near the archbishop.

The archbishop rose to his feet. "Welcome back to this special meeting of the *Witan*, *athelings* Edward and Ethelwold. Before I announce our decision, I want you to know that we had a most difficult task. We noted Ethelwold's maturity, but balanced against that, we had Edward's series of stunning victories against the Vikings. Ethelwold has perhaps the better claim, since his mother was a queen, but it is hard to ignore both tradition and the wishes of King Alfred. As King Alfred rightfully pointed out not too long ago, *primogeniture* has been the norm rather than the exception for over a hundred years. It is not, however, an immutable law. In the end, the balance was incredibly close. All members of the *Witan* were told to put aside personal feelings and decide impartially who would be best for Wessex. I think that is what we have done . . . Edward, son of Alfred, king of Wessex, your formal coronation will be at Kingston-on-the Thames, where your father and his father before him were crowned, in the spring, when the appropriate ceremony can be arranged. Let no man misunderstand. As of this day, Wessex has a king and you, Edward, have the right to wear the crown.' The archbishop paused. 'Is there any man here who can not or will not accept the decision of this august council?"

All eyes focused on Ethelwold, who went bright red. The archbishop continued.

"Then each man in this chamber will kneel and swear allegiance to King Edward, here and now! This oath, in the presence of God, is binding, and to break it will be considered treason and grounds for excommunication from Holy Mother Church. This is the last chance - if anyone cannot swear the oath, they may leave, now, unmolested, and they will have three days to exit Wessex."

Ethelwold suddenly stood and made for the door. The guards moved to detain him, but the archbishop's resonant voice filled the Great Hall. "The *ealdorman* is free to leave, unmolested. I have given my word!"

Edward watched his three closest companions file into his father's, now his, planning room. "Welcome, my friends! What news of Ethelwold?"

Polonius replied. "He gathered his escort, Sire, and was last seen riding hard for Dorset."

The young king was upset. "By the beard of Moses! I fear that we have not seen the end of him."

Ambrose spoke. "Nephew, he rules a *shire* of Wessex in the king's name. An *ealdorman* who does not accept your authority can not rule one of your *shires*. The Archbishop of Canterbury himself gave him three days to leave the country."

The king sighed. "I know, Uncle! I know, too, that if he does not leave Dorset voluntarily, we must eventually take it from him. The only question is - when? At this point, less than a day after my election, and before I have had a chance to consolidate my power, I hesitate to institute an armed conflict. I do think the time will come, however, eventually, for us to use force."

Ambrose sighed. "I think that day is sooner rather than later, my king."

CHAPTER 10

The Funeral

Archbishop Plegmund had done his job well. Hundreds of priests and monks, looking like a vast flock of crows in their black habits, followed the Archbishop of Canterbury and his bishops, whose clerical robes shone with peacock colors. Chanting and swinging thuribles, the bishops led the long procession toward Alfred's last resting place.

Following the clergy were the members of the royal family. Ealhswith, Alfred's widow, and her children marched with Ambrose, Polonius and their families. The king of Mercia walked solemnly beside his wife, Ethelflæd, who was Alfred's eldest daughter. The family was followed by an austere wagon, painted black. Here, the king's coffin rode in solitary splendor.

The wagon was followed by the *ealdormen* and other notables of the kingdom, and then came Alfred's Personal Guard. They were hundreds strong, and their carefully polished armor gleamed in the sunlight.

Finally, the thousands of garrison troops and Hampshire *fyrdmen,* who had been called up to guard Winchester, formed a long, long tail.

⚑

Archbishop Plegmund faced the many people crowded into Old Minster. The religious portion of the service complete, he turned to the family and spoke.

"It is time for me to turn this service over to a brave atheling who might himself have been king, but chose, instead, to devote his life to service in the name of the crown. This is a man who has met the Pope, refused to bow to the most powerful emperor in the world, and lived with the very Vikings who had originally enslaved him. I speak, of course, about a living legend - Ambrose, bastard prince of Wessex."

Ambrose stood in front of the many noblemen and clerics who had crowded into the church. He stared out at the audience for some time before speaking. At last he started.

"It is a great honor to be asked to speak at my brother's funeral. My brother . . . your king, Alfred, was fifth in line to the throne and intended originally to live the quiet life of a scholar.

I remember one time, when his mother offered her sons the chance to win a precious book. All they had to do was to be able to read it to her. Alfred, unable at that time to read, memorized the entire book, and he won the prize. This taught me, early in life, just how dedicated and stubborn Alfred could be when he put his mind to something. These qualities were to put him in good stead with what was to come.

The Viking Great Army arrived, and young Alfred put down his precious books and accompanied his brother the king into battle repeatedly. As some of you well remember, those were desperate times, and the kingdom reeled from the hammer blows of the pagan Danes. Alfred told me that they lost as many battles as they won. Then, in the midst of the chaos and strife, his elder brother died, leaving the throne vacant. The Witan chose a brother, a veteran commander, over a young and untried son because Wessex was fighting desperately for its life.

Alfred put down his books, picked up his sword, and proceeded to become a great general, defeating Viking army after Viking army. Perhaps even more important than that, he had a vision. He dreamed of a country where no one, churl, thane or ealdorman, would be more than a day's march from safety. Thus, in the midst of war, he established the burhs, along with permanent garrisons. They controlled the important fords, rivers and roads, and, very important, allowed Alfred to develop a mobile force that could travel anywhere, confidant that their loved ones were safe and protected. These fyrdmen were split into a summer and winter army, so we would never again be in the position of when King Guthrum invaded during Epiphany, when our army had disbanded for the winter.

Not content with that, he established a powerful navy, seizing dozens of stout vessels from the pagan Danes, but also, with the help of Frisian craftsmen, building new and larger ships that the Danish ships could not match.

If this is what my brother will be remembered for, he will have earned his place in the pantheon of great British kings - the only Angle, Saxon or Jutish king on the entire island to survive the Viking invasions. But he did so much more.

While fighting for the survival of this country, he quietly asked Lord Polonius, the renowned Byzantine scholar and linguist, to finish his education. Soon, my brother was translating original Latin texts into our language, codifying laws, and establishing a palace school where the children of members of the royal court could learn to read and write. Not content with the level of learning across the country, he insisted all ealdormen learn how to read and write. Much learning was lost due to the constant Viking incursions and the destruction of so many monasteries, but my brother still managed to attract famous people of learning to his court. I believe that his single greatest deed was to establish Wessex as a place of learning and education.

God has called my brother before his tasks were complete, and he had no choice but to go. Still, though I rejoice that his chronic pain has finally ended, yet I will mourn the loss of a dear brother and a great king. Alfred, *Bretwalda*, Consul of Rome, King of Wessex, Sussex, Kent and Cornwall, may you rest in peace!"

ᕈ

One by one, each member of the royal family walked to the

open grave, paused, and sprinkled a handful of dirt on Alfred's coffin. His wife threw in a flower she had been clutching all through the service, and burst into tears. Ambrose wrapped an arm around her and escorted her away. Their tears mingled together.

CHAPTER 11

AD 900: "Then Prince Ethelwold, the son of his paternal uncle, rode against the towns of Wimborne and of Twineham, without leave of the king and his council. Then rode the king with his army; so that he encamped the same night at Badbury near Wimborne; and Ethelwold remained within the town with the men that were under him, and had all the gates shut upon him, saying, that he would either there live or there die. But in the meantime he stole away in the night, and sought the army in Northumberland. The king gave orders to ride after him; but they were not able to overtake him. The Danes, however, received him as their king. They then rode after the wife that Ethelwold had taken without the king's leave, and against the command of the bishops; for she was formerly consecrated a nun."

.......The Anglo-Saxon Chronicles

When Polonius entered the room, Ambrose saw by his face that something was very wrong.

"What is it, Scholar? I have rarely seen you looking so upset!"

"I just spoke to one of my agents, Master. He almost killed several horses getting here. We have a very serious problem."

"Well, what is it?"

"Ethelwold has just seized both Wimborne Minster and Twineham. He has sent word to his fyrd to gather at their rallying points, and is strengthening all of his strongholds even as we speak."

Ambrose sighed. "Finally he makes his move, with Alfred just in the ground. I can't say I am surprised. We turned back his Viking supporters and the *Witan* voted for Edward. This is Ethelwold's last throw of the *bones* for kingship."

"That is the point, Master. A strong king is dead. Young Edward has yet to really prove himself, and he is not yet in full control."

"But the *Witan* has decided against Ethelwold and for Edward."

"Granted, Ambrose, but, as you say, that gives Ethelwold the impetus for one last throw of the *bones*. After losing the election, his only recourse now is to openly rebel and seize the throne by force of arms if he wants to be king of Wessex."

"Well, my friend, would you please grab your files, and let's go talk to a king!"

↩

King Edward looked up as his uncle and his spymaster invaded his planning room. He spoke.

"Welcome, uncle and scholar. The hour is late and I would have thought that you were both happily asleep by now. May I order a horn of mead for you?"

Ambrose spoke. "Unfortunately, King, we have an urgent

matter to discuss with you."

"More important than a horn of mead? It must be serious, indeed. Then speak, my friends. I am always available to listen to you two!"

Ambrose looked at Polonius. "Polonius . . ."

The thin Byzantine started. "Ethelwold has seized the two estates of Wimborne Minster and Twineham. His *fyrdmen* have been summoned from across the *shire*, and he is reinforcing the garrisons of his other *burhs*. There are more rumors of selective killings of various *thanes* throughout Dorset, but I have no names and precious few facts to substantiate these rumors."

"My God! What can he be up to?"

Polonius continued. "King, I think it is pretty clear that he is reinforcing his position militarily, and removing commanders who might feel their duty is to their king before their *ealdorman*."

Edward stared at Polonius. "You mean that he is murdering my supporters within his ranks."

"My king, Ethelwold is neither a nice nor an honorable man. I asked your father years ago for permission to kill the man."

Edward looked shocked. "I heard the reference to it when my father was on his deathbed. I was sure that my father would never have agreed to such a thing. Such an act would have lain heavily on his Christian conscience."

Polonius looked somber. "You are quite right, King. He did not agree."

"Polonius, why on earth would you have proposed such a thing so long ago?"

"King, sometimes it is necessary to put down a rabid dog. Now, instead of a single traitor's death, hundreds of innocent men are going to die, and, if the Danes become involved, perhaps thousands. Sire, kings must live with their Christian conscience, but they are responsible for much more than their own lives. You must make life and death decisions that will affect thousands of people. I understand your abhorrence of arranging for a man's murder, but what is more moral - the death of one traitor or of hundreds of innocent men?"

"It is customary, however, Polonius, to allow a man to commit a crime before you arrange for his execution. I must think on the issue, Scholar. It is quickly becoming more clear why my father preferred his academic studies and my grandfather wished for nothing more than a life in the bosom of Mother Church. . . . Polonius, tell me - why did you propose killing my cousin many years ago? You did not then know for sure that he would betray the kingdom and attempt insurrection."

"On the contrary, King, he proved himself a traitor a long time ago, when you were but a young lad. He has been actively working against you and your father since the day the *Witan* chose the youngest brother of the king over the young son."

"Scholar, you said that he was a traitor, but what exactly did he do, in your eyes, that you marked him for death?"

"Sire, he had every right to be bitter about the *Witan*'s decision, but it was not your father who pushed for the throne. The truth is as you previously stated - Alfred would have preferred to have lived the life of a scholar. The Danes were a great threat at the time, however, and your father, a proven warrior with several victories to his name, was chosen over a young and inexperienced boy."

"But that doesn't explain why you wanted to kill Ethelwold."

"King, he betrayed your father again and again. The list is almost too long to enumerate. When your father was chasing Guthrum across the country, the *ealdorman* of Dorset neglected to send adequate reinforcements to Wareham and Guthrum, naturally, seized it, and, from its stout walls, was able to defy your father. We had a long siege, and when Guthrum was running out of food, guess which section of ditch got miraculously filled in so the Danes could escape, and even take their horses with them? Ethelwold hung Delwyn, one of his own loyal *thanes*, to hide the truth from your father."

"Much of that I knew. I once even threw it in Ethelwold's face. But, between you and me, much of it is conjecture."

"There was room for doubt, King, and your father felt he did not have a strong enough case to present to the *Witan*. Soon thereafter, however, when Guthrum almost caught you and your father at Chippenham, it was Ethelwold who sent a hundred odd warriors in an attempt to capture your father when he was hiding in the forest of Selwood."

"I was young, but I remember a little of the times. The cold . . . and the panic, as mother got us across the river and through the ice in a leaky old boat. I can still hear the Viking warriors baying in frustration on the far side of the river as we slipped from their grasp."

"Hundreds of your father's *fyrdmen* perished that day, that you and the rest of the royal family could escape. When we had fled, and were in hiding in Selwood, the forest filled with spies. When put to the question, more than one admitted to being in the pay of your uncle."

"Why did Ethelwold not catch my father in the forest?"

"Ah, that was amusing. Ethelnoth, the *ealdormen* of Somerset, had left strict instructions that any men who wanted to see the king had to be blindfolded and taken to Alfred by a circuitous route. Seger, lieutenant to Ethelwold, arrived at one of the *vills* with the hundred warriors and demanded that he and his men be taken immediately to see your father. Instead, his men were provided billets and he was taken, blindfolded and alone, to the vill where your father was hiding. Seger complained bitterly of the rude treatment, but the truth is, it is a good thing that he never learned your father's exact location. I have no doubt that Guthrum and his army would have arrived in short order if Seger had not been blindfolded for that trip through Selwood Forest."

"Polonius, if my father had proof, why did he not move openly against Ethelwold when Guthrum sued for peace?"

"Sire, the list of betrayals I have enumerated is far from complete, but, as you say, much was circumstantial. You already know that Guthrum escaped that siege thanks to Ethelwold. We know that Ethelwold entered into negotiations with the Danes when Guthrum invaded, because your uncle here, in the guise of Hamar the *Rus*, saw him at Guthrum's camp! One of the Viking commanders there told Prince Ambrose that Ethelwold had a plan to capture King Alfred and, if that failed, he would bring his *fyrd* to the Viking side in the last minutes before battle. We know, years later, that he had his men waylay and kill royal couriers who passed through Dorset. Your uncle and I were attacked ourselves by Dorsetmen disguised as Vikings, when we made our way to your father's camp on the southern coast. King Eohric of East Anglia even admitted that he had powerful allies amongst the Saxon leaders of Wessex. We were forced to send a strong force to sit on Ethelwold's northern border, seized his capital, and even provided him with bodyguards who had instructions to kill him if he tried to raise his *fyrdmen* against the king. You might have noticed - the Dorset *fyrd* was conspicuous by its absence is several battles near Dorset. Ethelwold was forbidden to call them up, and when he was allowed to raise a partial force, his sons were required to live with the king's Personal Guard, along, not incidentally, with the heirs to Cornwall.

"But in spite of all that circumstantial evidence, my father would not act?"

"No, Sire. Ethelwold was his own nephew, and perhaps he felt guilty that Ethelwold had been passed over. Perhaps, too, he remembered what had happened in Northumbria and even in Wessex some years before."

"And what happened there, my Byzantine scholar?"

"It is what your father referred to in his speech to the Witan. Two rival kings, Aelle and Osberht, fought for the throne in Northumbria, and the Vikings simply waited until the two forces fatally weakened each other. By the time the two rival kings united to face the Viking invaders, it was too late. Their weakened armies were routed by the Danes, and once powerful Northumbria became the Viking possession now known as *Jorvik*. Even as we speak, the Franks fight each other for crumbs, and the empire of Charles the Great is no more. The same army that a hundred years ago conquered most of Europe, cannot even keep the Vikings pillaging their country from marching boldly where they please."

"Polonius, you mentioned my own family."

"I was in the wilderness of Asia at the time, Prince, but when your grandfather brought your young father home from his visit to Rome, he returned to find that Ethelbald, his own son and regent, had conspired with both *ealdormen* and church officials in order to keep the West Saxon throne for himself."

"I am told that my grandfather was a gentle and religious man, Polonius. Surely, however, he could have called on enough loyal *ealdormen* to have raised an army and crushed Ethelbald if he had so wished."

"He probably could have, but he knew that he could also throw the empire into a brutal civil war. There are no winners in a civil war, Sire. Instead, he accepted exile as underking of Kent."

Edward smiled. "I think, Scholar, that you are trying to tell me, in your own terse manner, that my father chose not to take the risk of civil war by moving openly against Ethelwold."

Polonius smiled in return. "Ethelwold was the son of a popular king. He had recruited men to his point of view, and, yes, there was a slight possibility that his followers would have risen in righteous indignation if he was blatantly assassinated."

"Then father tolerated the snake in his midst for the sake of peace. Polonius, if my father had agreed to Ethelwold's death, what would you have done? Surely you could not have used your magic throwing knives?"

"Sire, there are many poisonous herbs that mimic various illnesses. The Byzantine way would have been to quietly poison him. Instead, we had to post spies. As I said, we know he communicated with the Danes, and we were forced to tie up considerable *shire fyrdmen* from Devon in order to make sure that he did not march an army against us on the battlefield. Your uncle here even helped kidnap his sons and kept them hostage at your father's court. Ethelwold knew that his sons' lives would be the cost of betrayal, and so he never openly came out against your father. You may be sure, however, that he bribed a lot of the *Witan* to first put forward his name and then to vote against you."

"Then what happened? How did I win?"

Polonius smiled. "I spoke personally to most of the members of the *Witan*, Sire, and reminded them of your father's wish for you to follow him. I also used some of your treasury to bribe a few of the more venal conspirators. The vote, however, was closer than you know."

"I repeat. Why did they choose me?"

"Sire, Ethelwold is a more mature leader, but his military career isn't unblemished. I made sure to point out his military blunders in considerable detail to all who would listen. You, on the other hand, have had singular success, in spite of your tender age."

"Thank you for the kind words, Polonius, but you know as well as I do that my 'singular success', as you put it, is mainly due to Phillip, you, and Uncle Ambrose here!"

"You flatter us, King, but the truth is - several influential members of the *Witan* specifically asked if Ambrose and I would stay at your side if you became king."

"And what did you answer, Scholar?"

"As I hinted at some time back, Sire. That we are your loyal servants, but we have extensive business interests in the Viking north, and if Ethelwold was chosen, we would be moving back to the land of the *Rus* immediately."

"Thus removing the most successful military men in Wessex's history . . . and would you have really moved?"

"Sire, Prince Ambrose told you before that there are two Saxon dragon ships just waiting. They are tied up in a small bay on the coast, near Portchester. They are manned and ready to sail at a moment's notice."

"Polonius, do you not think that is a little alarmist?"

Ambrose spoke. "Nephew, we made sure there was room for you and your family on one of the ships. Unlike your father, Ethelwold would have had no compunction in clearing out his rivals. My guess is that you, and our entire families, would have died within days of his being crowned."

"Do you really believe that, uncle?"

"I can only answer that my family has their luggage packed and the best horses I could find are in a paddock on a farm just a little south of here."

"Surely Ethelwold would not have dared!"

"Dared what? A highly contagious disease swept through Winchester. The bringers of the metal illness would, in turn, fall to the mysterious disease. A liberal sprinkling of gold and favors, and perhaps a few more cases of a fatal fever, and our family is buried and forgotten. At worst, he is forced to pay a little *wergeld* and perhaps convert some particularly fine land into church *bookland*."

"But that would be blatant murder!"

"It is generally the winners who write the history, Sire."

Edward walked slowly around the room, staring at his advisor and uncle as if he had never seen them before. At last he spoke.

"God in heaven, what have I got myself into? Polonius, what are we to do?"

"You are king, Edward. Command and we shall obey."

Edward smiled suddenly. "Then if am king, I command my faithful advisors to tell a young and ignorant king what he must do!"

Polonius spoke. "Sire, Ethelwold is a festering sore that, if ignored, will find allies, or others may be encouraged to emulate him. Both of your faithful advisors recommend swift and decisive action."

"And what, exactly, do you propose?"

Ambrose spoke. "You, Nephew, should lead your Personal Guard against Ethelwold as soon as possible."

"Uncle, brave as the men of my Personal Guard are, they will not be able to overcome Ethelwold and his entire *shire fyrd* if he and his men retreat to their strongholds. Now you tell me he has now taken two more of mine!"

As he spoke, there was a knock on the door, and Phillip went to answer it. The big man took a note from a servant and passed it silently to Polonius.

At last, Polonius looked up. "It is a message from one of my agents. Ethelwold has now used armed men to break into a convent, where he seized a nun and carried her away."

Edward was aghast. "By the beard of Moses, why would he

kidnap a nun? Is the man insane?"

"It seems, Sire, that the woman spurned his advances some months ago. She fled to the convent and joined the order to escape his grasp."

Edward sighed. "I am trying to think like a king. Polonius, how can this matter be used to our advantage?"

"Now you are, indeed, thinking like a king, Sire. You should make sure this story spreads far and wide, and announce your displeasure to the ecclesiastical authorities as loudly as possible. It should help alienate any bishops that Ethelwold might have been counting on for support. I would suggest asking the archbishop himself for a Writ of Excommunication for this rash deed. His agreement would end any chance of church support for Ethelwold."

"Would the archbishop agree?"

"When the legitimate king of Wessex, duly chosen by the *Witan*, under the leadership of the archbishop himself, makes the request and attaches a generous grant of *bookland* to the request, why would he not? I can think of few things more upsetting to any prince of the church than to have one of his own snatched out of the sanctuary of a convent."

"Agreed. I shall speak with Archbishop Plegmund and get him moving on the matter before the sun sets. Now, what else do you have up your sleeve?"

Polonius looked thoughtful. "Well, if we agree to use the defiling of the convent to discredit Ethelwold in the eyes of the church and he is excommunicated, you could declare him to be outlaw."

The king nodded. "Hmm. That would make it a serious offense for any West Saxon to help him in any way. That I like, but in the meantime, what are we going to do about his outrageous seizure of two of my royal estates?"

"It is exactly that which makes me suggest that you take your Personal Guard and ride to Badbury Rings without delay!"

The king looked at Polonius with a puzzled look. "Badbury Rings? Is that not the ancient British hill fort near Wimborne

Minster? That was built even before the days of the ancient Romans!"

"Yes, Sire. It is in ruins, but the ramparts were partially rebuilt and used when our own ancestors landed on these shores. It is still a formidable defensive position. Ethelwold is apparently still at Wimborne Minster. Your very presence nearby will threaten him. You and your Personal Guard will be safe behind the ancient walls until we can gather enough *fyrdmen* to your side to be capable of large-scale siege operations against your cousin. If you agree, I will speak to Ethelhelm of Wiltshire, Edred of Devon and Ethelnoth of Somerset this very *night* and ask them to call up large contingents. Your possession of Badbury Rings will likely pin Ethelwold down, and it will not take long to gather an overwhelming host of loyal *fyrdmen* under your command."

"But Polonius, in the short term, his force at Wimborne Minster alone will likely outnumber mine. Should we not wait until we can gather enough loyal *fyrdmen* to form an overwhelming force before advancing?"

"Sire, he will not expect you to seize Badbury Rings. If he withdraws from Wimborne Minster after he has learned of your presence, than you have won one estate back without a fight, and, equally important, you are seen to be doing something decisive."

"That is logical, Scholar. Now what do we do about the rest of the Dorset *thanes* and their *fyrdmen*?"

"I would suggest you show mercy, King. The problem is not of their making, and they are caught in the middle, between you and Ethelwold. Thanes who obey and defend their *ealdorman*, are, in fact, only fulfilling their sworn oaths."

"What are you suggesting, Wizard?"

Polonius replied. "That you send messengers the length and breadth of Dorset, announcing the impending excommunication of Ethelwold and your decree that he is a traitor and outlaw. A new *ealdorman* is proclaimed, and all are required to come and swear obedience or face the loss of their lands."

Edward thought for a moment before replying. "Could we not send out traveling monks with the messages? Ethelwold will surely think twice before he harms any clerics."

Polonius smiled. "Now you are definitely thinking like a king, Sire. You welcome and forgive all the thanes in Dorset who ride to you and your new *ealdorman* at Badbury Rings and swear fealty to you there."

"And those who don't come?"

Polonius shrugged. "Those who refuse to come should be declared outlaw and their lands re-distributed. Ethelwold is a persuasive man. He will have retained the loyalty of at least some of his thanes, and this is the best chance you are likely to get to rid yourself of traitors within Dorset. Many of your father's older *drengs* have earned their share of gold rings and more. It is time to bestow land on the oldest and best of them."

"And I must choose a new *ealdorman*."

"Yes, Sire, but you have no end of brave men who have proved their loyalty to you or your father."

"Aye, I am thinking about Thane Ethelhere. He is a brave warrior, but, more important, he has shown an ability to organize and lead."

"Shall I fetch him, Sire?"

"Please. It will be a pleasure to honor the man. Oh, and Polonius?"

"Yes, King?"

"Right after him, perhaps in an hour, I would like to see Archbishop Plegmund."

"It shall be as you command, Sire."

Edward laughed. "That will be the day! Off you go, you rascal!"

The young thane on duty opened the door to Edward's planning room and stuck his head in. He spoke with a nervous quaver in his voice.

"Sire, Archbishop Plegmund is here and asks for

admittance."

Edward smiled warmly. "Relax, my boy! Saxon kings don't bite. Well, don't keep the head of the entire church in Britain waiting! Show the man in!"

As the prelate entered, Edward stood up, went over to his guest, and kissed his ring. "Welcome, Archbishop! Thank you for coming so promptly."

Archbishop Plegmund smiled. "You are king, and your messenger said that it was important."

"Aye, it is, Archbishop. And you know Lord Polonius, of course?"

"Of course, Sire."

"First of all, may I get you some mead or wine?"

"Why thank you. A little wine would not go amiss. It will help lubricate my tongue."

Edward nodded and Polonius disappeared. "Please, Archbishop, come and sit. Lord Polonius is a connoisseur of fine wines and will inevitably find the best of my father's stock."

Plegmund settled down on a comfortable chair and smiled at his king. "And what can I do for you, King?"

Edward paused before speaking. "It is a delicate matter, Archbishop."

"Come now, Sire. I have heard your confession, and I am bound by the confessional oath of confidentiality to die before revealing any secrets. There is little that will shock me at my age."

"Archbishop, we are about to invade Dorset."

"If you want my blessing, Sire, you have it. I watched Ethelwold the other day, and I saw a mad dog. I cannot help but think what he is doing to that poor nun he kidnapped. Did you know that he almost killed an aged nun who tried to stop him entering the convent? Jesus asks us to forgive, but he also said 'render unto Caesar'. We must forgive his transgressions, but that does not mean that he does not have to pay the price for what he did!"

"Archbishop, I want to minimize the killing when we invade."

"That is a noble desire, King, but I am not a military man. Just how can I help?"

"I want to send word ahead that Ethelwold has been excommunicated, declared outlaw, and replaced by Ethelhere."

"I have already agreed to excommunicate Ethelwold for his outrageous behavior. I repeat, Sire. How can the church help in this noble cause?"

"I need to send people to Dorset who will be trusted, and people Ethelwold would hesitate to interfere with."

"It is an interesting idea, King. I suspect that you are thinking of priests and traveling monks."

"You are reading my mind, Archbishop. It may be dangerous for whoever goes. I have no wish to add to your already long list of martyrs."

"There will be risk, Sire, but I will only send volunteers. If my people can save the lives of good Christians, then it is their duty. It might help, however, when I present it to God's shepherds, if I can offer them some sort of incentive."

"That sounds like an interesting idea, Archbishop. What did you have in mind?"

"Oh, I don't know. Perhaps you could help me found a new monastery somewhere, maybe in Dorset. The monks could light candles and pray daily for any monks or priests who fall victim to Ethelwold's wickedness."

"I am sure, Archbishop, that I could find a choice piece of land for you."

"And I would need help with some money to build the monastery itself."

"Of course! I don't think that would be a problem. If the monks would also promise to pray daily for my father's soul, then I would be pleased to pay the entire cost."

"That would be very generous of you. I shall scour the ranks for volunteers. They will be on their way within two *nights* at most. I hope that is satisfactory?"

"That is more than satisfactory, Archbishop. It is better than I could have hoped . . . I see that Polonius has brought us a fine wine. Perhaps we can drink to our little project."

Archbishop Plegmund smiled. "With the utmost pleasure, Sire!"

CHAPTER 12

The Cousins Meet at Wimborne Minster

Three hundred West Saxon warriors rode in pairs through the open Winchester gate. Their destination was to the south and the east. Ambrose and his nephew stood at the side of the old Roman road and watched the armored host exit the royal *burh* and wheel south.

The men grinned and saluted their young king and the legendary warrior-prince known as Ambrose the Daneslayer. Most were young men, *drengs*, eager to prove their prowess. The bravest men of the Personal Guard were rewarded with gold rings, and the lucky few who won many gold rings were eventually called before their king for a greater award. Those who had showed courage and integrity were rewarded with several *hides* of land, each *hide* being large enough to support a family. The newly promoted thane then joined the ranks of the *duguos*, the veterans who held land and no longer lived with the king at his court as part of his Personal Guard, but were still required to provide military service when the king called upon them.

The *drengs* were excited, because it was only in war that they could win fame, gold, glory, and land. Scattered amongst the column were the old veterans, the *duguos* who had been visiting the royal court, or were close enough that they had been called up to swell the ranks of the eager young men.

Edward was going to war, and he, with his Personal Guardsmen and a few scrounged garrison troops from Winchester, were invading a hostile *shire*. The move was calculated to put pressure on Ethelwold, but it was a risky maneuver. The Dorset *fyrdmen* under Ethelwold's command far outnumbered the few brave men who constituted the young king's small force.

Once across the border into Dorset, the king led his force southwards at a reckless speed. Three *shires* were gathering their *fyrdmen* to ride in support of their king, but the *fyrds* assembled slowly, and it would be a week or more before appreciable numbers of loyal *fyrdmen* would reach the king's side. Thus Edward drove his men hard. He knew he had to reach a secure defensive position before Ethelwold caught him in the open with his numerically inferior force.

The young king stared in awe. The fortification that loomed before him had been old when the ancient Romans landed their all-conquering legions on the foggy coast of Britannia. Whatever part of the immense structure that had been made of wood was long gone, rotted into nothingness. The massive ramparts of rock and dirt, however, still towered over the countryside. Even eroded, they were impressive. Edward stared in admiration and then turned to Ambrose.

"Your mother's ancestors built well, Uncle. This is clearly the labor of many men working for many, many years!"

Ambrose nodded. "My mother's people, the Durotriges, lived just to the west of here and built Maiden Castle. The ancient Celtic hill-forts were well-nigh impregnable, Edward . . . at least until the Romans came, with their advanced techniques of siege-craft. Still, ruined as it is, the ramparts and heights give the defenders a major advantage, and all we have to do is to be able to hold off superior numbers of Ethelwold's *fyrdmen* until the armies of Wiltshire, Devon and Somerset arrive to join us. Meantime, we are close to Wimborne Minster and can flood the area with scouts. I have no doubt that Ethelwold will soon know of our presence if he does not already, but it is unlikely that he knows our real numbers. Our presence here should therefore at least unsettle him.

The sound of the horns brought Edward running. He clambered up the steep embankment to where the sentry was still blowing his horn.

Polonius was already there, and he turned to greet the king. "Good morning, Sire!"

Edward scanned the land below, and then spoke. "Why the alarm, Scholar?"

"King, if you look almost due east, you can see a dust cloud and the glint of metal. It is still distant, but my guess is that a column of mounted and armored men is approaching."

Edward looked back at his encampment where the men had not yet formed into ranks. "Then I guess we had better get the men into position as soon as possible! If this is Ethelwold approaching, we had better get ready for him."

"And if it is the men of Wiltshire approaching?"

The king smiled. "Then we practiced a very important maneuver."

On the king's command, the signaler changed from blowing the warning note to blowing the impatient blasts that sent the men scrambling to their defensive positions. While the men snatched their weapons and ran for their positions on the heights, Edward anxiously watched the dust cloud resolve itself into a massive column of mounted men.

The column broadened into long lines of armored horsemen, and Edward chewed his nails in anxiety. Even a quick scan told him that the advancing horsemen outnumbered his little force by at least three or four times. The column became a line, and the men slipped from their saddles and formed a shield-wall. At last the ranks halted, and a small group of men in glittering armor rode forward.

Ambrose spotted the banner first, and he smiled at Edward. "King, it is Ethelnoth of Wiltshire! The first of your reinforcements has arrived."

Edward sighed in relief. "By the many-colored coat of Joseph! I was afraid that Ethelwold had decided to take us on before we could receive our reinforcements."

Polonius spoke. "Ethelwold probably still has no idea how many men we have inside these walls, King. We have killed several of his scouts who were trying to find out."

Edward seemed to come to a decision. "Well, it no longer matters if he finds out our numbers. Tomorrow we will personally show him. Polonius, would you please arrange the details? I want all but a small garrison to ride with me to Wimborne Minster tomorrow at dawn."

"Are we attacking, Sire?"

"Let's just call it a reconnaissance-in-strength. Did not your good Chinese friend, Sun Tzu, say not to besiege walled cities if it can possibly be avoided? I concede that we might have to eventually besiege the tun, but I think an actual attack should wait until we also have the men of Devon and Somerset in our ranks."

Polonius smiled and started down the steep embankment. "Understood, Sire."

⚑

The little column of officers and messengers broke free of the forest, and a cacophony of enemy signal horns commenced immediately. The small group advanced, and suddenly, behind them, a long line of *fyrdmen* appeared all along the periphery of the woods. The long line of men stood still and silent, while the little force continued to advance.

The gates of Wimborne Minster swung open, and a small group of horsemen emerged. Led by a man wearing a crown, the little force stopped an easy spear-cast from the other group. Edward recognized his cousin Ethelwold.

Ethelwold called out. **"Have you come to bring me my proper crown, Cousin?"**

Edward responded. **"Ethelwold, you have been excommunicated and declared outlaw. Any West Saxon may** freely take your life without penalty, and the Archbishop of Canterbury himself has commanded that you are to be shunned until you make amends with Holy Mother Church for your many sins. Nevertheless, I am going to give you one chance and one chance only. If you swear to put down your arms, tell your followers to do the same, and agree to return the nun you kidnapped to her convent, I will allow you three days to collect your family and leave Wessex peacefully. This is your last chance to end all this peacefully."

Ethelwold grew furious. Spittle flew as he yelled. "Cousin, you know as well as me that I am the rightful king of Wessex! My father is buried here, at Wimborne Minster, and, as God is my witness, I will live my life and die here! Flee while you can, false king, or I will turn all Wessex into a charnel house!"

Edward sighed. "Then I guess there is nothing further to be said between us . . . I now command all loyal subjects of Wessex to strike down Ethelwold, former *ealdorman* of Dorset! As a traitor to Wessex, his life is hereby forfeit!"

Edward then spoke quietly to his cousin. "Two more shire armies march to join their king. I will be back soon to claim your head. Run while you can, coward!"

CHAPTER 13

Ethelwold Flees Wimborne Minster

Ambrose was half-asleep and thinking longingly of his beloved Gretchen as the first probing tendrils of the early morning sunshine pushed his mind toward full consciousness. Suddenly, a Saxon signal horn sounded from nearby and Gretchen faded from his arms. His consciousness instantly recognized that the call was the strident summons to arms, and his body responded. He groaned, rolled out of his cocoon of blankets and called out to Ambrose and Phillip.

"Wake up, sluggards! Some fool with a horn took my Gretchen from me along with my sleep, and now we are being called to arms! Rise and shine! There is no sense in me suffering in this morning cold all by myself."

In spite of the bantering, the three old veterans dressed within seconds, and, less than five minutes after Ambrose's dream had slipped from his grasp, the three stepped, armed and armored, out of their tent into the dawn light. Officers were rushing toward the main gate, so Ambrose and his companions followed. They climbed the tower that Edward had ordered constructed next to the new gate, and from the high vantage point they saw a force of mounted Saxons, armed, silent, and just out of arrow range.

The mysterious riders made no hostile move, but seemed to be waiting patiently. Suddenly, the cluster of men and officers along the wall was disturbed by the arrival of their young king, Archbishop Plegmund, and a score of assistants. Edward strode over to where Polonius was and looked down at the armed strangers.

"Well, Scholar, I see armed men, but we do not seem to actually be under attack."

"There are not enough to be a serious threat, Sire, unless there is another force sneaking up on us elsewhere."

"After that noise, all of our sentries should now be on the alert, Polonius. Do we know who these men are?"

Polonius looked through the aperture formed by closing his finger tight, in an attempt to cut the glare. Only then did he speak. "No, Sire. I cannot make out who they are, though they look like Saxon *fyrdmen* to me. They fly no banners."

"Then by the many-colored coat of Joseph, what are they doing here?"

"Sire, that much I can partly deduce."

"Well deduce away, my Byzantine friend!"

"They rode through the night either to attack us, join us, or parlay. I can think of no other good reason why they would be sitting outside our gates."

Edward nodded. "If they were our reinforcements, their *ealdorman* would have ridden right up and identified himself. I see no identifying banners flying, and no commanders that I recognize."

Ambrose interrupted. "Nephew, may I suggest that you order your personal banner raised high?"

The king stared at his uncle. "I am puzzled by your request, Ambrose, but I long ago learned that it is generally advisable to follow your sage advice, early morning or not. Edward turned to the thane who had been given the honor of carrying the royal banner. 'Kenward, you heard Prince Ambrose. Raise my banner high so that our mysterious visitors can know that it is indeed the rightful king of Wessex who adorns this tower!"

As the royal banner was raised into the gently blowing morning breeze, two riders broke away from the mass of mounted warriors and rode slowly toward the gate. One raised a white shield, and Edward turned to his Personal Guard who were busy nocking their arrows.

"Let no one draw their bow until I give instructions! Let us hear what our visitors have to say before we shoot them out of their saddles!"

The two riders rode to within an easy spear cast before they stopped. The warrior on the left, a big man mounted on a big roan, called out.

"I wish to speak to King Edward!"

Edward called out. "You are speaking to him. What is it that you and your men want?"

"Is it true, Sire, that *Ealdorman* Ethelwold has been relieved of his position?"

"It is true. He had three days to either bend his knee to me and swear an oath of obedience, or leave Wessex. He chose to do neither, so I have replaced him."

"Is it true, Sire, that he has been excommunicated from Holy Mother Church?"

Edward looked stern. "Just who am I talking to?"

"If it please you, Sire, my name is Oswin of Beamminster, *thane* to Ethelwold."

"Well then, *Thane* Oswin, to answer your question, Archbishop Plegmund himself, the archbishop of Canterbury and the very man who stands by my side, excommunicated Ethelwold for refusing to swear an oath of obedience to his rightful king, for kidnaping a consecrated nun from a convent, and for arranging to kill an innocent girl. He has been cast out of the church and is to be shunned by all good Christians until he rights these very serious wrongs . . . Why are you here?"

"What you have told me was reported to us by traveling monks. Sire, we are the garrison of Wimborne Minster. We are loyal *fyrdmen* of *Ealdorman* Ethelwold, sworn to an oath of obedience. As the sun set last night, Sire, Ethelwold called us together, and ordered us to hold the *tun*, even unto death. He then took his captive bride, his entire Personal Guard, and rode north, leaving us to man the walls and await your attack."

"But you are not manning the walls of Wimborne Minster, *Thane*, and you are armed for war. I repeat, why are you here?"

"Sire, we are honorable men. Our oath was to Ethelwold,

and we will obey his commands, yet the monks told us that no command of his is lawful any longer. We would like to pay our respects to our new king and bend our knee to the new *ealdorman* of Dorset, Sire, but we need assurances from the man-of-God at your side that our previous oath can be absolved."

Archbishop Plegmund looked to the king, who nodded assent. "*Thane*, I am the Archbishop of Canterbury, head of the Christian Church of all Britain. It is I who excommunicated the former *ealdorman* Ethelwold, and I now declare, in front of man and God, that you are absolved of any and all oaths to Ethelwold. Dismount, kneel before your king and Ethelhere, your new *ealdorman,* and show them the same loyalty and obedience you were prepared to show Ethelwold!"

When the two spokesmen knelt, the other *fyrdmen* dismounted, approached, and knelt with the first two. Soon several hundred former enemies were kneeling before the gates.

Edward turned to his group of advisors. "Let us open the gate and meet our new followers."

Phillip blocked his way. "Are you sure it is a good idea, King? You risk your life by going out amongst the Dorset men."

"It was you and my uncle who taught me the meaning of bravery, Phillip. I am more than a little nervous, but this is a unique opportunity to recruit Ethelwold's men to our side. If word gets out that the Dorset *fyrdmen* who come to swear allegiance are accepted and welcome in my camp, it will diminish the chances of us being forced into a long and bitter struggle against our own countrymen.' Suddenly Edward smiled. 'Come, my friend. Bring your over-sized sword, and fetch *Ealdorman* Ethelhere so we can all go and meet our new recruits."

Polonius, Phillip and Ambrose all walked close behind young King Edward. Polonius' hand hovered near his deadly throwing knives, but no member of the Wimborne garrison made any threatening gesture. To a man, they kneeled to their king and their new *ealdorman*. Archbishop Theomund raised both his arms, and there was sudden silence.

"I said before and I say again, as head of the Holy

Catholic church in Britain, I hereby absolve you of any sin in disobeying your former *ealdorman's* commands. Ethelwold is both excommunicated and declared outlaw! Before you stands Ethelhere, newly appointed *ealdorman* of Dorset. King Edward has asked me to witness your solemn oath, here and now, that you will obey *Ealdorman* Ethelhere as your legitimate ruler. When I give the command, I expect to hear the following. 'Here, in sight of king and God, I will obey all lawful commands of my *ealdorman*, Ethelhere.' Any man who does not wish to so swear may stand and leave. No one will stop or harm you, but King Edward has informed me that any *hides* of land you hold in the *ealdorman's* name will be forfeited."

Ambrose watched, his hand on ***Victory-Maker***, but no man stood, and all spoke the oath. There were still thousands of armed Dorsetmen out there, but Wimborne Minster had fallen without a fight. It was a start.

⚑

King Edward escorted the former garrison commander, Oswin by name, into the ancient and massive ring-fort that had provided temporary security for Edward and his small band of *thanes* until the *fyrdmen* from the neighboring *shires* arrived to swell the king's numbers. As they walked, he spoke to the earnest officer.

"Oswin, I need to know where Ethelwold is going. He cannot be left loose or we are going to see a civil war and thousands of innocent people are going to die."

"Sire, you are my king! I will tell you all that I know."

"And what is that?"

"Sire, two days ago, the *ealdorman's* Danes requisitioned horses and rode out of Wimborne Minster."

"Danes? Ethelwold had a force of Danes at Wimborne Minster?"

"Aye, King. There were perhaps a hundred. They were very

arrogant, but Ethelwold favored them over all others."

"Oswin, where did they come from?"

"I do not know, King. I would guess that they had a long-ship tied up somewhere on the southern coast."

"And where did they go?"

"Sire, that I do not know. They left Wimborne Minster on horseback and took the northern road. Our gates were then barred, and none of us were allowed to exit the *tun*."

"And then the next day?"

"That, Sire, is when *Ealdorman* Ethelwold told us to stay and fight to the death, while he took his treasure, his wife, and his Personal Guard, and they, too, took the northern road."

ᚱ

King Edward was young and energetic, and his mortal enemy was somewhere ahead. He pushed his horse into a cantor, and his officers were forced to increase their pace to keep up.

Ambrose pulled alongside and spoke to his nephew. "Edward, you seem keen to catch up!"

"I am, Uncle. The sooner my cousin's throat is slit, the happier I will be. I know now that he is going to cause us nothing but grief until he is put into the ground."

"On that, dear nephew, we wholeheartedly agree! I am just puzzled why his Vikings rode out ahead of him, and hope we can catch up with our errant *ealdorman* before he slips across the Thames into East Anglia.

Polonius sent his winged messengers out first thing this morning. He has asked that the entire garrison of both London and Southwark be stripped and sent to patrol the southern bank of the Thames, along with as many local *fyrdmen* as can be scrounged together."

ᚱ

On the second morning, an excited scout rode his lathered

horse straight to the king. The man was clearly exhausted, but he slipped off his horse and kneeled before King Edward.

"Sire, we have them!"

"Easy, man. What are you talking about?"

"There is a group of some eighty riders ahead, Sire! They are heading north, so they are not likely to be your *fyrdmen* answering your summons. I cannot be sure, but I think I saw *Ealdorman* Ethelwold's banner flapping in the breeze. They seem to be escorting three stout wagons."

Edward turned to Polonius. "What are our most current numbers, Scholar?"

"Your Personal Guard numbers perhaps a hundred and fifty, plus the hundred you scrounged from the Winchester garrison. You must have another two hundred of the Wiltshire *fyrdmen*, and at least fifty more from Devon joined us around noon today.

"Then we have around five hundred warriors with us?"

"That is an approximation, King, but the number is not too far off."

"Then let us push the horses and get this over with! How many of my Personal Guard have you trained with your pig-stickers?"

Polonius grinned. "All, Sire, but only a hundred are currently equipped with the long lances."

"Then let's give them the honors. I am almost embarrassed to suggest it, but I would like to propose a simple battle order. We close. We fight. They die. How does that sound?"

Polonius nodded. "They have barely enough men for a single line, so they will be very vulnerable to horsemen. In this particular situation, and with the numbers so much in our favor, I cannot think of a better plan, Sire."

Phillip, riding nearby, spoke up. "Sire, we must give them the option of surrendering before we cut them down."

Edward responded after a little hesitation. "Very well, Weapons-master, you may make the offer, but I do not want your offer to give any of them the chance to slip away."

"Understood, Sire!"

As the mass of mounted Saxons cleared the wood and

became visible, the men escorting the wagons reacted swiftly. While the wagon horses were whipped into a gallop, the rest of the men dismounted and formed a single line that stretched across the road and the open ground from woodland to woodland.

Phillip led the *thanes* with the lances, but stopped once he got within a few hundred Roman feet of the shield-wall. He called out in his stentorian voice.

"You are *fyrdmen* of Wessex, and your king, duly chosen by the *Witan*, is before you! Until now, you have kept your honor by obeying the lawful commands of your *ealdorman*. Ethelwold has been both excommunicated and declared outlaw, his life forfeit. The Archbishop of Canterbury himself has released you from your vow of obedience to him. Bow before Ethelhere, your new *ealdorman* of Dorset, and your king, and there will be no need for killing today."

In response, a tall, gaunt warrior stepped forward. His beard was long and black, and he carried a massive battle-axe that many would have trouble even lifting.

"I am Ethelwold's man, and I will die Ethelwold's man. I will not bend my knee to a young pup who is just out of diapers. Do your worst, Phillip the Weapons-master. I will teach you how a real man fights!"

With that, the tall warrior spat on the ground and then stepped back into the thin shield-wall. Phillip did not hesitate. His arm lifted above his head and then swung down. The hundred lancers kicked their mounts into a gallop and aimed the long lances at the single line of men forming the shield-wall.

The hundred lancers struck with the sound of thunder, and they tore through the hastily formed wall of men like a hot knife through butter. On the heels of the riders with the long weapons came wave after wave of mounted infantry. The Dorset warriors fought bravely, but they were simply overwhelmed by the horde of attackers. Within moments, the shield-wall became a mangled line of dead or wounded *fyrdmen*.

Ambrose personally led a force of fifty well-mounted riders through the gaping hole in the shield-wall and rode after the wagons. He had not seen Ethelwold in the battle line, and he was worried that the slippery *atheling* would manage to escape yet again. The last of the riders passed through the gap in the line cut by the lancers, and then continued along the road after the wagons.

They caught up within one or two Roman miles and surrounded each wagon. Two of the three wagon-drivers, accepting the inevitable, brought their horses to a halt and then raised their hands, but one driver continued to flee blindly. Finally, two riders leapt to the back of the lead horses and pulled at the reins, while a third speared the driver.

The third wagon was brought back to join the first two, and Ambrose dismounted to see what so many had died for.

The massively-built wagon contained a quantity of silver and some gold, while the second contained food and supplies. The third contained a very upset woman who was chained by the ankle to the frame of the wagon. When she saw Ambrose's face, she cried out. "God has answered my pleas! I have been kidnapped and made a prisoner by *Ealdorman* Ethelwold! I pray, sir, that you will set me free so I may return to my real vocation."

Ambrose smiled at the beautiful woman so incongruously wearing heavy fetters. "And what is that, my lady?"

"I am a bride of Christ, sir, ripped from my convent, raped and forced to marry a vile man or see my mother tortured and killed right before my eyes.'

She burst into tears. 'Who are you, sir, and may I go home?"

"I am Ambrose, *atheling* of Wessex and uncle of the king. You are safe, Sister, and I will personally arrange an escort to take you wherever you wish to go, but first I need information."

"Ask what you want, Prince. I have heard the ballads about you and will help you in any way that I can."

"Good. Most important, I need to know where Ethelwold is!"

"I only wish that I could tell you, Prince Ambrose. The truth is - I don't know."

"What is your name, Sister?"

"I am Sister Mary-Eve, Prince."

"Well, Sister Mary-Eve, how is it that you do not know where your husband is?"

"In God's eyes, he is no husband of mine! Do not think that I do not want to tell you, Prince. She held up her shackled leg. He took me from my convent cell, kidnapped me, stripped me naked, raped me repeatedly, and chained me when I tried to escape. I hope that God will forgive my wicked thoughts, but I want him to suffer the torments of hell for what he did to me!"

"Then when did you see him last?"

"He was in camp last night, sir, but he called his men together and had them swear an oath to protect me from King Edward's men. With that, he took a little gold and a dozen of his favorite *thanes*, and they rode into the darkness."

"Sister, do you know where he was heading?"

"He did not say, sir, but he said two days ago that he was sending his Danes ahead to prepare his boat."

"Do you know where this boat is?"

"No, Prince, just that it was somewhere along the southern coast of Dorset, beached beside the 'drinking dragon'. I do not know what or where that is."

"Then you think this column was just a feint to throw us off his scent?"

"I think he hoped that we would make it into Viking territory. He told me that he couldn't wait to use the kiss of the whip to teach me proper manners. He was afraid that King Edward's northern garrisons would effectively block the river, however, so he made alternate plans for himself. He left several hundred of his loyal *fyrdmen* to defend Wimborne Minster to the death. He made them swear not to surrender. Then, last night, he ordered us to ride hard for the Thames, steal a boat, and cross into East Anglian territory. He then abandoned us, with the same instructions to the men to fight to the death if any of the king's forces caught up with us."

CHAPTER 14

Ambrose, Polonius and Edward Meet

King Edward watched Ambrose approach from the north. He called out when the prince neared.

"Did you have any luck, Uncle?"

"The wagons will arrive shortly, Sister Mary-Eve is safe, and we only had to kill one driver. And you?"

Edward gestured toward the battleground. "Most of Ethelwold's men died in the initial charge. They killed eight of our men, and wounded another twenty. Most fought bravely, and I was saddened to see good men on both sides die.' He paused.

'Was there any sign of Ethelwold?"

Ambrose nodded. "There is a little news, but you are not going to like it."

"Uncle, what did you find out?"

"Ethelwold left late last night with a dozen of his best men. Sister Mary-Eve thinks he turned south and headed for a Viking long-ship tied up somewhere on the southern coast beside a 'drinking dragon'."

"By the many-colored coat of Joseph! Then this was a diversion for us while he rode in the other direction! Damn the man! He is too clever by a half . . . You said 'drinking dragon'?"

"That was the phrase Sister-Mary-Eve used."

"Several years ago, when I was riding along the Dorset coast, we came across a strange rock formation. It has a large arch at one end, and kind of looked like a 'drinking-dragon'. I think the locals called it the 'Durdle Door'."

Ambrose nodded. "Then, my king, we have a destination! If we ride hard for this Durdle Door, we just might have a chance to catch up with Ethelwold."

Edward sighed. "Let's do a *Long Ride*! Innocent men died today because of Ethelwold. I want his head separated from his body, and the sooner the better. Uncle, what about this Sister Mary-Eve? What are we going to do with her?"

"Ethelwold had her chained in one of the wagons. It is pretty clear that she was forced into this marriage. Ethelwold threatened to torture her mother if she refused to marry him. I think we should ask the archbishop to annul the marriage, and then we should return her to the convent. She has been through quite enough."

"Agreed, Uncle. Perhaps Phillip can take her back to Winchester for now, while the rest of us go after Ethelwold."

"Nephew, you know that Phillip will be upset if you send him back."

"Uncle, there is no more steady warrior anywhere in Wessex, but the real truth is, he looks to be in a lot of pain. A slow ride back, escorting the three wagons, should be a lot easier on him then a mad dash across the entire *shire* of Dorset."

"Then let it be a king's command. He would be heartbroken if I sent him back."

Edward smiled. "And you were the one who taught me what bravery was!"

Ambrose smiled in return. "There are limits to every man's bravery, oh great king! I owe no man in the world more than I owe that great walking oak tree!"

ↄ

Ambrose's voice boomed across the field. **"All men form into pairs . . . Every other man hand his horse over to his partner! We are going on a *Long Ride*, and I want no wounded or sick with me. Decide between you who is most fit. Throw the *bones* or flip a coin if you must. We ride in two minutes!"**

Edward spoke to his uncle. "Ambrose, half leaves you with but two hundred men. You just might find yourself outnumbered when Ethelwold reaches his Viking allies."

"Then, my favorite nephew, I guess we had better catch up before Ethelwold reaches his allies! I intend to at least damn-well try!"

"Then I ride with you. I cannot send men into danger that I am personally unwilling to face."

Ambrose smiled. "It is an exhausting maneuver, Edward, and you will have cause to regret volunteering, but I can hardly say 'no' to the king of Wessex."

Edward grinned. "I should think not, and I will match you stride for stride."

"Then steal another horse from somewhere, my king. It is time to ride!"

෴

The chosen warriors, two hundred strong and leading an equal number of spare mounts, moved south at a fast trot. Ethelwold had some hour's head-start, and the riders were eager to catch up.

The long riders stopped only occasionally, to pick up supplies from the royal estates scattered across the land, to ask about any riders that might have passed recently, and to trade in any lame horses for fresh ones. The warriors pushed south at a breakneck speed.

As the force caught the first glimpses of sea far ahead, Ambrose ordered a halt. Edward, looking exhausted, moved close to Ambrose. "Well, Uncle? What do we do next?"

"Is it impolite to tell a king that he looks terrible?"

"Is it impolite for a stiff and sore king to complain? I can hardly move."

"I told you that you would have cause to regret coming along, Edward."

"You did, Uncle, but I perhaps foolishly thought that resilient youth could overcome any obstacle."

"I will ask Polonius to find you some of his famous liniment.

You father went through a great deal of it on our *Long Ride* through Wales."

"There is the coast in the distance, Uncle. What do we do?"

"Nephew and king, the coast is long. I suggest we split into two forces of a hundred. One can follow the coast starting here, while the other makes a dash for this 'Durdle Door'."

"That hardly gives us overwhelming superiority of numbers."

Ambrose shrugged. "It is a risk, King, but the numbers are sufficient if we catch up before Ethelwold joins the Danes. It gives us two chances instead of one. Ethelwold cannot be far ahead."

Edward sighed and rubbed his behind. "So be it. I am for the Durdle Door. Split the men, and let's ride!"

The two forces split and rode for their designated targets. Ambrose, Polonius and Edward led their little force toward Lulworth Cove, stopping only to question any people they met.

At the fourth little fishing settlement they came across, Ambrose rode alone through the open gate and into the area that served as a square for the local inhabitants, while the others waited nearby. Seeing a tall thin man pushing a two-wheeled cart, he called out to him.

"You there, sir! Have you seen any Danes hereabouts?"

The tall man set down the handle of his cart, then looked Ambrose up and down before replying. "And who is asking?"

"I am Ambrose, *atheling* of Wessex."

The man hesitated. "Are you the bastard brother of old King Alfred?"

Ambrose twisted a bit, trying to find a portion of skin on his buttocks that did not feel flayed. "Aye, I am that Ambrose. Can you help me?"

"Prince, I am sworn to *Ealdorman* Ethelwold."

"Ethelwold has been excommunicated by the church and declared outlaw by the king. You owe the man no further obedience. Ethelhere is now master of Wessex, and any men who do not swear allegiance to him will be dispossessed and driven from this *shire*."

"Aye, that is what the traveling monks told us. I do not know either *ealdorman* personally, but I know of you, sir. You are a legend in these parts. If you can assure me that God will forgive me for breaking a sacred oath, then I will answer your question."

"The Archbishop of Canterbury himself stated that all followers of Ethelwold are absolved of their oaths of loyalty to him."

The tall man suddenly smiled. "Who would not believe Canuteson of the Rus? Prince, there is a Viking long-ship beached not far from here, near Durdle Door."

Ambrose smiled. "That name is familiar and is, in fact, where we were trying to head, but we do not know the exact location of Durdle Door. Where exactly is it?"

"About three Roman miles along the coast."

"You let a Viking long-ship beach on your coast there?"

"Prince, *Ealdorman* Ethelwold's men were present to make sure that no one made a hostile move, and when the Danes came through several days ago, they had a pass direct from the *ealdorman* himself."

"Several days ago?"

"Aye, Prince. Prince, do you think that King Edward will come this way?"

Ambrose smiled. "I know he will. Do you see that man on the roan over there?"

"Aye, Prince."

"That is your very tired and sore king. He has not left that saddle for more than a few minutes in more than twenty-four hours."

"May I give him my obeisance?"

Ambrose nodded. "He needs to catch his breath and, truth to tell, he needs all the friends he can get in Dorset. Go ahead."

The tall thin man strode through the gate to where the *fyrdmen* waited with their king. As the villager approached the king, Polonius edged his coat back, and his fingers slipped close to his throwing knives. When Ambrose shook his head, however, Polonius did nothing further.

The villager slipped to his knees in front of the king. "Edward, king of Wessex, I took an oath of loyalty to your father when I joined the shield-wall at Wareham. I now pledge my loyalty to you. I am your man."

Edward smiled through his pain. "I thank you for those words, sir. What is your name?"

"I am known as Tall Eric, King. I am a fisherman and headman of this little *vill*."

"Well, Tall Eric, I am glad to know that I have at least one sworn man in Dorset!"

"You will soon have many more, Sire. Ethelwold was not universally beloved. We are stubborn people, though, and most remain loyal to their oath. You will have to make it clear that Ethelwold is no longer our rightful leader."

"Speaking of Ethelwold, Tall Eric, have you heard of or seen him recently?"

"His henchmen, the Danes, came and requisitioned food just yesterday. The arrogant devils took what they wanted without recompense. When we complained, they just laughed and said that King Ethelwold would come and pay for the supplies."

Exhausted as he was, Edward perked up. "And have you seen Ethelwold recently?"

"Aye, King. I thought that that might be the reason you are here. He passed by just after sunrise."

"And do you know where he was headed?"

"He did not stop and said nothing, Sire, but he had a Dane with him, and he headed in the general direction of the long-ship."

"With how many men?"

"Not more than a dozen, King."

"Then spread the word for me, Tall Eric. Ethelhere is the rightful *ealdorman* of Dorset, and we must try and catch Ethelwold before he escapes to wreck havoc elsewhere! Can you show us where that Viking ship is?"

"Aye, King. T'would be a pleasure!"

"Can you ride?"

"I served in the *fyrd*, Sire. I had to learn to stay on a horse to keep up with your father."

"Excellent. Take my spare mount here, and let's ride!"

☙

The land was gently undulating and very open. The riders, exhausted as they were, made excellent time. Suddenly, Tall Eric reined in, and the riders found themselves on the edge of a cliff. Far below was a beach, and then the sea. To the left was a giant rock formation that looked to Ambrose as if a dragon was dipping its snout into the water.

Ambrose turned to Tall Eric. "Is that rock formation what you call the Durdle Door?"

"Aye, Prince. That is it."

Polonius had dismounted and walked close to the edge. Suddenly he pointed.

"There is the ship, Master! It is just below us!"

The men scrambled to the very edge of the cliff, and the Viking long-ship came into view when they looked down. The ship had been launched, and the Viking crewmen were just sliding their oars into the water.

Even as Edward and Ambrose watched, the lithe vessel slipped through the surf and into deeper water. The crew pulled for the open sea. The captain looked up and saw the West Saxons silhouetted on the top of the cliff. He waved his hand in farewell.

Edward was furious. "By the many-colored coat of Joseph! My cousin escapes justice yet again!"

Polonius spoke. "We can only hope, Sire, that a squadron of our navy comes across them and sinks them."

The king sighed. "I guess dead is dead, though that was not the death I envisioned for him!"

CHAPTER 15

Ethelwold Escapes

An exhausted rider swayed before his king and Polonius, who was generally known as the 'scholar', but was sometimes known as 'spymaster'. The Byzantine handed the rider a horn of water and encouraged him to report.

"Lord Polonius, King Edward, lookouts at Lands-End report spotting a single Viking sail far out to sea, clearing the point and heading north."

Ambrose turned to Edward. "It makes sense, Sire. Ethelwold must have been on that ship we saw near Durdle Door. No one else has been able to get so much as a glimpse of him, in spite of our little feathered messengers and relays of riders spreading out in all directions. Tall Eric swore that it was Ethelwold who passed his little vill."

Edward looked puzzled. "What, exactly, are you thinking, Scholar?"

"That we were on his trail, but we were too slow. After abandoning the wagons and most of his men, he turned south and rode to the coast. His trick of throwing us off the scent by deliberately sending a majority of his men, the wagons, and his new wife, north toward the Thames and East Anglia was quite successful. It bought him the time necessary to reach the ship. Do you realize that in order to obscure his tracks, he first abandoned his followers in Dorset, then his men at Wimborne Minster, and finally his wife and most of the rest of his loyal followers?"

"Scholar, aside from the search parties we had out, I had the entire West Saxon fleet on the lookout for any Viking craft off our southern coast! I am surprised that he dared take the water route north."

"Aye, Sire. You did - but the fleet moved mainly between Dorset and Portsmouth. Few ships went as far west as the Durdle Door. We had over fifty vessels, armed and ready for battle, but if the Viking ship sailed west by night, or, more likely, used a *sunstone* and sailed far out from shore, it would likely have encountered few of our ships and had clear passage all the way to the west coast of Northumbria."

"Then, by Christ's beard, we must assume that he was on that ship. That must be how he got away from us!"

CHAPTER 16

The Coronation

Archbishop Plegmund, as spiritual leader of all Christian Britain, was used to having his way. As Ambrose listened, the learned church leader matched wits with Edward.

"Sire, I have the scroll in my hand. This is the procedure your father followed, and his father before him! You cannot interrupt the solemn march to the church with these . . . these theatrics."

"My good Archbishop, I am not being crowned king of just Wessex. I am going to be crowned king of all the free Angles and Saxons of this island, and I expect your words to emphasize that! The Jutes of Kent are already part of the procession. The symbolism of the Angle Mercians crossing the river and joining with the West Saxons and Jutes for the Grand March to the church is crucial. A sovereign king, and his queen, who just happens to be Ethelflæd, my beloved sister, will fall in behind the West Saxon nobility, both lay and ecclesiastical. Together, united, the Angles, Saxons and Jutes will march to my coronation."

The archbishop tried another tack. "But, Sire, the church is small! There is barely room inside for your family, the *ealdormen*, my bishops, the clergy and a choir. Now you are telling me to make room for another king and his retinue!"

"My dear Archbishop, there are also ambassadors from the Welsh kingdoms and the Continent. The bishops can stay. The many priests you have brought will have to join my own Personal Guard outside the church. We will, of course, make room for the choir."

"Sire, you are recklessly changing a time-honored tradition! I simply cannot approve."

Edward grew annoyed. "Archbishop, if anyone deserves to be by my side for my coronation, it is King Ethelred and my own darling sister, who have been, it should be noted, staunch defenders of Holy Mother Church, and have fought steadfastly and faithfully at our side for years. No one has paid more in lives and property for freedom than our northern Angle cousins. Ethelred has acknowledged me as over-king, and the symbolism is vital for my future plans. We must welcome our Angle cousins into the West Saxon empire, not insult future countrymen."

Plegmund sighed. "Very well, Sire, I understand the politics of what you request, but I must insist that a bishop of Mercia lead the column across the river."

Edward smiled his dazzling smile. "I am sure I can persuade Ethelred to allow a bishop to ride with the royal party, Archbishop, and I will talk with King Ethelred about a generous donation to Mother Church. I do believe you have found a solution, and for that I thank you!"

The archbishop pursed his lips. "Your 'solution' would be a terrible insult to the bishop who will be relegated to such a secondary role. I am not sure, Sire, that I could ask it of anyone."

Edward looked thoughtful. "Perhaps if I could persuade King Ethelred to offer some prime Mercian land as *bookland* . . ."

The archbishop sighed again. "I suppose that I could ask. It would have to be a generous donation to Mother Church and a choice piece of land, however. It is a big insult for a bishop to swallow . . . Very well, King Edward. If you meet those conditions, I will bow to your request."

⚑

The Archbishop of Canterbury smiled at the nervous young king. "Sire, all is ready."

"Then pray let us start, Archbishop."

Plegmund gestured silently, and two bishops positioned themselves on either side of the king. Their task was to lead Edward by the hand to the church. With incense and sonorous chants filling the air, the archbishop led the glittering column of churchmen and noblemen out of the Great Hall that was being used as a gathering place for the procession, and toward the church that sat near the winding river.

As the column approached the river ford, horns suddenly sounded from across the river. The Archbishop of Canterbury halted the royal column while the king and queen of Mercia, followed by dozens of important noblemen and officials, followed by Ethelred's entire Personal Guard, rode directly to the ford and crossed the Thames River into Wessex. Edward smiled and waited while the glittering column splashed across the river and joined the rear of the column. Once in position, the entire retinue dismounted, and young stable hands, who had been waiting excitedly, stepped forward to take the reins of the many horses.

At last the two columns were joined, and the solemn procession continued. As Edward neared the door of the church, the two bishops began to chant a hymn.

"Let thy hands be strengthened,

Glory be to the Father, and to the Son, and to the Holy Ghost . . ."

As the hymn continued, Edward was led the length of the church, and then the Archbishop signaled that he was to prostrate himself in front of the alter. As the king lowered himself to the ground, the archbishop led the entire assembled crowd in a second hymn.

"We praise thee, O God, we acknowledge thee to be the Lord . . ."

As the hymn ended, the archbishop and several *ealdormen* helped raise the king to his feet. Archbishop Plegmund's voice filled the church. **"Edward, descendent of Cerdic, the bishops and the people of Wessex have chosen you as their next king. As such, they raise you to your feet, and to your position. In return, we ask that you promise to keep three laws, and to declare so before God and all the people of Wessex."**

Edward had practiced for hours, and he did not even look at the parchment he held in his hand. He spoke the words.

"In the name of Christ, I promise three things to the Christian people - my subjects. First, that the Church of God, and all the Christian people, shall always preserve true peace through our arbitration. Second, that I will forbid rapacity and all iniquities to every condition. Third, that I will command equity and mercy in all judgments, that to me and to you the gracious and merciful God may extend his mercy."

The Archbishop recited another prayer, and then lifted Edward's crown above his head. He then prayed.

"Almighty Creator, everlasting Lord, Governor of heaven and earth, the Maker and Disposer of angels and men, King of Kings and Lord of Lords, who made thy faithful servant Abraham to triumph over his enemies, and gavest manifold victories to Moses and Joshua, the prelates of thy people, and did raise David thy lowly child to the summit of thy kingdom, and didst free him from the mouth of the lion and the paws of the bear, and from Goliath, and from the malignant sword of Saul and of his enemies, and who didst endow Solomon with the ineffable gift of wisdom and peace; look down propitiously on our humble prayers, and multiply the gifts of thy blessing on this thy servant, whom with humble devotion we have chosen to be king of the Angles and the Saxons; surround him everywhere with the right hand of thy power, that strengthened with the faithfulness of Abraham, the meekness of Moses, the courage of Joshua, the humility of David, and the wisdom of Solomon, he may be well pleasing to thee in all things, and may always advance in the way of justice with inoffensive progress. May he so nourish, teach, defend, and instruct the church of all the kingdom of the Anglo-Saxons, with the people annexed to it, and so potently and royally rule it against all visible and invisible enemies, that he may never desert the royal throne and scepter of the Angles and Saxons; but that he may keep their minds in the harmony of the pristine faith and peace. May he, supported by the due subjection of the people, and blessed by thy love through a long life, govern and establish it, aided with they united mercy and glory. Defended with the helmet and invincible shield of Thy protection, and surrounded with celestial arms, may he obtain the triumph of victory over all his enemies, and pour the terror of his power on all the unfaithful, and shed peace on those joyfully fighting for thee. Adorn him with the virtues with which thou hast decorated thy faithful servant; place him high in his dominion, and anoint him with the grace of thy Holy Spirit."

Ambrose watched as Archbishop Plegmund anointed Edward with oil, while a choir of priests sang another hymn.

When the hymn finished, the Archbishop turned to the assembled noblemen and began another prayer.

"O Christ, anoint this king with the power with which thou has anointed priests, kings, prophets, and martyrs; who, by faith have conquered kingdoms, enforced justice, and gained Thy promises. Let Thy most sacred unction be poured on his head, and descend on him internally, and penetrate into his heart; and let him be rendered worthy of Thy grace and promises, which the most victorious kings have obtained, so that he may reign happily in the present life, and may join their communion in thy heavenly kingdom."

As the ceremony continued, Ambrose's mind wandered. Alfred had achieved much in his years as king, but Wessex still shared an island with fierce Viking warriors who were ever land-hungry. He knew that the West Saxons were still not masters of the entire island, and feared that much more blood would be shed before the contest was settled. He roused again when Archbishop Plegmund plucked a gleaming sword off a silken cushion and began yet another prayer.

"Receive this sword, given to thee together with the blessing of God, with which, through the virtue of the Holy Spirit, you may be able to resist and throw down all your enemies, and all the adversaries of the Church of God; to defend the kingdom entrusted to thee, and to protect the most invincible Conqueror, our Lord Jesus Christ, who with the Father, in the unity of the Spirit, lives and reigns."

Ambrose 's mind wandered again as the archbishop handed Edward the sword and immediately started another prayer. Next

Plegmund reached for the royal scepter and then the staff. A prayer preceeded and followed each presentation to Edward. While Ambrose's eyes took in the spectacle, he thought about Ethelwold. Somewhere, presumably in Northumbria, was an angry and ambitious man who would do all he could to dispossess Edward and take his throne. Ethelwold had sworn that he would die defending the seized estate where his father was buried, but he had abandoned his followers and ran like a coward when Edward had brought his small force to Badbury Rings.

Ambrose snapped back to attention when Archbishop Plegmund began a speech to Edward.

"Stand and retain now the state which you have held by paternal succession with the hereditary right, delegated to thee by the authority of Almighty God, and by this our present delivery, that is, of all the Bishops and other servants of God, and insomuch as thou hast beheld the clergy nearer the sacred altars, so much more remember to pay them due homage in suitable places, so may the mediator, God and man, confirm thee the mediator of the clergy and the common people on the throne of his kingdom, and make thee reign with him in his eternal kingdom."

After one last prayer, Edward's consecration was complete, and Archbishop Plegmund led the royal party out of the little church to thunderous applause from the several thousand *thanes*, *churls*, priests and common folk who had gathered outside the church. The procession retraced the route it had taken earlier, but now it was lead by a consecrated king. The real celebration was about to begin!

CHAPTER 17

A Visit from an Old Friend

The burly Viking walked slowly along the main street of Westchester. He was old, and by his costume, he was from far away. Ambrose turned to Polonius. "By the beard of sweet Jesus, that old man approaching reminds me of an aged version of our old friend, Hammar of the *Rus*."

Polonius turned and stared at the shambling man. The old man wore a *Rus* costume, and his features were disturbingly familiar. The puzzle was solved in an instant. The man saw Ambrose and Polonius, and called out in the *Rus* tongue. "Can it really be little Ambrose and the Byzantine strategist?"

Ambrose closed the distance and hugged the old man tight. This was the brave captain who had risked his life to allow Ambrose and his friends to escape the clutches of Grand Chamberlain Basil, one of the most powerful men in the Byzantine world. They had parted on the docks of Constantinople, Hammar playing decoy to the imperial Byzantine navy and heading north into the Black Sea, while Ambrose and his companions sailed south in a tiny boat. Now, almost thirty-five years later, they were re-united on the streets of Winchester.

Ambrose finally let go and Polonius squeezed him tight in turn. At last, as Polonius let go, Ambrose spoke. "Hammar, my friend, what are you doing here?"

The old man grinned, revealing several teeth still proudly jutting out of his gums. "Don't you have a cargo ship arrive from Gunnarson yearly?"

"Yes, but the ship docks in London, and every time I asked about you, I was told that you were still out somewhere in the wilderness, plying the Asian rivers."

"Aye, that would have been true, until a few months ago. A man gets old and wants to return to his homeland.' He grinned again. 'The truth is, I am old and tired. I am not sure that I can join the *skjaldborg* and hold my own any longer. I thought of being a berserker in my next skirmish, and so earning my way to *Valhalla,* but then I decided it was time to see my homeland one more time, while I still can."

Ambrose smiled. "But the land of the *Rus* is still a very long way from here, my friend!"

"Aye, but I had been home for over a week and was already getting restless when Gunnarson let it slip that he had a stout *knarr* heading for Wessex, taking a cargo to an old Dnieper River trader by the name of Canuteson. The ship is a pig in the water, not like the sleek long-ships I captained on the eastern rivers, but there are no portages or nomad raiders to deal with, and, besides, I wanted to see some old friends, so I asked Gunnarson if I could captain the ship - and here I am!"

"Well, whatever the reason that you are here, I am glad! I never had the chance to thank you properly for the gift of the *sunstone* and for sailing north to draw off pursuit. It probably saved our lives. Come now! I am a poor host. Come to the king's Great Hall, and I will order both food and drink until you disappear under the table."

"Ho! We shall see who slips under the table first! I hope that Polonius and Phillip can join us in our heroic endeavor to single-handedly empty Winchester of its entire mead supply!"

Polonius smiled and answered. "I would consider it an honor, and Phillip will not forgive me if I do not send for him!"

Hammar clanked his horn cup with Ambrose's, and then spoke. "And what goods have you collected for me to take back to Gunnarson?"

"The cargo is waiting for you in London, my friend. I have a large cargo of good Anglish wool, several hundred ingots of tin, and a load of linen."

"Excellent, Gunnarson will be pleased. He asked, however, for as much more wool as you can find. It is presently in short supply back home and selling dearly."

"Then I will ask my buyers to scour London, my friend. I will arrange for local merchants to make the purchases so the price is not driven up unduly. If they see your face and hear your accent, the price will triple."

"It is not necessary for you to go to all that trouble, Canuteson. I will take what you have."

"It is the least I can do for my old *Rus* friends. A messenger with the instructions will be winging his way to London with the rising of the sun, and the goods will be waiting for you when you return to your ship. Now let me pour you another cup of that mead. It is from the king's own stock."

Ambrose lifted his cup of mead and smiled at Hammar. "And what cargo do you have for me this year, my friend?"

"Gunnarson sent a load of what I am told you ignorant Saxons like to think of as unicorn horns. I have two dozen narwhale horns, a mountain of walrus tusks, and hundreds of feet of whale-hide rope."

Polonius asked eagerly. "Do you have any amber this year?"

Hammar smiled, exposing his few remaining teeth. "So it is amber you covet, is it? Well, Gunnarson told me that he has sent you the best collection he has amassed in years."

"And the most important goods of all?"

"Gunnarson tells me that you have already imported most of the *sun-stones* in the Viking lands . . . No, do not look so sad, my friend. I am only teasing you. I have over a dozen more for you."

"You know, my friend, the one you gave me as we parted saved my life. I owe you a debt of gratitude for that."

"Did it allow you to escape a sea fog?"

"No, it actually saved my life on land."

Gunnar looked surprised. "That is unusual! How did it help?"

"Well, we joined a camel caravan and were on our way home along the coast of North Africa, when our route west was blocked by a hostile Byzantine naval contingent. The only way past them was to ride into a trackless sand desert that even the local tribesmen would not enter. The cloud cover was almost continuous, and without the *sun-stone*, we would never have found our way out again."

Hammar belched loudly. "Then I am glad that it was of use to you."

"And now you tell me that you have more for me! I will pay for them in gold, Hammar."

"No you won't, boy! They have already been paid for, in full."

Ambrose looked puzzled. "How is that possible?"

Hammar grinned. "Gunnarson tells me that you pay double the weight in gold."

"That has been our agreed price, for several years."

"And the cost has already been deducted from the gold that Gunnarson holds for you."

"And I had enough gold to cover the cost?"

Gunnar snorted. "It barely dented your hoard. Canuteson, you are a very wealthy man! Some day you must come north and collect all your treasure - or let me bring it south for you."

"I don't understand, Hammar."

"Prince, Gunnarson's trade routes now extend beyond Constantinople - all the way to Alexandria. He bypasses the greedy Greek merchants of Byzantium completely, and trades directly with your old friend Hakim. The direct trade has been extraordinarily lucrative, and Hakim insists each year that five percent of his profits goes to you, Polonius and Phillip via Gunnarson."

"I knew that Hakim had sent money north in my name, and I have always told Gunnar, and now his son, to re-invest our earnings in his trading company."

"They both did so, Canuteson. We now also do a lot of trade down the Volga River, all the way to the Caspian Sea. Gunnar, and now Gunnarson, have done extraordinarily well. Your share makes you a very rich man."

"Hammar, my old friend, you have no idea how close we came to moving back to your homeland just a few months ago."

"You would leave this land, where you are a prince and a

great hero? Even I have heard the ballads they sing about you and your exploits. The *Rus* are proud that you lived with us and laugh, but I have noticed that the Danes are not always so amused. You have made several of their kings and jarls look like rank fools."

"A few months ago, my brother Alfred died."

"I have heard of this Alfred. I am told that many already call him Alfred the Great."

"He was indeed a great man, but after his death, the son of his older brother tried to sway our council into appointing him king, and when that did not succeed, he rose in armed rebellion."

"Canuteson, I am an old man and speak with an old man's bluntness. Forgive me for saying so, but I never knew you to run from a fight."

"Hammar, if the Witan, the council of noblemen and advisors, had selected the *atheling* over Alfred's own son, I would have left for the north within days. I had two dragon ships prepared, crewed, and ready to leave at a moment's notice. I firmly believe that my entire family would have been murdered within a month or two after Ethelwold took the throne."

"So this Ethelwold is the villain of your tale? That is a familiar name. Give an old man a moment to dig into his memory . . . Ah, I remember now!' Hammar reached deep into his pouch and pulled out a newly-minted silver coin. 'Canuteson, I think I told you that I stopped in Jorvik on the way south. I did a little trade in walrus tusks and was paid with a few new coins.' He tossed a shiny silver coin to Ambrose. 'Have you ever seen its like before?"

Ambrose examined the coin closely, then got up and walked closer to the window so that the coin was lit by the direct sunlight.

Ambrose spoke excitedly. "Hammar, do you know the implications of this new coin?"

"I know that it was struck to honor the crowning of the new king of Jorvik."

Ambrose looked stunned, and Polonius silently reached out for the coin. When he read the words, he exclaimed. "By the robe of sweet Jesus! The inscription says 'Rex Ethelwold!'"

Phillip looked at both of his friends and spoke. "What does

this mean?"

Ambrose replied. "It means that the man we chased away, declared outlaw, and arranged to have excommunicated from Holy Mother Church, has been made king of Jorvik!"

Phillip's jaw dropped. "Ethelwold king of Viking Jorvik! It is not possible!"

Ambrose replied. "It seems to be true, nevertheless. Phillip, would you please send one of the sentries for King Edward! He has to see this coin and hear what Hammar has to say."

Hammar looked confused. "Canuteson, is this truly the man of which you speak?"

Ambrose sighed. "I pray that the name is a coincidence, but our southern fleet turned back several ship-loads of Jorvik's Vikings just before my brother's death, and we believe Ethelwold escaped north on a Northumbrian long-ship. It is more than likely that my dear cousin is now ruler of the most powerful Viking kingdom on the island of Britain!"

Polonius nodded. "Then Wessex will inevitably be going to war."

Hammar looked puzzled. "You proved yourself to be a great scholar, Polonius but can you also see into the future?"

"No, my friend, but the only reason the Danes of Jorvik would crown a Saxon as their king is because they know it would split the *thanes* and *ealdormen* of Wessex. Once brother fights brother to a bloody standstill, then the Danes can step in and easily finish off the battered remnants of the West Saxon army. It is how they conquered Northumbria - the land they now call Jorvik."

"Then I bring you bad news. I am truly sorry."

Ambrose smiled at the old man. "No, my friend. What would be truly bad is for us not to know while Ethelwold and his Danes prepare for invasion!"

CHAPTER 18

Alba

Ambrose smiled across at Polonius as the scholar entered the king's planning room. The gaunt Byzantine had been called away to meet with one of his couriers, and he was out-of-breath from rushing back to the meeting with King Edward.

The king spoke. "Perhaps we should hear the news first from our illustrious spymaster. Polonius, what news did you receive today?"

"I have just received word from King Constantine of *Alba*, Sire."

"And are the Scots and Picts willing to send sufficient numbers of their warriors into Northumbria?"

"Neither the Picts and the Scots have much love for the Saxons, Sire. They still see your ancestors as savage invaders."

"Our ancestors invaded several centuries ago, Scholar, as pagan barbarians. Now, as fellow Christians, we must put old spats aside and unite in the face of a common foe!"

"King Constantine is well aware that we want to use his young men to distract the Vikings of Jorvik from our shores. He is no fool, Sire."

Edward sighed. "I know, Polonius. That is why we are offering him large sums of gold and a ship-load of weapons. His men do what they have done for centuries, he gets paid in silver and gold for it, and, not incidentally, we arm a large numbers of his warriors with the best of weapons."

"But he could pay a terrible price if the Vikings decide to retaliate and invade his northern lands again."

"Polonius, I think you are trying to tell me that our offer has been rejected."

"Not exactly, King."

"I am afraid you are confusing a king. Does he accept the offer or not?"

"The answer is yes - but there are conditions."

Edward was beginning to look exasperated. "I humbly await your explanation, Scholar."

"The Picts raided before, in alliance with your father, but you are an unknown to him, and Constantine doesn't know if you are able to handle the Danes. He made two suggestions."

"Yes, Polonius?"

"First, that you journey to their land and fight alongside them."

Edward snorted in derision. "I hardly think that possible, Scholar. What of the threat of East Anglia? And what of the various Viking fleets that dog our shores? And we know that somewhere in Northumbria is my cousin, plotting to replace me on the throne of Wessex."

"As I said, Sire, he had two proposals."

Edward sighed. "I am listening, my Byzantine friend."

"He said that since he had heard all of the ballads, he would also accept three famous and legendary heroes in your place."

"Three legendary heroes? And I assume that all three must still be alive. Hmm. I can only assume that he means Phillip, Ambrose and you."

Polonius smiled. "The words he used embarrass me, Sire, but they are a direct quote from his letter."

Edward sighed. "An attack by the Scots and Picts is the only way I can think to tie down a large body of Northumbrian Vikings. It is possibly vital to our defense . . . are you, Phillip and Ambrose willing to make the journey?"

Ambrose replied for the three of them. "We have sworn to serve Wessex. If you need us to go, then go we shall!"

CHAPTER 19

Ambrose Is Intercepted by Danes

The two sleek long-ships pushed northward. When possible, they raised the great square sail and used the wind, but when it stopped, or blew contrary, the men pushed out the oars and rowed. With a good breeze and stops only on uninhabited islands, Ambrose and his two crews made good time. Wales was far astern and the ships slipped past the Norse holdings with no challenges. Soon after reaching the Scottish coast, however, three long-ships rounded a headland and altered course toward the Saxon vessels.

The Viking ships were in front of Ambrose's two vessels, so the prince gave no orders to flee. Instead, he ordered the sails to be lowered, and then sent the rowers to their benches. The other three long-ships approached gracefully on oars, and then, in unison, pulled them in. The three boats floated serenely in front of Ambrose's two.

The captain of the first vessel called out through a speaking trumpet. **"Well met, stranger! Who are you and where are you going?"**

Ambrose picked up the speaking trumpet. **"I am Canuteson of the Danes. Who wants to know?"**

"I am Godwulf, *jarl* to Ivar the Fat"

"Well met, *Jarl* Godwulf. We are free men heading for the coast of *Alba*."

"Then you are almost there, Canuteson, but if you are looking for loot, I suspect that you will be sorely disappointed."

Ambrose yelled back. **"How so?"**

"The Scots and Picts have been raided so often that they

have become a tough nut to crack. Except for a few well-fortified sites, there are no more settlements near the coast. They have both moved inland and set up an efficient system of coastal watchers."

Ambrose shrugged. "That is bad news, but we have come far, and will pray for *Odin* to guide us to prosperous and unguarded towns."

"You might try a day or two further north, but don't expect too much."

"Thank you, *Jarl*. Your advice is appreciated. Good hunting, yourself!"

As Ambrose was signaling Phillip to get the vessels underway again, a tall blond warrior approached the *jarl* and spoke quietly to him. The *jarl* raised his speaking trumpet again and called out.

"One moment, Canuteson!"

"What is it, *Jarl*?"

"The dragon carving on the bow of your ship seems to have been badly damaged."

"This ship has seen war more than once, *Jarl*. The dragon head was damaged and we have not yet found a master woodcarver to replace it. What of it?"

"My lieutenant here tells me he has seen its like before."

"I am not surprised, *Jarl*. The ship is over twenty years old and has been many places."

"He tells me that your ship was at Benfleet during the war against Wessex."

"That is possible, *Jarl*. I do not know, however, as I was not captain of this vessel at that time."

". . . where its crew was forced to abandon the ship and the Saxons seized it, along with many others."

Ambrose felt a cold sweat. This was not going as he hoped. He shrugged again. "It is possible, *Jarl*. I told you - I was not captain then."

"But how can it be manned by Danes if it was taken as spoil by the West Saxons?"

"The Saxons sold it? It was recaptured? *Jarl*, you will have to ask the ship owner. I am merely the captain and paid to do as I am told."

"I think, Canuteson, that I would like to come aboard and inspect your ship, myself."

"I am a free Dane, *Jarl*. Danes of East Anglia are not subject to your authority. I only answer to King Eohric. I therefore don't much care what you want to do. Neither you, nor any of your men, are boarding either of my vessels."

"Be careful, Canuteson. There are three of us and only two of you. You have little choice."

"I will only warn you once, Godwulf. If you attack us, we will fight, and if the gods are just, then we will destroy you. Sail away, while you yet can."

꙰

Ambrose, a veteran of many skirmishes when he fought alongside the *Rus* Vikings, knew exactly what the long throbbing note meant. The *jarl* had just ordered an attack! The Danish warriors ran to man their oars. The battle was on!

Ambrose turned to Phillip and Polonius, standing nearby. "Phillip, we need the bolt throwers mounted, now! Polonius, would you be so kind as to break out your famous substitute '*Greek-Fire*'?

Ambrose turned next to the pair of burly men who manned the huge and unwieldy steering oar, and then, finally, to his old friend and former mentor. "Steersmen, turn us south as quickly as possible! Phillip, send the men to the oars!"

The Saxon crewmen were, with *Frisian* instruction and years of practice, almost as well trained as the Viking crews. All five vessels came alive within minutes, but by the time the three Viking ships were ready to attack, the Saxon ships had also turned and were fleeing south. Ambrose signaled Phillip to bring the bolt-throwers to the stern. They were quickly brought up from their hiding places, maneuvered onto their mounting posts, and

Phillip told the crews to ratchet them tight. A small firepot was hung on gimbals, and the crewmen responsible for the weapons ran to retrieve the special darts Polonius had designed.

The three Viking vessels surged forward, and Ambrose turned to the ship commander. "Captain Osred, slow the beat enough that this vessel takes the stern position."

The wind brushed against the prince's hair, and he realized that it had both picked up and shifted until it was now coming from the starboard. Ambrose deduced that the angle was such that the sail could probably catch it. "Captain, let the wind kiss our sail. Set the crew to hauling the sail into place!"

With the help of both wind and oars, the two Saxon vessels slowly gathered speed, and the Vikings copied the move.

It was what Ambrose had been hoping for. He turned to Polonius.

"Scholar, can your crews hit the first ship's sail?"

Polonius smiled. "With a missile on fire and filled with volatile oil? It would be my distinct pleasure, Master. Why, at Rochester . . ."

"Now, my friend!"

Polonius spoke to the two bolt thrower crews one at a time, and each crew loaded his specially designed darts. They only had a limited supply of darts, so both crews waited until the first Viking vessel approached closer.

When Polonius was satisfied, he called out to the two crews. **"Release!"**

The twin darts arced directly into the heavy woolen sails of the leading Viking long-ship, but the sharp point, designed to lodge in wood, just tore through the wool, and the containers of oil and chemicals, designed to break on contact, followed through the holes without shattering.

Polonius was very disappointed. He knew there were few things more calculated to distract a crew than a rapidly burning sail on a ship at sea. He called out to Ambrose. "No luck, Prince! I think I can fix it by adding two small crossbars, but I have no time to try it now!"

Ambrose nodded. "Then let's go for the decks, my Byzantine

friend!"

"Aye, Prince! **Bolt thrower crews, you heard Prince Ambrose! Aim for the bow of the big one closing on us, and don't miss! Archers, light your fire-arrows and loose. I still want to see that sail go up in flames!"**

Arrow after arrow arced into the woolen sails that had survived the first bolts. The heavy bolts, now aimed lower, slammed into the side of the ship, and this time they spilled their cargo of flammable liquids over the planks. The flames on the trailing material, however, had gone out.

Polonius called directly to the line of fire archers. **"Light up that oil!"**

The barrage of fire arrows had managed to produce only desultory flames in the square sail, but the effect on the bow of the Viking vessel was much more dramatic. The oil caught eagerly, and the flames began to lick the decks. Two more bolts thudded into the bow with their liquid cargo, and the already intense heat caused the oil to burst instantaneously into raging fire. The ship dropped its sail and dozens of crewman abandoned their oars to grab wooden buckets and throw sea water onto the now roaring fire.

Ambrose smiled grimly. While Polonius had never managed to learn the top-secret formula for the Byzantines' *Greek-Fire*, yet his version was at least pernicious, and he knew that the fire would spread before the crewmen could put it out. If the ship survived the fire, it was at least out of the chase.

The second and third vessels slipped by their stricken comrade, and Ambrose could hear the Viking drummers beating a killing pace. As the two ships closed the gap, Ambrose had the three strongest men aboard grab globes attached to five-foot ropes. The men spun them around and around, and then let them go arcing up and onto the enemy decks. The glass bulbs shattered on contact, leaving pools of oil on the ship's deck. One captain understood the significance of the pools of oil on his deck, and ordered a sharp turn, but the other had finally got within spear range, and he attempted to close.

Polonius called out from behind his shield. **"Fire archers, release!"**

The puddles of fluid erupted into solid flame. Within seconds, the long-ship was ablaze, and Ambrose could hear the screams of men being roasted alive on the deck.

Polonius turned to his friend and master. "Do we fire on the third ship? The captain is attempting to flee."

Ambrose sighed. "I think they have had enough. Let them go rescue their friends on the first ship."

Polonius nodded. "They will report our position, Master."

"They will report where we were, since we are about to come about and head north again. And what are they going to report? 'Two rogue Viking ships, flying the crest of East Anglia, refused to be searched and fought back with fire weapons when attacked'."

CHAPTER 20

Ambrose Lands in Alba

As the sleek Viking vessel slid closer to the old stone jetty, the warriors on the shore formed a defensive line and loudly hammered their weapons against their shields. The resulting thunder brought a smile to Ambrose's face. He turned to his Byzantine friend.

"Let us hope that they keep such enthusiasm for what comes next. I might suggest that we slow a little, and ensure that we are welcome ashore. I would not want to be mistaken for a real Viking."

"We fly the banners of the house of Wessex at the top of our mast, Prince, and I think that all this fuss is but bravado. If it would make you happy, however, I will talk with them before we get within range of their spears."

Ambrose smiled again at his comrade. "It would ease an old man's fears, Scholar."

Polonius spoke a few curt words, and the ship commander instructed the rowers to slow the boat, until it floated just a spear's cast from the dock. Polonius picked up a speaking horn and called out to the waiting Picts.

"We are a royal delegation from your ally, Wessex."

A big man, covered in expensive chainmail armor, strode in front of the line of waiting spearmen and called back with a booming voice. **"Whether you be allies or enemies of good King Constantine remains to be seen, stranger."**

Polonius called back. **"We are here at the request of your king! Have your men stand down and we will tie up our ship."**

"My men do not like the shape of your boat, stranger. The appearance of such craft on this coast is generally a

precursor to grievous pain, misery and even death."

"It means the same on our coast, sir, but the original owners of these particular vessels were all killed by good Saxon *fyrdmen*. The ships are no longer a threat to you and yours."

"I was told to expect a ship from Wessex, but I did not expect you to arrive in a Viking long-ship."

"Can you think of a better boat to use when you have to coast through waters controlled by the Norse and Danes?"

"You have a point, stranger. You and a delegation of two more from your ship may come ashore." As soon as the burly giant had finished speaking to Polonius, he turned to his men and waved them off the ancient stone jetty.

Polonius frowned and then called out. **"I will bring ashore my entire delegation, or I will return home and let you personally explain to your king why a friend and ally was so rudely turned away!"**

The big man looked suddenly nervous. **"If you feel so strongly about it, then I give you permission to land your entire delegation. My men, however, will stay close-by!"**

"I would expect nothing else. Then we shall land."

Ambrose signaled Phillip, and with a minimum of words, the long blades began to dip again in unison, moving the vessel backward and forward until it just kissed the jetty. A sailor at either end took a rope and leapt ashore, expertly whipping the ropes around the waiting stone bollards so the long-ship was tied fast.

As soon as the ship was fastened, Ambrose, Phillip and Polonius leapt ashore. They were met by the big man.

"Welcome to the land of the Scots and the Picts. I am Lord Andrew, commander of the garrison of *Ayr* tun."

Polonius spoke. "I thank you. I am Polonius, advisor to King Edward of Wessex, and this is Prince Ambrose, uncle to the king. Behind him is Thane Phillip, weapons-master to the royal court."

The officer, a big man, looked up to Phillip. "Weapons-master, I do not look up at many men in this world. You are a giant, and if you can actually swing that giant blade hanging down your back, then you are a strong man indeed. My instructions are to help your crew unload considerable cargo from your ship."

Polonius spoke. "The cargo will be unloaded just as soon as we and your king come to an agreement."

The big man looked stubborn. "That's not what I was told!"

"That is what I am telling you. We are wasting time arguing. Your job is to take us to your king; not tell a foreign emissary what he has to do!"

The big man's face went red and he put his hand on his sword. Polonius spoke quietly.

"Draw that in the presence of my master, and you will be dead before it clears its scabbard."

The burly officer looked shocked. "You dare stand on Alban land and address a king's officer so? You scrawny little foreigner, you do not even wear a sword. I should have you whipped for your impudence!"

Ambrose spoke in his Irish-accented Gaelic. "Lord Andrew, you have insulted the king's own high advisor. Be grateful that Lord Polonius has decided to let you live!"

"Prince Ambrose, this strutting popinjay dares to threaten me! I only let him live because he is not man enough to wear a weapon!"

"You are wrong, Andrew. He is armed and could easily kill you before your sword could leave its scabbard. Just be thankful he is in a good mood and does not want to create an incident today."

"Kill me? With what? His bare hands?"

"Polonius, show the man."

Polonius waved his hands in the motions used by magicians, and, suddenly, each hand held a shiny steel throwing knife. He made a second pass, and just as mysteriously, they disappeared.

Ambrose smiled. "Now do you understand, Andrew? I have never known Polonius to miss with his throwing knives."

Andrew looked thunderstruck. At last he spoke. "Our bards sing of a giant named Phillip and a Greek named Polonius who has an uncanny skill with throwing knives. Polonius is a very uncommon name. Are you the three of legend?"

Ambrose smiled. "Yes, we sailed to far-off Constantinople and met the Byzantine emperor. We escaped an entire Imperial fleet sent after us, and yes, we freed princesses from the Vikings. My wife was one of the captives. We fought for the Viking *Great Army* and we spied on the Danes."

"But the stories are of long-ago!"

Ambrose nodded. "And we are getting old, but yes, Andrew, we are the three that your bard sang about."

"Forgive me, Prince, I did not know! I will leave an honor guard here to help protect your ships, and then I will take you direct to the king."

"I can ask for no more, Lord Andrew. We are ready to travel. By the way, do you know a good wood-carver?"

CHAPTER 21

They Meet the King at a Hunting Lodge

Ambrose, Polonius, and Phillip all bowed to King Constantine. The young king smiled at his new guests and then spoke. "Ah, the proud prince who refused to grovel before an emperor, the Byzantine scholar and the king's weapons-master. Well met! I have heard the ballads about you three since I was a wee bairn, but never thought to have the pleasure to meet you in person."

Ambrose replied. "And it is a pleasure to meet you, Sire."

"Come, sit beside me, and we can quench our thirst!' The king turned to the tall thin warrior at his side. 'Tell the serving wenches to bring mead at once!

Please sit down. This is a hunting lodge, and not my royal court. Here we can relax the etiquette. Prince Ambrose, you have come a long way to see me."

"I came, Sire, because you rejected our last embassy and specifically asked for us."

The king sighed. "Aye, I did. The truth is, I have little reason to love or trust Angles, Saxons, or Jutes. Your Anglian cousins have been attempting to push us out of our ancestral lands for centuries. We have conquered and made peace with the Britons that your people drove northward, but now, with the Vikings seizing all the islands off our coast and trying to push up from the south, there is nowhere left for us to retreat to!"

Polonius spoke. "I might point out, Sire, that your Pictish ancestors have been raiding south for even more centuries. The ancient Romans built not one, but two walls to try and keep your tribesmen out of the south. And need I mention the many raids the Scotti made along the western coasts?"

Constantine smiled. "The Roman walls were not very successful, and for many years after the founding of Dál Riata, the Scotti were truly daring sailors and raiders. Now, however, both peoples face a terrible new foe, one that has sundered our ties with Ireland, swept my people from the sea lanes and threatens our very existence. I assume that is the reason your king sent a delegation north in the first place."

Ambrose spoke. "It is, Sire. Like you, King Edward is new to the throne. His ascension has caused a rift in our country. Ethelwold, the king's cousin and son of a former king, tried to claim the throne for himself, but when the *Witan* chose Edward, Ethelwold rose in rebellion and sought out allies both in Wessex and amongst our enemies. He fled the country when King Edward marched against him. Then, less than a month ago, a trader brought us a coin from Jorvik. Apparently the Northumbrian Vikings have made our runaway *atheling* their king!"

"So a Saxon prince, driven from what he thought to be his rightful throne, is now king of a powerful nation of warlike Danes. I would say that, if I was a West Saxon, would be cause for considerable alarm, Prince. What, however, does it have to do with my country? We are not the ones who denied this man what he obviously thought was his right."

Ambrose took a deep breath before he spoke. "Sire, we would like you to send a strong raiding party into Jorvik's lands."

"Prince, we have the, what do our Irish cousins call them, the *finn-galls* holding an enclave on our west coast, and the *dubh-galls*, apparently led by your cousin, looking north. Now you are asking me to start a war with a very strong and hostile nation who has already cast more than one covetous glance in our direction. Why would you ask such a thing?"

"Truthfully, Sire? The *jarls* of Jorvik are less likely to commit to an outright invasion of Wessex if there is unrest on their own borders."

"You also have Eohric's East Anglian Vikings to deal with, Prince Ambrose."

"True, Sire, but we do not currently see them as a problem."

"Thousands of fierce Viking warriors, sharing a long border

with your subject kingdom of Mercia and eager for more land? How can that not be a problem?"

"Sire, we have the entire Mercian army sitting on their border, while the *fyrds* of half a dozen West Saxon *shires* are formed up and ready to ride if and when needed."

"Stripping your home *shires* of any protection, Prince!"

"Not so, Sire. Many years ago, after he was forced to hide in the forests and swamps of his own land, King Alfred started to build a system of *burhs* - of fortified *tuns*, each with its own permanent garrison. Our crops and homes may be at risk during an invasion, but the people, their treasures, and their herds - all have a safe haven while the *fyrds* ride, free to go where they are needed. Not incidentally, most of the major roads, fords and rivers are now defended by these *burhs*."

"Prince Ambrose, I can see the advantage for Wessex of having thousands of my ragged northern barbarian tribesmen pour across the border into Jorvik, but as sure as dusk follows dawn, it is going to provoke retaliation. My people will pay a terrible price for such an action."

"King Constantine, you do not have to love Saxons, but you should care about what happens to Wessex."

The king looked puzzled. "Really? The Angles, Saxons and Jutes have not been kind to my people, Prince. Just why should I care what happens to you and yours?"

"King Constantine, in our grandfather's time there were almost a dozen nations on this island. Most of them now have Viking rulers. In fact, aside from the Welsh kingdoms and Mercia, who are now the firm allies of King Edward, the unconquered nations are Wessex - and you."

"I know the history of this island, Prince. What are you trying to tell me?"

"Edward rules the last Saxon kingdom. If it falls, you will probably have a false peace for anywhere up to several years. Once Wessex has been thoroughly pacified, however, the Danes will unite to conquer the last parcel of land they don't control, and they will conscript the young men of every conquered country to do it. You will face an army far larger than you could possibly manage if you called up every man in your country, and all their cousins from Ireland.

King Constantine, the Welsh accepted King Alfred, and now King Edward, as their *bretwalda* - their supreme ruler. Now, when a Viking army lands anywhere in Wales, Mercian or West Saxon *fyrdmen* are dispatched. The Vikings were supremely successful when they could use surprise and land more warriors than a local community could match. With our defensive positions secure, and controlling both the rivers and the old Roman roads, we are now able, given some time, to gather sufficient *fyrdmen* to outnumber them anywhere, anytime. They can land, but they cannot take our fortified *burhs*, we obstruct their movement, and they are eventually driven back.

Combined Viking armies invaded five separate times less than ten years ago, with, at one point, over five thousand warriors, but each time we both drove them out and inflicted huge losses. In fact, we seized an entire Viking fleet, and much of their treasure plucked with so much blood and effort from all of Britain and *Frankland*."

The king of the Scots and Picts looked thoughtful. "I can understand why the Welsh have traded their independence for security, and, with Viking nations both to their north and east, the Mercians. It was their choice, and considering their limited numbers of warriors and their locations, it may have been a wise choice. I am a long way from the borders of Wessex, however, or even Mercia. Why should I stir up a hornet's nest? I can hardly count on your Saxon *fyrdmen* to come and rescue me if I am attacked!"

"True, Sire, but we can help you financially, and even now we have a shipload of the finest weapons just waiting for your young warriors.' Ambrose smiled suddenly.

'And the truth is, Sire, your young men have crossed that border almost every year since time immemorial. You are going to raid anyway. We will just help you buy supplies, hire mercenaries, pay compensation to widows, and we will help provide weapons."

"Then you will not reciprocate with men when we are hard-pressed?"

"Sire, if you ever decide to declare Edward to be *bretwalda*, then I can guarantee an army crossing the southern border of Northumbria each time Jorvik moves against you. As a matter of fact, there is a Welsh army moving north to the border even as we speak."

"And there is a reason for that?"

Ambrose smiled again. "Should you decide to send a force of men across the border, we would propose you head due south."

"South is all well and good, Prince, but even if we foolishly agreed to your invasion plan and go deep into Northumbria, the Vikings would likely move a large enough force between us and the northern border that we would be trapped. I am not going to send my young men to certain death, even if it would help the cause of Wessex."

"But that is the exact point, Sire. The Danes gather a force that outnumbers yours, and then pursues, driving you ever south. At last, trapped near the southern border, you make a last, desperate stand. The Vikings form their vaunted *skjaldborg* and prepare to destroy you. Suddenly, a thousand of the finest archers of Wales come out of hiding, and the Vikings are decimated."

"And if the Welsh have gone home, or are a little late in arriving, my men are the ones who are decimated."

"King Constantine, if you feel that you might lose, or have not found the Welsh reinforcements by the time you reach the south, you simply cross the border into Mercia. There you will be treated as honored guests, and all your needs will be taken care of until we can arrange for our fleet or a Mercian army to escort you home safely."

"We, Prince Ambrose?"

"Do you think I would ask you to send off your young men and then slip back to safety? Polonius here just aches for the excitement of combat - isn't that so, Scholar?"

Polonius, who hated physical combat more than anything else he had done in his life, just smiled wanly. "You, of all people, know, Prince, how much I enjoy having some barbarian thug trying to take my life with a rusty blade."

Ambrose smiled. "You see, King Constantine? It is all I can do to hold the man back."

King Constantine stared at the three men for a long time. "Prince Ambrose, I was not sure that I would agree to your proposal, even though I knew that my immediate predecessors, Giric and Eochaid, had made a similar arrangement with King Alfred and Lord Polonius here. The Good Lord knows that my treasury could use the gold and silver you offer, and my young men are always in need of better weapons, but I had no intention of letting you hurt Jorvik with the bodies of innocent Scot and Pict warriors. That you wish to ride with the raiding party, and have already arranged for a surprise for the Northumbrian Vikings, makes me rethink my position.'

The king smiled. 'I know from the ballads that Lord Polonius abhors physical combat, yet he is willing to risk his life to ride with you. I do not see that I can do any less. Who knows - perhaps the bards will then sing ballads about me, too."

"Then you will send a raiding party south?"

Constantine smiled. "No, Prince Ambrose. I will **lead** a raiding party south. The Danes have been testing the resolve of a new king by harassing my border lands for months, and it is time to teach them respect for my *Alba* and its people. The fact that you are going to help pay for my adventure just makes it the sweeter."

The king of the Scots, the Picts, and the remaining northern Britons, looked at Ambrose over his horn of mead. "Prince, I seem to remember a ballad where you took a Welsh city with a heroic ride through the night."

Ambrose smiled. "I think that you are referring to the *Long Gallop* or the *Long Ride*, Sire. The trick has been known by both names."

"That sounds like it. Just what, exactly, is it?"

"It is a trick we learned from the *Pechenegs*, a savage tribe of nomad warriors, who live far to the east, on vast grasslands that stretch so far it takes months of riding to cross them."

"And just how did it work?"

"The *Pechenegs* sent a strong force into *Varangian* - Viking and Slav - territory disguised as traders. At the allotted moment, they systematically set up roadblocks on every road that might be used to bring the city of Kiev warning of an impending attack. At the same time, they turned on and killed all the Varangians at a watchtower south of the city, which had been designed specifically to send word of any impending attack by means of boatmen, riders, or signal fire."

"That prevents word from being sent, but it hardly takes the city, Prince."

"True, Sire. That's where the ride comes in. Some miles to the south, out of sight of our scouts and traders, a massive force of mounted warriors formed up. With two spare horses apiece, they began the ride north. The secret is to never stop once you begin the ride. The Pechenegs are master horsemen. By switching horses as they ride and even urinating without dismounting, they move toward their target faster than word can travel. Any man who slows down for any reason is left behind. Of course, if someone does manage to see them coming and get ahead of them, the messengers they send will run into the roadblocks set up specifically to stop them. *Kiev* was where I lived at the time, and it was the destination of the *Pechenegs*."

Constantine was excited. "And did the city fall?"

"No, Sire, but it was a very close thing."

"If they killed your lookouts, and outrode the news of their coming, how did you not lose the city?"

"A river *long-ship* arrived from downriver just after the *Pechenegs* destroyed the outpost, and the *Varangians* almost killed themselves rowing through the night. They arrived at *Kiev* literally minutes ahead of the long riders, who had had to ride along narrow forest trails in the dark. The gates to the city were closed only seconds before the first of the long riders arrived."

"And if the *Pechenegs* had got there a minute earlier?"

"If the *Pechenegs* had reached the gates before they could be closed, then the city would have fallen without much of a fight.

The *Pechenegs* attackers greatly outnumbered the *Varangian* defenders. Once the gates closed, however, it was a different story. The *Pechenegs* were forced to besiege the city and the *Varangians* controlled the river with their Viking craft."

"Prince Ambrose, in the ballad of you rescuing your beloved, there was mention of Carnarvon and an ox cart."

"Aye, Sire. While the Saxon long riders made their *Long Ride*, a group of us, in disguise and with a massive hay wagon, joined a line of farmers going to market. As the wagon was passing through the main gate, the wheel was pushed off, and the immobilized wagon now prevented the gates from being closed. Saxon archers crawled out of the hay, and, along with a small force already smuggled into the *tun*, proceeded to hold the gate until the larger force of galloping horsemen arrived."

"And so the *tun* fell?"

"The Welsh put up a good fight, but not being able to close the main gate, it was an easy matter to take the *tun* without having to resort to a long siege."

"What you say is very interesting, Prince."

"What are you thinking, Sire?"

"When we raid the Viking lands, we burn crops and houses, but, once word spreads that we are coming, most of the wealthy jarls take their families and their treasures and retreat to their major *tuns*. We simply do not have the time or training to stop and besiege the bigger *tuns*. Even if we tried, it would just give the Danes time to gather forces large enough to defeat us. Like the Vikings who raided Wessex, our success is because we move quickly through an area, hit hard, and leave before they can gather overwhelming numbers to counter us."

"Then you are thinking of a *Long Ride*?"

"Why not? You want to scare the Danes into keeping all their warriors at home. What could be more effective than the taking of one of their large *tuns*?"

Ambrose smiled. "I can think of few things that would cause more fear and consternation, Sire. King Alfred built dozens of fortified *tuns*, which he called *burhs*, and provided them with permanent garrisons, specifically so the mounted troops of *fyrdmen* would be willing to ride far away from their families, secure in the knowledge that their families and their treasures back home were safe. Without such security, few warriors are willing to ride far or leave their families for long."

"The taking of such a Northumbrian *tun* would then send a strong message to all Jorvik, Prince, and the plentiful loot would, not incidentally, make my warriors very happy. Stealing from Saxon and Viking *thralls* is not very lucrative."

"Then by all means, Sire, let us plan a *Long Ride*! First of all, however, may I borrow a dozen of your blacksmiths for several days and several hundred pounds of iron?"

Constantine looked puzzled. "And this will help our *Long Ride*?"

"Not so much the *Long Ride*, but it will help us achieve victory over the Danes."

"Then you shall have as many smiths as you need, but can you tell a curious king why?"

"Of course, Sire. Polonius!"

The Byzantine stuck his head in the room. "Yes, Master?"

"Can you get me a *caltrop* from our luggage? I want to show King Constantine their use."

"Your wish is my command, Prince!"

Within seconds, Polonius returned with a strange metal object. Ambrose held it up to the Scottish king. "Sire, I could use as many of these as your smiths can make and we can carry without slowing us down."

Constantine pricked his finger on it as he picked it up. "It is made of iron, with many points, which, I can say from personal experience, are sharp. Do I throw it? If so, a handle would help a lot."

Ambrose smiled. "You could, Sire, but that is not its best use. Polonius here tells me that the ancient Romans carried them in all their campaigns."

"So what do I do with it?"

"Throw it on the ground a few feet in front of you."

Constantine gave it a gentle toss. "Interesting. One spike sticks straight up."

"Throw it again, Sire."

"Again the same spike sticks straight up. No, that is another spike. The upright one has a bit of a leaf that it picked up from the ground on the last throw."

"Now envision us in a line, Sire. Between us and the enemy, hidden in tall grass, are hundreds or even thousands of these *caltrops*."

"And we are facing the dreaded Viking *skjaldborg*?"

"It doesn't matter, Sire. The *caltrops* are just as effective against men or horses."

Constantine thought about it for a few moments. "Hmm. They would be devastating against an enemy who did not expect them, but your cousin would surely warn the Danes to look for them as the *skjaldborg* advanced."

"Then the Danes must pause and take the time to collect or move them. The key is - they must pause, well within range of your spearmen and crossbowmen. Even the bravest warriors cannot run through a field of *caltrops* without taking many casualties."

"Then the zone where these are placed becomes a killing ground!"

Ambrose smiled. "Either hundreds are crippled by the spikes, or we kill them while they are busy getting past these nasty little devices."

"Prince Ambrose, you may have as many blacksmiths as you need! The more we injure with these, the less we have to kill when they finally hit our shield-wall."

CHAPTER 22

Phillip Teaches a Lesson

Polonius spoke to the young king. "King Constantine, I am puzzled."

"Tell me what puzzles you. It would be a pleasure to be able to enlighten a scholar as esteemed as you."

"I noticed that your horsemen carry crossbows."

"That is true, Polonius. What of it?"

"It is not a weapon I have seen much in Britain."

"Because few others seem to favor it. It was copied by the Picts from the ancient Romans, and our horsemen find them useful. A longbow, such as Thane Phillip carries, is too unwieldy to be of much use on a horse. To get a bow equivalent in strength to one of our crossbows, it must be at least the height of the man using it."

"Sire, the nomad tribes of the Asian steppes fight almost exclusively from horseback, and they use a short compound bow with enough penetrating power to go through even heavy armor."

"Polonius, it has been my experience that the power of a bow increases with the length. By what magic can the nomads use a short bow, yet achieve such penetrating power?"

"Their compound bows are of wood, but the wood is strengthened with pieces of thin horn that are carefully glued in place."

"And this gives the bow sufficient power to send an arrow through armor?"

"Easily, Sire."

"And why could we not make such bows here?"

"We can, Sire, but there will be several problems."

The king looked intrigued. "Which are?"

"Your men are trained to the crossbow, not the nomad compound bows."

"All of my warriors are familiar with hunting bows, and it has been my experience that any warrior will happily learn a new skill if it will give him an advantage over an enemy. What is your next concern?"

"The nomad tribesmen spend years developing their muscles to be able to draw the bow."

"My warriors are as strong as any others I have ever met. Why could they not draw this compound bow you talk of?"

"Sire, why do I not show you? If you would choose several of your strongest men, I will ask Phillip to get his equipment and we will test the hypothesis . . . Oh, and can we have some old shields to use as targets?"

King Constantine grinned. "I will send for some captured Viking shields. Call your champion, Scholar, and I will show you Pictish weapons skills!"

~

Polonius stared at the round Viking shield that was propped against a stump. Finally, he turned to Phillip. "Weapons-master, would you put a shaft through the shield?"

The giant Saxon pulled the arrow back until it almost touched his ear, and then swiftly loosed. The arrow struck the shield right below the *boss*, and the long *bodkin* point easily punched through the leather and wood. When a Pictish warrior sent to retrieve the shield attempted to lift it, he found that the point was buried deep inside the stump.

King Constantine walked the length of the range in order to see for himself. He turned to Polonius.

"If I had not seen it, I would not have believed it. That is a shield that is proof against both our crossbows and our hunting bows."

Polonius nodded. "Would you have one of your men put a quarrel or two into the shield, Sire?"

At Constantine's gesture, a warrior handed the king a crossbow. He walked back to the shooting line, took careful aim, and the quarrel struck right next to Phillip's arrow.

Ambrose smiled. "Well shot, Sire. Now pick your best and strongest archer. Philip will lend the man his bow. It is not a compound bow, but it has a similar draw."

To cheers from the Pictish warriors, a young man, with shoulders even more broad that Phillip's, strode arrogantly forward. Phillip silently handed the man his bow and a pair of arrows.

The man smiled as he attempted to draw the bow. His smile quickly disappeared, however, and, in spite of great effort, he was unable to bring the arrow even close to his ear. The bow wobbled uncontrollably, and when the arrow leapt forward, it was with nowhere near the power of Phillip's shot, nor was it even accurate.

King Constantine looked at Polonius. "I think there are lessons to be learned in this demonstration, Scholar."

Polonius smiled. "You are right, Sire. Most of your men could shoot Phillip's bow - if they practiced diligently, on a daily basis, for several years. Few men who have not trained for years can shoot such a bow. The nomads trained regularly from when they were young boys."

"Then a horn-reinforced wooden bow is not going to be of much use to my men, at least in the near future."

"Perhaps not, Sire, but I wonder if we could use the horn to give the crossbows more penetrating power. The firing rate of a crossbow is slow, but if the quarrels can penetrate both shield and armor, then you can stop a Viking force cold."

"But Polonius, if we make a crossbow as powerful as Phillip's longbow, the men will not be able to cock the string on it."

"A crossbowman can use both hands if he is standing on the ground, Sire. My ancient Romans ancestors also developed several devices for cocking a crossbow. I don't know how effective they would be on horseback, however."

King Constantine smiled. "Can we make a few prototypes and find out?"

"Of course, Sire. Phillip is our master bowyer, so I will draw up a list of what we need, and the two of us will get to work on it first thing in the morning."

The king looked pleased. "Excellent. You just make the list, and everything will be ready for you before the dawn breaks!"

CHAPTER 23

Northumbrian Invasion

Constantine smiled at his royal guest. "Ambrose . . . that is not a Saxon name."

"No, King. My father was a Saxon king, but my mother, though of ancient Celtic royal lineage, was a beautiful slave that the king took to his bed."

"One of the ballads about you talks about a birthmark saving your life."

"The story is true, Sire! After the Viking conquests in Ireland, the Christians were very suspicious of any strangers. When they caught us passing through their territory, they planned to torture us to find the truth about who we really were. When I told them my story, however, the headman sent for an ancient crone who knew the old ways. It was amazing! She actually knew of the Celtic tribe which my mother's ancestors had ruled. I showed her my birthmark, in the shape of an oak leaf, and after that the Irish treated us as honored guests."

"Celtic. What tribe did your mother's ancestors rule?"

"The Durotriges. They lived in southern Britain, but were defeated when the Romans landed."

"I am not sure that Ambrose is Celtic, either."

"You are right, Sire. My mother's ancestors lived under the rule of the Romans. Over the centuries, the family intermarried with the Roman occupiers."

"Now I begin to understand. Your mother gave you a Roman name to remind you of your ancestry."

"Precisely, Sire. That is why she chose Ambrose. My ancestors remained an important family in southern Britain until the pagan Saxons arrived."

"What happened then?"

Ambrose shrugged. "My mother's ancestors were reduced to slavery and forced to work the fields they once owned."

King Constantine smiled. "But a lusty king saw a beautiful woman and would not be denied."

"True, Sire. The king, however, was kind enough to acknowledge me when I was born. I was thus brought up as a royal atheling instead of a field slave."

"Then you could possibly have become king of Wessex!"

"King, when I was kidnapped by Vikings, I was a spoiled youth. After I wore a slave collar and then lived in the east, I had a very rude awakening and grew up very quickly. I still think someone, possibly one of my half-brothers, arranged to have me taken by the Viking slavers. When I returned to Wessex after an absence of over five years, I swore to the king that I would serve in any way I could, but I had no interest in being considered by the Witan, our council, as a possible ruler. Now, after all these years, I have not changed my mind. Just a few weeks ago, the king of East Anglia personally offered me a Viking army if I wanted to seize the throne. I have lived as a warrior and I will die as a warrior. I have forsworn any claim to the throne."

Ambrose smiled at his old mentor. Phillip had saved his life more times than he could count, and the guidance and hard training of the tough thane had made Ambrose the warrior that he was. Together they had faced Vikings in *Frankland* and Britain, steppe raiders on the Asian grasslands, Byzantine soldiers on the Bosporus, savage pirates in the Mediterranean, slavers in Northern Italy, and ferocious Tuaregs in North Africa, but Phillip was finally showing his age. Arthritis was making movement more and more difficult.

Ambrose spoke. "Old friend, why do you not go back with the ship to Mercia? I need someone I can trust to march north with the Welsh archers. If they do not reach their destination in time, then our ambush will fail and if we can't withdraw quickly enough, then we will get a lot of Picts and Scots killed unnecessarily."

"Now, Prince, I promised your father . . ."

Ambrose put his arm on Phillip's shoulder. "I know old friend, but you are not up to the rigors of a *Long Ride.*"

"Prince, I am not going to go sit idly at home until I die. I can still remember old Viking warriors demanding that their sons carry them to the *skjaldborg* so they could die as warriors. I am not interested in earning my way into *Asgard*, but I do now understand how they felt. The pain gets ever greater as my body betrays me. I would rather die in battle than end up a helpless cripple."

"Old friend, I am not sending you home! I need you to go to Mercia by ship and make sure the Welsh archers get in position before our raiding party reaches the southern border. The arrival of the Welsh troops is a pivotal part of our plan, and I really need someone leading them who I can trust."

The old warrior sighed. He knew that Ambrose was right, but, even after all their years together, he still felt a responsibility for the bastard prince. He knew that Ambrose and Polonius together were a team that was virtually unbeatable. More than once, however, in spite of their remarkable military prowess, it had been his massive broadsword that had saved their lives. He hated for his prince to go into battle without him at his side. He also knew that he would not be able to complete the *Long Ride.* His body was just too old and stiff for that kind of punishment. Reluctantly, he agreed.

"A good soldier knows when to take orders without argument. I will do as you say, Prince."

⚐

Polonius bowed to King Constantine, who smiled at the Byzantine scholar. "Good morning, Lord Polonius."

"Good morning, Sire. Prince Ambrose said that you were

asking about the trick we used in Wales to keep the gates of Carnarvon open."

"Yes. I was thinking about the *Long Ride*. I was wondering if there was a way we could guarantee that the gates of our target would be open when our long riders arrive."

"There are few guarantees in combat, Sire, as you well know. Where do you wish to attack?"

"There is a fortified tun, called Blackpool, perhaps ten miles along the coast. It is a staging center for the Danes whenever they invade Alba. We have never retaliated against it because it has formidable defenses and an attack on it would just bog us down and give the Danes time to gather their warriors."

"You say it is along the coast?"

"Yes, there is a sandy beach there that stretches for miles."

"Sire, what would happen if a ship beached during the night and quietly let off a hundred warriors near the tun?"

"Alas, Polonius, any ship of ours that is seen is snatched from the waters and the crews enslaved. Many of our best sailors wear chains and now work Viking farms or mines. None captured have made it home. The great fleet of Dál Riata is no more. We are hopelessly outmatched by the Viking vessels."

Polonius looked thoughtful. "But what if the ship we used was a Viking long-ship?"

"Do you mean the one you arrived in?"

"Exactly! Phillip took one to Wales, but the other is still hidden in the creek not far from here. No one is likely to question a Danish ship heading south. We could even fill it with Pict and Scot slaves without causing any suspicion. Would the people of Blackpool have sentries looking out to sea?"

Constantine smiled. "Not likely, and if they saw a long-ship they would probably not even sound an alarm. You can be sure, however, that there are many sentries looking northward. They know that we will eventually respond to their raids."

"Sire, send your Angle and British scouts south. Give them a week. Their job is to find any sentry posts with a signal pyre and ensure that they are not lit on the night your main force rides south. Others must infiltrate quietly and set up ambush points on any tracks between the border and Blackpool."

The king of Alba thought for a moment. "Hmm. Using the long-ship would give us a hundred or more warriors, unseen and near the tun, and, if the scouts do their job, our riders should be able to get at least near the tun without raising an alarm. Then what?"

Polonius shrugged. "Perhaps a dozen Danes walk openly to the gate. They might even be leading a coffle of Pictish slaves."

"And then?"

"If the gate is opened, then the 'Danes' seize it, supported by the rest of the crew who rush from hiding. If the timing is good, then the riders arrive soon thereafter, and the *burh* inevitably falls."

King Constantine posed another question. "And if they don't?"

"Then our brave men either die or fight their way back to the ship. I cannot offer you guarantees, Sire."

"But you believe in the plan?"

"Knowing my prince, I fully expect to be in the forefront of the attack!"

King Constantine smiled. "I cannot ask for more of a guarantee than that, Lord Polonius."

ౡ

As the Viking long-ship coasted into Northumbrian waters, another long-ship slid out from behind an island. The crest on the sail was Northumbrian, so Ambrose made no effort to escape. He called out to his men in Danish. **"Let the sail down! Lively now, you lazy lubbers! Oars in!"**

The Danish vessel slid closer, and the captain or commander, wearing thick arm bands and a massive gold *torque*, called out through a speaking horn. **"Welcome, strangers! Who are you?"**

"We are free Danes of East Anglia, doing a little hunting in Alba."

"You are far from your normal hunting grounds."

"The Saxons on the south and east coast grow more wary of strange ships."

"Well, it looks like you had good luck in Alba!"

The clank of chains could be heard even as Ambrose spoke. "The gods were good to us. We took two ships laden with strong men."

The captain replied. "I can see that. What is to be their fate?"

"I am returning to East Anglia. My jarl has need of many more miners.' Ambrose smiled suddenly. 'These scum will be given the opportunity to spend the rest of their lives digging and hauling rock."

"Have you seen anything of a long-ship that has a damaged dragon attached to the bow?"

"I can't say that I have. Should I be on the watch for it?"

"A patrol of three long-ships approached two strange ships several weeks ago. One had the damaged dragon-head. Our ships gave chase when the captain refused to allow a search. Somehow, these two ships managed to start serious fires on two of the three attackers! We have been looking for the ships along this coast ever since."

Ambrose stared at his carved dragon prow. The paint was fresh and the oiled wood glowed. **"Thank you for the warning. I will be on the lookout for such a ship."**

"Well, may *Odin* grant you a safe journey!"

Ambrose smiled. "And you!"

The sleek long-ship slipped through the surf and crunched onto the long and sandy beach. Instantly, a dozen sailors leapt over the side with sturdy ropes and struggled against the tidal pull to stake the vessel to the shore. Within a minute, the ship was securely staked and over a hundred and fifty warriors leapt over the side and stood on the sand. The men, British, Saxon, Angle, Jute, Scot and Pict, gathered together for one common purpose.

With the wan light of the moon shining down on them, a warrior who had traveled several times to Blackpool to trade, led them toward the defensive walls.

ꝑ

The men lay in the shelter of the little woods. Some managed to sleep a little, but all waited for dawn. When the sun's rays finally tickled the horizon, a dozen warriors dressed as Danes followed Ambrose toward the gate. In their midst a sullen group of Scots and Picts, linked together by chains attached around their necks, staggered along under their burdens of large bundles.

The little group was spotted almost immediately, and the two guards at the gate rose to their feet, spears in hand. The bigger of the two, dressed in dirty homespun and wearing an ancient leather cuirass, called out.

"Who are you, and where did you come from?"

Ambrose spoke in Danish. "Look down at the beach, friend, and you'll see our ship sitting on your beach. We arrived during the night, but thought that you would rather see our handsome faces in the light of day. These fine thralls are bringing you a treasure trove of the finest goods you are likely to see for a long time! I understood that today is your market day."

"Aye, that it is, and we have had very few traders pass through recently."

"Then, friend, today is your lucky day! Open the gates a little wider, so our human pack animals here can get their burdens through. If you do that for Canuteson the Trader, I will save a small jug of my finest ale for you!"

The guard hesitated. "Well, I suppose a dozen warriors are not too great a threat to our *jarl*. You may enter, but don't forget your promise to me! I will come looking for you when I am off duty."

As Ambrose reached the middle of the entranceway, he drew **Victory-Maker** and spun around. "I will be easy to find, friend! I will actually be right here! Drop your spear or I will ram three feet of incredibly sharp steel right through your throat!"

As the shocked guard dropped his weapon, the *'thralls'* threw down their bundles, cast off the lengths of chain that had held them together, and then burrowed into their packs. Within seconds, each man had strapped on an axe or sword, and held a loaded crossbow at the ready. There were few people about so early in the morning, but several early-risers saw the weapons in the hands of strangers, screamed, and ran for shelter.

Ambrose cursed. He knew that it was now all a matter of timing. He whistled shrilly, and a small avalanche of Scottish, Pictish and Saxon warriors rose from hiding and ran for the gate. A few Danes, attracted by the noise and screams, started to arrive, weapons in hand. The Viking warriors started to form a shield-wall, but the powerful crossbows punched right through their armor and killed them where they stood.

As the mass of Constantine's warriors reinforced the first small group, the Viking horns on the walls started to blare. Ambrose had heard the sound many times, and he knew that all of the Danes of the tun were being called to war. Constantine's spies had reported there were several hundred men in Blackpool capable of combat. He had achieved surprise and was inside the walls, but he knew it was only a matter of time before the discrepancy in numbers and the sheer fighting ferocity of the Danes would drive him and his men from the gate. Now, above all, he needed Constantine and his hard-riding long riders!"

The Danes gathered nearby, and this time Ambrose knew that he would soon be facing a far more numerous and determined enemy. He could already see them forming up into a much more substantial shield-wall formation. When a crossbow quarrel took down a warrior, two stepped forward to take his place.

Suddenly, the sentries with horns redoubled their efforts. Again they blatted the warning notes. Ambrose smiled in relief. He knew that it could only mean one thing. Somewhere out on the rolling land, a massive force of mounted raiders must be visible and galloping toward the tun. Only that could cause such an uproar.

Ambrose ordered the warriors to exhaust their supply of

quarrels. The massive volleys discouraged the Danes from advancing, and Ambrose counted on the reinforcements arriving before their situation became desperate.

The Danes were brave warriors, and they knew that if they could not close the gate within a very short time, then the fate of their tun, and their women, children and treasures, were in the hands of some actively hostile strangers. Their shield-wall, their famed *skjaldborg,* resumed its advance just as thundering hooves announced the arrival of a much larger enemy force. As the Danes hesitated, an avalanche of screaming Scots and Picts poured through the open gate.

Ambrose hugged the young king. "Constantine, you are a sight for sore eyes! Your timing was impeccable!"

As they spoke, the continuous flood of warriors finally broke the Vikings' resolve. The Viking mass broke, and the brave mass of warriors became frightened individuals who ran to try and protect their homes and loved ones.

The king grinned at Ambrose. "How so, Prince?"

"We shook them up, but they were about to get serious when you showed up. Your arrival shattered their confidence, and now they have run for their homes."

"Then we have won!"

"We now outnumber them, Sire, but, man for man, these are some of the bravest men you will ever face. We must keep up the pressure. Your warriors should go after them right away. If you give them time to think and form up again, they could still do terrible damage to your army. Did you know that when I was ambassador to the great Eastern Roman Empire, Byzantium, the Byzantines positively drooled over the possibility of hiring the Rus Vikings as mercenaries?"

"Prince, why would they want to hire ignorant northern barbarians?"

"They had seen the Rus and their cousins stand up to the finest cavalry in the world - and win! They saw big, powerful men who were not afraid to die, and men who were not involved in or interested in the politics of the Byzantine Empire. I have been away from Byzantium for a long time, but I understand that thousands of Vikings have served in what they now call the Varangian Guard. We would not be wise to ease the pressure. Given time, these men will figure their best defense is a united one, and, man for man, there are few better fighters anywhere in the world."

Constantine drew his own sword. "Then let us go, Prince! I have not yet had a chance to dip my blade in Viking blood!"

"King, many of the men of the town are not your enemies - they are but Angle and British peasants, enslaved by the Danes."

"I daresay you are right, Prince Ambrose. I have already instructed my warriors to kill only the Danes, unless provoked. I do not pay my warriors, Prince, so I have to give them the right to loot and rape.' The king shrugged. 'Tonight they will slaughter enough animals to feed us all, and then they will lay with the most comely women. Tomorrow we will move on. It is the way of war, Prince, and it is what you paid us to do. At least we do not enslave the population, and we do not kill women and children."

"And the slaves?"

Constantine smiled. "That is a part I enjoy, as should you! Did you not once seize and free an entire long-ship of captive princesses?"

Ambrose smiled in return. "Not all of the women were actually princesses, but it is true that all were of noble birth and exceeding beauty. My wife, Gretchen, was amongst the captives."

"Well, Prince Ambrose, if the slaves are Scots or Picts, then we will tell them to run northward to freedom. In your honor, I will give orders that the Angle and Saxon slaves may join them if they wish. Let us be clear on one thing, however. If anyone so much as lifts a weapon against us, we will kill that person."

As the sun rose on the following day, hundreds of Scots and Picts and Saxons staggered out of the houses they had commandeered for the night and gradually made their way to the open square that served as meeting place. Many walked gingerly, or tried to hold their heads together with their hands. All, however, wore or carried their weapons. Most also carried a bundle of goods. After taking the youngest and comeliest women, they had thoroughly looted the tun.

Their king looked at the piles of material on the ground beside his army, and spoke. **"I just want to say that you did brilliantly yesterday. With few casualties, you seized an important tun that has been used over and over to marshal raiding armies against us. Your stomachs should be full, you made heroic efforts to drain the tun of all of its mead and ale supplies, and I just know that your peckers were well exercised last night! I see mountains of looted goods that you want to take home, but remember, we have just started our invasion. We are going to drive deep into Northumbria, and if we are not able to keep ahead of the gathering Viking army, we are going to die. Take what is lightest and most valuable, and throw the rest of that junk into the fires!"**

One burley warrior, struggling to stand upright, dared interrupt his king. "Begging your pardon, Sire, but what fires?"

Constantine grinned. "A good question, Warrior. Finish eating and start packing, for in less than an hour, I want you on your horse - and I want this tun burned to the ground! We must teach the heathen Danes that it is a dangerous proposition to raid Alba!"

Many of the horsemen had trouble staying in the saddle, but they were ready within the allotted hour. As flames licked greedily at the wooden palisade walls and wooden structures of the tun, the army of vengeance rode south, led by a Scottish king, a Saxon prince, and a Byzantine scholar.

The army continued south, until scouts reported a small vill not more than a few miles ahead. Oddly, although a few signal pyres burned far to the north, the villagers appeared to have either not seen or had ignored the warnings. King Constantine gave the order, and a large force of mixed Scottish and Pictish horsemen erupted from the main force. Yipping madly, the riders galloped toward the little vill. The sudden arrival of hundreds of screaming warriors from the north sent the people of the poor village into a panic. They abandoned their livestock and goods, and ran desperately for the shelter of the nearby woods. The riders had anticipated this move, however, and galloping riders arced around the refugees and turned them back.

Ambrose rode close to Constantine. "You said, Sire, that only the Danes would be killed. "

"Aye, I did, Prince, along with anyone else who raises a weapon against us. Most of the inhabitants here seem to be slaves, but mixed in will be the Viking masters. Once we separate the masters from the slaves, we will let the men and children go immediately. The women will have to pay a price for their lives today and freedom tomorrow. Sadly, we are going to have to slaughter a lot of this vill's livestock if we are to eat tonight."

The army of vengeance rode steadily southward. They paused for a day or two at a time, generally when they were lucky enough to seize a vill or tun, but both Polonius and Constantine drove them on. Both knew that in their wake thousands of fierce warriors gathered their weapons and rode or marched along the path of devastation. The army of the Danes, once it gathered its many components, would be enormous, and it was likely that a hard-riding vanguard was already nearing.

At last they neared the border of Mercia. Ambrose spoke to the young Scottish king who rode at his side. "King Constantine, Polonius has to ride ahead with the hundred Saxons and perhaps two hundred of your men. It is time for him to move against the border and prepare a battlefield."

"And what do the rest of us do?"

"We raid any farms we find, attack any small groups of

Danes, and in general provide a screen for his preparation. When the pressure grows - more Danes are approaching every day - we will fall back to the prepared defenses."

"Tell him to pick whichever of my men he needs. I just pray to Almighty God that your friend Phillip will be there with those vaunted Welsh archers of yours when the time comes!"

"I, too, Sire. If they are late, however, we will just cross the river and retreat into Mercia until we find him. The archers are the key to defeating the Danes.

┝

The army of vengeance burned several coastal vills, and then rode eastward to avoid the Norse settlements that were just south of their position. Scouts reported multiple contacts to the north. Clearly, King Ethelwold's army was nearing.

A Saxon scout, one of the few men Ambrose had kept with him, returned from patrol at a hard gallop. He rode directly for King Constantine and Prince Ambrose. "King and Prince, they come!"

Ambrose replied. "Easy, man! Who comes?"

"Danes, Prince! Danes come!"

"Take a deep breath, and we will try again. How many men did you see?"

"It looked like a scouting party, Prince. I counted about fifty mounted Danes in the next valley."

"And were there signs of any more?"

"Not that I saw, Prince!"

"Did they see you?"

"I don't think so, Prince. I dismounted as I had been taught and looked through bushes so that I would not be silhouetted on the crest."

Ambrose turned to King Constantine. "Sire, may I suggest a little trap?"

"Suggest away, Prince."

"Let us get your seven hundred men lined up, quietly and

with crossbows in hand, just below the crest of the hill. Then ten of your Picts will ride over the crest, see the Danes, turn their horses and gallop back this way."

"And if the Danes are foolish enough to follow?"

"The valley will run red with their blood."

King Constantine smiled. "I like it.' He turned to his captains. 'Hamesh, take nine men and crest that hill. Look like you are snooping about, are surprised when you see the Danes in the valley below, and then ride back here like you are in a panic. Go now!"

The Danes whooped when they saw Pictish horsemen top the rise. The sound carried all the way back to Ambrose. The Picts sawed at the reins to turn their horses, galloped their horses back over the crest of the hill and plunged down out of sight. With blood-curdling yells, the Viking riders followed.

Fifty horsemen crested the rise at a full gallop. Suddenly, they found themselves facing seven hundred of Constantine's men. Hundreds of crossbow *quarrels* flew at the hapless riders, and most just tumbled from their mounts. The few remaining riders, who had been inadvertently protected by their comrades' bodies, found themselves facing a horde of charging Pictish spearmen. Not a single Dane survived the attack.

Ambrose and Constantine surveyed the scene of the massacre. The king spoke. "I hope that will send them a message."

Ambrose replied. "I can tell you that they won't be pleased. I do think that it is about time for us to go and find Polonius. He has had enough time to prepare a site for battle, and I have no doubt that Ethelwold's main army, or at least a large vanguard, will be here within hours."

Constantine smiled. "I do hate to run from the Danes."

Ambrose smiled in return. "We are not running, King. We are luring the Danish army into a killing ground."

"That does sound better. I must admit, Prince Ambrose, I didn't think that I would learn anything new from Saxon barbarians, but I was wrong. You and your Byzantine scholar are teaching me interesting new ways to kill Danes."

⚑

Ambrose spoke to King Constantine. "Sire, we must stop and tell the men to form into a single column."

Constantine looked puzzled. "I am afraid that I don't understand, Prince."

"Sire, do you see the flags ahead?"

"Yes, of course. What do they mean?"

"Polonius has marked a safe path through the killing ground. If a man strays far from the marked path, he is liable to step in a man trap or find our *caltrops*."

"Then single file, from flag to flag, with no deviations?"

"Ambrose smiled. "Exactly, Sire."

"But won't your Ethelwold know to do the same?"

"He would if the flags remained, Sire. They will be removed when the last of your men are through the killing ground."

⚑

Ambrose hugged his Byzantine friend. "It is good to see you, Polonius! How goes the construction?"

"The killing ground is prepared, Master. Now I am constructing a bridge of boats across the river."

"But Polonius, I thought you said that we should fight on this side?"

"I did, Master, and we should."

"Then why the boats?"

"We will never complete the task. Prince, the Danes are no fools. We must do everything we can to egg Ethelwold on. I want him so angry that he will not take the time to think things through thoroughly. We are apparently trapped against a river, and have no room to use the Pictish horsemen. If he was smart, he would just sit and wait for reinforcements. The boat bridge is to encourage him to attack. I suspect that the last thing he wants is for us to slip across the river and escape. We are then in Mercian territory, the advantage will inevitably shift to us, and he knows it."

King Constantine looked around curiously. "Polonius, you seem to have all the men busy doing something. What are you up to?"

"Sire, I have put the men to making ballistae."

"Ballistae? What are they?"

"Sire, think of one of your crossbows. It is bigger, and generally mounted on a frame. Instead of the flex of a supple branch giving it power, however, it uses the power of twisted rope."

"And this will help us against the Danes?"

"Sire, the weapons can shoot spears or rocks up to the size of your head for several hundred paces. Few Danes will survive a hit from one of these."

Constantine looked excited. "Then we can massacre the Danes!"

Polonius replied. "Sire, we can punch holes in their line, and we can kill at long distances, but the weapon must be cranked after each shot, and that takes time. More, I have little in the way of iron, competent blacksmiths, or other supplies. We will not finish too many before Ethelwold and his men get here."

CHAPTER 24

Ambrose and Ethelwold Meet in Jorvik

King Ethelwold stared in shock at the slim man who accompanied King Constantine forward under the flag-of-truce. "You! You dare ride with these God-cursed Alban raiders!?"

Ambrose smiled. "And British, Pictish and Saxon. There are even a few Angles in the ranks. Good morning to you, too, Cousin. I see that you have finally managed to find a crown that fits."

"Ambrose of Wessex, I will curse your name for all eternity. You have no idea just how many of my plans you and your devious little friend have ruined!"

Ambrose grinned. "I think I do, Cousin. I know you had an agreement with King Guthrum to turn over Alfred and his family to his tender mercies - except we made sure that you couldn't locate them. Polonius and I arranged to have your sons called to court so they could serve as hostages - and it worked. Invasion after invasion, you remained a loyal *ealdorman*. You were very wise. Your loyalty saved your sons' heads. Do you think we were not aware of your plans to switch sides and join the Viking host at the last moment? Guthrum himself warned me about you. You are a traitor to your country, Ethelwold. I am only sorry that I did not persuade Alfred to let Polonius slit your throat when you first showed your traitorous intent."

"Ambrose, you are a fool! If you had not interfered, Jorvik and Wessex would now be one. Mercia is already a puppet and Wales subservient. East Anglia could not have held out for long, and all *Angleland* would have quickly become one nation, ruled by a Saxon king! Then, united, we could have easily rolled up the Pictish and Scottish lands of this king you ride with. Our dream of one united Britain was within my grasp - until your scheming Byzantine clown interfered. **That** is the dream that you have destroyed, and for that I can never forgive you."

"And you are a bigger fool than me if you believe that the Danes would have really let you rule! You are nothing but a puppet to them. They would have used you to divide the West Saxons, and, when the Danes controlled everything, you would have had an unfortunate 'accident'. A *blood-eagle,* or perhaps being used as an *archery target,* like good King Edmund - you can be sure that they had something special planned for you after you had served your purpose. Ethelwold, you are a fool! To divide and conquer is the Viking way, Cousin! I know - I lived amongst them for years. They appointed puppet kings in East Anglia and Mercia - until they were ready to rule directly. Guess what happened to the puppet kings then?"

"Why are you here, Ambrose?"

"Jorvik sent Viking warriors to join you in Dorset, Ethelwold. That is an act of war and we thought that we should show your new countrymen that it would be wiser for them to keep their young men at home."

"Jorvik sent Viking warriors to honor their new king, as is their right and obligation!'

Ethelwold turned toward Ambrose's companion. 'You! By the banners I see and the crown on your head, I am going to assume that you must be King Constantine."

"You are very observant, King Ethelwold."

"Do you not see that this man is coldly manipulating you? You will pay dearly for this little adventure - with the lives of your men. I intend to see to it personally. Turn this man and his Greek toady over to me and ride back north today, and I will see that the reparations are not too burdensome."

"King, when a boulder is rolling downhill, and a little voice pipes up and squeaks 'stop', should it suddenly stop? **Can** it suddenly stop?"

"I am a simple man, King Constantine. I do not like parables. Just tell me simply what you mean."

"The Scots of Dál Riata, the Picts, and the last of the free northern Britons have faced half a dozen invasions in the last ten years, King - all from Jorvik. My country has already been devastated by your warriors. Your warriors have been violating the border for months. We are already at war. Are you so surprised that we would finally strike back in force? This is just a taste of what will happen to Jorvik if you do not respect our borders."

Ethelwold suddenly smiled. "You know, I am glad that you are both here. Your vicious raid has, indeed, caused considerable anxiety amongst the *jarls* of *Jorvik*. Because of what you have done, thousands of veteran warriors are gathering to join the host you see behind me. King Constantine, you have let a fool lead you! You are trapped far south of your border, and my entire army now sits between you and your homeland. I have to admit, your *Long Ride* was masterful, yet in your greed you have pushed much too far from your frontier. No matter. You have given me an opportunity to get rid of two thorns at one time, and that I appreciate."

Ambrose smiled. "Cousin, that is Mercia on the other side of the river."

"It is very difficult maneuver to cross even a little river in the face of an implacable enemy, Ambrose, and, in any case, your precious little bridge is not even half complete. You should know the folly of escape across a river while under enemy attack. In any case, Mercia is subservient to Wessex, and, as you have so carefully pointed out, Jorvik is at war with Wessex. I therefore do not find the thought of crossing a boundary to hunt down any survivors the least bit daunting."

"The Mercians are battle-hardened, Cousin. They have to be - they have long lived trapped between your new warriors and those of King Eohric."

"A good try, Cousin, but I happen to know that the Mercian army is far away to the south and east. Except for a few garrisons, Ethelbert seems to have concentrated all of his forces along the border with East Anglia, no doubt to intimidate King Eohric. Unfortunately for you, they will do you little good there."

Ambrose nodded. "I knew that you would appreciate that maneuver, Ethelwold. We wanted to make sure that we used a force that had not been corrupted by your foolish promises and your gold."

Ethelwold spoke bitterly. "In the end, my gold and promises did not buy me the loyalty in Wessex that I expected."

Ambrose replied. "The *Witan*'s vote was unbiased, Ethelwold, but after that, your lack of allies arose because you broke the sanctity of a convent.' The prince smiled. 'And it didn't help that we had a list of your supporters and collected their elder sons as hostages. Where that didn't work, or when loyalty to Wessex was not sufficient, Polonius either sent armed men or offered bigger bribes than you had."

Ethelwold's face grew red. "I hope my warriors catch that interfering little bastard today! I look forward to inflicting many long hours of grievous pain on him before he is allowed to expire."

Ambrose spoke. "You are more than welcome to come and get Polonius! I understand that he has saved a dagger just for you."

"Oh, you may be sure that I am coming - for both of you!"

"First you have to defeat the army, Cousin."

Ethelwold shrugged. "You are trapped against a river, have a dense forest on your right flank, and the land between us is flat meadow, which will favor my *skjaldborg*."

"Horsemen like grasslands, Cousin, and the Picts do love their horses."

"Horses are useful only if the riders have the room and freedom to maneuver. It is puzzling to me why two such wily commanders as you two would make such a foolish strategic mistake. Don't think I am not grateful, however. I do not want my army to be too bloodied today. This army is soon going to put me in my rightful place in Wessex, and then I will be visiting Eohric of East Anglia. Well, I will put down your foolish choice of location to old age, Cousin. You and Polonius are getting too old for this sort of adventure. You have, what, perhaps a thousand lightly armed horsemen and less than a hundred West Saxons, against almost fifteen hundred of my best veteran Viking warriors, while massive reinforcements follow the trail of destruction you left behind you. I would counsel you to surrender now, except that I would not accept it. It would deprive me of the opportunity to watch my men carve their way through you."

Ambrose turned to King Constantine. "Sire, did I ever tell you the difference between a man and a coward?"

"I don't think so, Prince."

"Well a man stands by his comrades, even unto death. A coward runs and leaves his followers to fight his battle and die. A man asks for a woman's hand, and accepts her answer with grace and dignity. A coward uses armed men to break into a convent and steal away the woman who refused him. He manages to overcome and hurt an aged nun who protests. Then, the coward finds that he has to put his wife in chains to keep her from running away."

Constantine smiled. "And a man stands up for his honor when his reputation is besmirched. Among my people, that is more important than life itself."

Ethelwold was so mad that he spit as he spoke. "I had thought to give you an honorable death, bastard prince! Now you will suffer alongside your Greek friend. You are going to beg me to let you die!"

"First you have to defeat us, Cousin!"

"Return to your barbarian Albans. I am coming for you!' Ethelwold looked at the angle of the sun. 'Sunset is close. Dream tonight of what I am going to do to you. Admire the stars for the last time. Tomorrow at dawn we finish you!"

Ambrose stared at Ethelwold. "And we will meet you face to face. I guess that there is nothing further to say. I do think you will find us harder to digest than you imagine."

"Hah! Do your worst. Tomorrow I will be rid of several thorns in my side!"

⚑

Ambrose hugged the giant thane. "Phillip, it is good to see you! I was beginning to worry."

"We crossed the river upstream with the *coracles* and rafts two nights ago, Prince, and moved directly into the forest. I can see why you are worried, however. Ethelwold has you neatly trapped against the river and the forest. If I had not arrived, you would have been massacred."

"I know, old friend, and Ethelwold sees it the same way."

"Yes, I watched you talking with him. You took a serious risk in choosing this particular meadow, Prince."

Ambrose nodded. "It was carefully chosen by a brilliant military strategist for specific purposes. There is always slight risk in war, but I think it minimal. After all, I had you leading the Welsh here. Moreover, the reward is that the Danes are marching onto our prepared ground, and Ethelwold seems willing to attack before his reinforcements show up. Polonius started tying together boats as if we are trying to build a pontoon bridge. He thought it might encourage Ethelwold to be precipitous. Above all, my cousin does not want us to escape. I expect that he will commit his full force tomorrow, thinking that he has a large advantage."

⚑

Phillip stood before King Constantine and Prince Ambrose. "I have a proposal, King and Prince. May I speak?"

Ambrose smiled. "Since when does the greatest warrior in all Wessex need leave to speak? Say on, old friend."

"Thank you, Prince. Last night, after the Welshmen were settled in the thickest part of the forest, I went scouting. I was drawn to the smell of smoke and then the light of many campfires. They led me to Ethelwold's camp a few miles north of here.

The defenses were minimal, but I had no men with me to take advantage of the situation. Tonight could be a different proposition."

Polonius spoke. "Weapons-master, are you saying that you think they will return to that camp, and we could launch an attack against it?"

"Why not? The camp is a natural strongpoint, and they seem too lazy to build one of Polonius' old Roman marching forts. With their overwhelming numbers, they are probably not too worried about an attack from us."

King Constantine spoke. "Just what are you thinking we should do?"

"I understood that we are pushing Ethelwold so he will rush into battle. I can think of few things more likely to upset him than an attack on his camp."

Ambrose spoke next. "Even with the advantage of surprise, we would risk much by attacking in the dark. We might find we are unable to disengage, and that could destroy us."

Phillip smiled his slow smile. "I was thinking more of lobbing stones from a safe distance, using a couple of Polonius' infernal machines."

Polonius looked concerned. "But we would have to abandon our ballistae when they discovered our location."

Phillip replied. "We will lose several machines. A few ballistae one way or the other will make little practical difference in the battle tomorrow, but their use tonight will definitely make Ethelwold furious!"

Ambrose grinned. "Well, Polonius, what do you think?"

The walking oak tree is right. "Let's do it!"

༄

The many porters put down their loads and then headed back to their own encampment. The men Polonius had trained soon had the five ballistae bolted back together again, and they preceeded to scavenge as many appropriately sized rocks as they could. The Danish camp was in a natural saddle of land, and Viking sentries walked the perimeter, but the defenses were minimal. The many campfires gave away the location of the camp, and Polonius had each ballistae painstakingly maneuvered and aimed for maximum damage. The little group tried to sleep, but most were too excited. Just after midnight, the moon rose and threw a gentle light across the land. It was the time that Polonius had been waiting for.

They were forced to shoot blind, because of the natural height of land between them and the Viking camp, but the ballistae were accurate and the approximate distance was easy to estimate. Five at a time, large rocks, each capable of instantly killing a man, arced high in the sky. They landed with a ground-shaking thud, and screams of pain and surprise soon emanated from the camp.

As expected, the Danes quickly organized themselves. Once they figured out what was probably happening, armed groups began spiraling out of their camp, looking for the perpetrators. Phillip and Ambrose cut down one small knot of warriors, but the noise drew others, and Ambrose was forced to order the withdrawal. The crews slashed the ropes that provided the power to the bars, and poured oil on their weapons. Within a minute, the Saxons left behind five roaring blazes. The exultant *fyrdmen* rode for the edge of the forest, where men waited with torches to guide them safely through the killing ground.

Dawn's early light had just started diffusing itself across the landscape when the sound of drumming brought the Albans and West Saxons to full alertness. The raiders abandoned their breakfasts, exited their own rudimentary fort, and raced to form into their shield-wall. The noise was quickly explained. Viking warriors marched out of the early-morning mist. They were dismounted and already formed into a long and menacing *skjaldborg*. The Danes were rhythmically slamming their weapons against their shields. Backed by the rest of their army, the big men slowly advanced.

Ambrose swallowed and the butterflies raced around his stomach. The Danes, having looted the battle sites of many victories in many lands, were well-armored as they marched into battle. The prince looked at his own force. A hundred *fyrdmen*, thanes all, and equal to any Viking, held the center. On either side stretched a shield-wall of lightly armored Scots, Britons, Picts and Angles. By choice, the Picts fought mounted, throwing their light spears and then retreating. As light horsemen they were formidable, but the limited space and advancing *skjaldborg* left them no room to maneuver and they had been forced to abandon their horses. Ambrose knew that, in a contest of shield-wall to shield-wall, they were no match for the advancing foe, even if they were not outnumbered.

Ambrose yelled so Phillip could hear him over the din. "Phillip, the signal is a long climbing note, repeated! You had best return now to our Welsh friends."

"Aye, Prince. I will see you soon. May God bless you and keep you!"

"Go with God, old friend!"

Ambrose watched Phillip's retreating back as he hurried toward the sheltering forest. The big man was too proud to say anything, but Ambrose could see the stiffness in his gait. The thane quickly disappeared into the shelter of the trees.

Constantine spoke in his ear. "They are slowing, Prince. Your cousin Ethelwold must have told the men to check the ground for *caltrops*."

Suddenly, the advancing Danes found the series of man-traps dug in the ground and carefully camouflaged. One after another, warriors fell screaming into pits lined with sharpened stakes. A few stepped on *caltrops*, but the Danes had been warned about them, and most slid their feet along so that the sharp metal spikes were ineffective. They did have to stop, however to move the nasty spikes out of the way. It was what the spearmen were waiting for. The previous Viking losses had made little breaks in their shield-wall, but the veteran warriors from the second line just advanced and filled the empty spaces.

King Constantine had his signalers blow a deep note, and the sky filled with light spears. A few struck home, but most were stopped on the uplifted shields the Vikings carried. In return, and in response to a strident call from Viking horns, spears and axes were thrown at the allies.

Ambrose watched the entire line waver as the ranks were struck by the hurtling missiles. He spoke hurriedly to the king who stood beside him. "Sire, now might be the time to try out the crossbows! Polonius, the ballistae!"

Constantine looked at Ambrose as if he was in a daze. "Yes, of course. Signaler, blow the signal."

The mournful note echoed over the din, and the entire allied line stepped back two measured paces. Suddenly a veritable wall of sharpened stakes, previously hidden in the tall grass, were propped up and facing the advancing Vikings. The first rank of Pictish spearmen dropped to their knees, and hundreds of crossbows rose as one. The Viking had faced Pictish crossbows many times before, and did not much fear them. Their shields rose to protect their faces, and they continued to advance.

The rocks hurled by Polonius' weapons crushed each man struck, punching holes in the shield-wall, but there were only a few *ballistae*, and each took time to reload. The heavy *quarrels* from the crossbows were far more numerous. They struck the Viking shields and many penetrated. There were screams up and down the Viking *skjaldborg*, as the Danes found, to their surprise, that their shields could not stop a *quarrel* fired at close range. The crossbows were also slow to re-cock, however and the shock was quickly lost. The Pictish second and third ranks hastily swapped weapons, and a second volley thudded into the Viking line, along with a few more rocks. More Viking warriors from their second and third ranks filled the new gaps, however, and the Danes sped up their pace, wanting to close before more warriors fell to the powerful but slow-firing Pictish weapons. The sharpened stakes broke up their formation slightly, but the veteran Danes flowed around them and kept advancing. While a few found more *caltrops*, the main force hit the allied shield-wall with a terrible crash. Wherever a battleaxe hooked a Pict's or Scot's shield, another Viking axe or sword quickly followed. Dozens of Picts and Scots, and even a few Saxons, started to fall. The Vikings had accepted the losses necessary to close the distance, but they excelled in hand to hand combat. Their weapons began to tear great holes in the allies' shield-wall.

Polonius yelled so Ambrose could hear. "Prince, the Picts, Scots and Britons will break soon. They cannot take this pressure much longer. They just don't have the armor to hold for long against the Danes!"

Ambrose nodded. "Order the signal, Scholar!"

The signalers' rising notes reverberated across the battlefield. Phillip had clearly been waiting, for within seconds thousands of long arrows arced high from the forest and plunged into the unprotected Viking flank and rear. The arrows, driven by the powerful Welsh longbows, dropped like rain upon the Viking warriors. The barrage of arrows continued unabated, until most of the Danes not in active combat were forced to duck down and hide under the shelter of their shields.

The Danes were dying first by the dozen, and then the hundred, but they could do nothing about it. Some tried to advance toward the forest and close with their tormentors, but any who attempted it became the targets of dozens of arrows which, when fired directly at close range, were capable of penetrating the best-made armor. Meantime, the well-armored Saxons, sensing a weakness, started pushing back the Viking front rank. Suddenly, as if a dam had burst, the Viking warriors broke and ran. Ethelwold's ferocious army suddenly became a loose collection of dazed and terrified individuals who turned and ran for their lives.

While the Saxons, Scots and Britons charged after the running Danes, the Picts ran for their horses. Next came the part they lived for. A broken army ran as individuals, and thus were easy prey for even the lightly armored mounted spearmen from the northern lands of *Alba*. Hundreds of Danes fell from wounds in their backs. The hard-riding Picts showed no mercy.

Ambrose yelled at Polonius. "Scholar, let's mount up the Saxons and see if we can catch us a would-be king!"

Within minutes, the two commanders had mounted up and collected a force of Saxons. The band spurred after Ethelwold and his officers, ignoring the hundreds of running Danes. The Northumbrian commanders were well mounted, however, and had kept their horses beside them during the battle. The hard-riding officers made it safely to a border fort before the prince and his men could catch up. Ambrose cursed as he watched the fort's gates swing shut. He turned to his companion of many years and almost as many battles.

"Damn it, Polonius! He was almost in our grasp! I know that we are going to be sorry that we did not manage to kill him today."

"Prince, we shattered his army and the Danes will now have little faith in their new king's judgment. That is at least something."

℞

King Constantine took the horn of mead that Ambrose offered him. He smiled for the first time and sat down on the tree stump that Phillip had placed next to the campfire. The dead had been buried, and the wounded had been seen to. Amongst the Danes, there were no wounded. The Picts and Scots had simply slit their throats.

The Alban king raised his horn. "Here's to the brave men who gave their lives teaching the Danes the meaning of fear!"

Ambrose, Polonius and Phillip raised their mugs in tribute. Constantine then turned to Ambrose.

"Prince, you said that you actually visited this New Rome, this mystical city of Constantinople?"

"It is not mythical, Sire, but it is a very long way from here. After an audacious attack on Constantinople, the Vikings of Kiev sent us south as joint ambassadors to the royal court at Constantinople."

"Is it really as big as they say?"

"It is so big that the Vikings who travel there from their frozen lands in the far north just know it as Miklagard, or 'big city'."

"It has been said that no army can conquer the mighty city." said King Constantine.

"The three of us were actually part of a joint Viking-Slav attack on the great city. Together, they called themselves

Varangians."

Constantine grew excited. "And did you actually manage to take it?"

"Sire, by either great good fortune or very clever timing, both the Byzantine army and navy were away at the time. We sank the few ships they had, and defeated a force of cavalry who attacked us on the shore, but we never faced their main forces. We fled before they could return."

"Were you able to break through the walls?"

"We seized hundreds of trading craft and raided and burned the farms and settlements around the city for perhaps a hundred Roman miles. There was no hope of taking the city itself, and, in fact, it wasn't necessary. Viking traders had been abused, and the Vikings were trying to teach the Byzantines a lesson. I cannot begin to list the treasures that were taken from the Byzantine territory outside the walls. On the way back across the Black Sea, many ships sank because they were so grossly overloaded with treasures. Every member of the expedition who survived went home very, very rich."

"Then you are saying that this 'Varangian' army could not take the city itself?"

"A large enough army could take it, Sire, but it would involve a siege of several years, and vast numbers of warriors. There are three separate walls, each one towering over the next, and the smallest as great as the greatest wall I have ever seen on the island of Britain. These mighty walls stretch for many miles, and enclose vast harbors. I watched just a few byzantine naval vessels attack us, and, with their dreaded *Greek-Fire*, it is safe to say that they have the most powerful fleet in the world. As long as they can keep control of the sea, the city will never fall."

"And is it as rich as they say?"

"I had golden lions roar at me, and had gilded songbirds in metal trees sing to me. The emperor's throne rose high into the air while I was talking with him. Entire roofs were covered in gold, and the number of people who live within the walls is possibly greater than the population of this entire island."

"The city sounds incredible. Where does such wealth come

from?"

"The Byzantines live to trade, Sire. They are at the crossroad of trade between the east and the west, the frozen north and the African south. They take a percentage of all the trade that passes through their lands. As well, Byzantium has a system of guilds. Only men certified by the appropriate guild are allowed to sell their goods, and the standards are extraordinary. Constantinople exports its crafted goods to all parts of the world."

"Prince Ambrose, I am puzzled. You said that these Varangians sent you and Polonius as ambassadors?"

Ambrose smiled. "True, Sire. I am a prince and Polonius is an expert linguist and negotiator, but I do not think those were the real reasons we were chosen."

"Oh, then what were they?"

"We represented the Varangians - the mixture of Viking tribes who had settled along the northern rivers, plus the Slavs who had allied themselves with the Viking interlopers - but we were not Viking ourselves. Thus we were relatively neutral, and, if truth be told, the Byzantines had killed us, well, that would not automatically have caused an immediate blood feud, since we were foreigners."

"But the ballads say that you managed to negotiate a treaty."

"Aye, Sire, we did. The emperor was most gracious to us."

"Then you could have stayed and amassed a great fortune."

"We actually might have, except that the Grand Chamberlain, now Emperor Basil, attempted to involve us in nasty politics and expected Polonius, with his unique knife-throwing skills, to kill the reigning emperor for him! I was expected to kill an old but very rich man after he caught me cuckolding him. Rather than get caught up in their sordid affairs, we fled the city."

ᙏ

King Constantine climbed down from his horse and hugged Prince Ambrose and then Polonius. "Thanks to your Welsh archers, the path home is clear. It will take the Danes time to reconstitute an army. I will ride east to avoid the bands of vengeful Danes still moving south, and then I will push north. I intend to be safely across the Alban border before they even realize I am heading north again."

Ambrose smiled. "May God watch over you, King Constantine. I hope that we are never enemies. I very much enjoyed riding with you."

"I, too, Prince.' He smiled suddenly. 'For old men, you and your Byzantine friend are worthy companions. I am proud to have ridden with you. Go with God, my friends."

CHAPTER 25

A.D. 902. This year came Ethelwold hither over sea with all the fleet that he could get, and he was submitted to in Essex.
..........Anglo-Saxon Chronicles

Polonius stood before Edward, Phillip and Ambrose, a tiny sheet of parchment in his hand and worry on his face. "King, this urgent message has just arrived from Rochester. More than two hundred Viking craft have already passed the *burh*, with more on the horizon! All seem to be flying the banner of Jorvik."

Edward had a look of alarm on his face. "Ethelwold! By the many-colored coat of Joseph, where can they all be heading?"

"The report just says that they are heading up the Thames estuary. Our ships pulled back to Rochester to send this warning and await further instructions."

Edward rose to his feet and started pacing. "And just what are we going to do about this possible invasion?"

Polonius spoke. "Sire, I would suggest that we should alert the London garrison immediately! If that is the target, then they must be warned! As well, we could send several of the ships based in London downriver, with instructions to scout around, but to retreat in the face of any hostile ships. Come to think of it, the **Black Arrow** is presently in London, and it is the fastest ship in the fleet. Let us send it downriver with one of Jorvik's captured banners on its mast. Ethelred might also wish to start calling up his *fyrdmen*."

"And us?"

"Kent is mobilizing as we speak, but, beyond that, we need

more information, Sire."

"Polonius, it is clear that the attack is aimed at us, at Mercia, or at East Anglia. There are no other targets up the Thames."

"Then let's start with calling up *fyrdmen* from Berkshire, Wiltshire and Surrey. If Ethelwold is coming south of the Thames, they are the most likely *shires* to be invaded."

"And you say Kent has already mobilized?"

"The fleet has by-passed Kent, Sire, but they are ready for any trouble."

"And the other *shires*?"

"I would suggest that we send messengers with warnings to at least alert their *ealdormen* to the potential danger."

Edward paused in his restless pacing. "I don't know what I would do without you all. Polonius, can you make all that happen?"

"The birds will leave within the hour, Sire, and the human messengers with the dawn."

"Thank you. May God be merciful to Wessex today!"

⮊

Three days later, Polonius arrived at the king's planning room with the latest message from Ethelred of Mercia. Edward glanced eagerly at the little slip of parchment.

He spoke. "Well, Polonius, out with it! The suspense is killing me!"

"Sire, a massive Viking army has invaded Essex. Word has it that the jarls there are already suing for peace."

"Then there has been no invasion of Wessex or Mercia?"

"None reported as yet, Sire."

"Then the good news is that we are notfacing immediate invasion. The bad news is that we now have Ethelwold as a neighbor."

Polonius nodded. "True, King. It is not a matter of **if** we will be attacked, but **when**."

Ambrose interrupted. "I don't doubt that he is coming, but I think we have some time to prepare."

Edward was intrigued. "Uncle, why do you think so?"

"Ethelwold has just stolen a province from Eohric of East Anglia. I think he will have to see to its defense against East Anglia before he can turn to the invasion of Wessex. That being said, I do not think it a bad idea to send Ethelred several thousand *fyrdmen* to help with defense. Mercia has born far more than its share of the burden over the last few years."

Edward considered the words. "Perhaps we could call on Cornwall, Devon and Somerset this time. They are the least likely to face invasion."

Polonius bowed. "It shall be as you say, King!"

CHAPTER 26

A.D. 903. "This year Ethelwold enticed the army in East-Anglia to rebellion; so that they overran all the land of Mercia, until they came to Cricklade, where they forded the Thames; and having seized, either in Bradon or thereabout, all that they could lay their hands upon, they went homeward again."
......The Anglo-Saxon Chronicles.

Ambrose looked down at the map while King Edward pointed with his *sax*. "Ethelwold's men are right here, but the latest scouts indicated that they appear to be in full retreat."

"Surely that is not such a terrible thing, Nephew."

"Uncle, Ethelwold knows almost to the day how long it takes us to gather a host sufficient to meet him in open combat. The *fyrds* of Wiltshire, Devon, Sussex and Somerset are here, here, here, and here! A strong force of Mercians and Welshmen are approaching the Thames. The circle is almost complete and in just a few more days we would have had the traitor greatly outnumbered and thoroughly cornered!"

Ambrose spoke. "But not a single *burh* has fallen to Ethelwold and Eohric. Our women and children are not wearing slave chains, most of the livestock was moved out of their way, and the loot that Vikings crave so much is safe behind the same *burh* walls. I would count that a great success, Edward."

"They have burned hundreds of farms, Uncle! We could

well be facing starvation come winter."

Ambrose replied. "Nephew, the crops can be planted again next year, and buildings can be rebuilt. If you feel particularly guilty, you can open the crown's coffers a little, and help the people recover."

Edward turned to Polonius. "Can we afford to do that, Scholar?"

Polonius hesitated. "The treasury is not bottomless, but I think we could spare some silver . . . We did take an unholy lot of treasure from the Vikings when we took Benfleet and the Viking camp near Rochester, my king."

Edward sighed again. "Then arrange it, please, Polonius - once the war is over."

Polonius smiled. "It will be my pleasure, King!"

Ambrose spoke. "So what are we going to do about Ethelwold and his allies?"

Edward spoke angrily. "I want to follow the traitor king and his Viking subjects, and make them pay for what they did to Mercia and Wessex!"

Ambrose nodded. "The war arrows have already been sent and the *shire fyrds* have already gathered. It would be a shame not to lead that force into East Anglia."

Polonius suddenly smiled. "Let us not be too hasty!"

Edward was puzzled. "But Scholar, they must be punished. East Anglia is long overdue for a lesson, and I would, frankly, like Essex returned to the fold. My father only gave it to Guthrum under duress, and now that Eohric has torn up our covenant with him, I have no problem taking it back from him."

"Except you now have to take it back from the warriors of Ethelwold."

Edward paused. "I have no problem with that! Of the two Viking kings, however, I am most upset with Eohric. I expected nothing less from Ethelwold. We must, therefore, punish Eohric and East Anglia."

Polonius spoke. "And so they shall be punished, King!"

Edward smiled in return. "Out with it, Scholar! I know

your devious mind is coming up with something."

"Sire, what happens if we snap at their heels all the way back to the border?"

"They could turn and fight, but as our numbers swell on the march to the border, that will be less and less likely. More likely they will cross the border with their loot intact and then man their border forts against us."

"Which would mean?"

"Once we have crossed the border? We would be forced to bypass strong positions, which would leave our supply lines extremely vulnerable, or we stop to besiege their fortifications one by one."

"And that would mean?"

Edward sighed. "We would need ten to one odds to be assured victory, they would have time to muster overwhelming forces of their own . . . and we would still suffer huge losses . . . Unless?"

"Unless, my king, we follow them to the border, but with only a small force."

"What are you thinking, Polonius?"

"The small force, of perhaps five hundred warriors, harasses them all the way to the border."

"And?"

"And once we reach the border, we start on the construction of an old Roman marching fort."

Edward grew impatient. "So they will think that we are going to build a static defense against further incursions. They will think that we are going to once again respect the boundary, but we will not?"

"Sire, We move all those other *shire fyrds* to perhaps a half day's ride from near the border, but quietly. We send out a thick screen of scouts to keep the enemy blind and guessing. If it looks like we are not massing our *fyrdmen*, they might even disband some of their warriors once they re-enter home territory . . . Meanwhile, the fleet slips its moorings from London and Rochester, while the massed *fyrdmen* ride for the border."

"I am listening, Polonius."

"The army crosses the river in a lightening thrust. We might have the Welsh archers line our side of the river. The ships ferry men, while others try to ride across at the ford. Whatever rearguard the Danes left at the river border will move to the river bank to cut us down as we attempt to land."

"We know they will, Scholar, archers or not. They would be loathe to lose such a large advantage."

"But the other half of the fleet moves, by night, quietly to the river shore a few Roman miles from the ford and disgorges its cargo of Kentish *fyrdmen*. The *fyrdmen* march the few miles and hit the Danes from behind, while our main force tries to force its way across at the ford, We kill all we can. If we can sufficiently shatter their border force, it will take weeks for them to throw together another force that is capable of threatening us. Meanwhile, we use Ethelwold's lightening tactics. We ride north through both Essex and East Anglia, perhaps as far as the northern fens, burning and pillaging all the way."

Edward nodded. "Both Essex and East Anglia will be like a beehive with a bear's nose stuck in it. Thousands of furious Viking warriors will march to the sound of battle."

"Which is why, Sire, we move quickly, ignore any strongholds, have limited objectives, and then withdraw before the Viking bees can swarm in sufficient numbers to threaten us - just as Ethelwold and Eohric did to us. We might also consider exiting via northern Mercia. It would mean, as long as we keep moving, that we do not have to cut back through the territory we have already raided, and the gathering Danes will have to chase us all the way."

Edward smiled. "I think we have a plan!"

⚑

The long-ships appeared with the dawn. Dozens of ships fought the current and moved steadily up the Lea River. Ship-mounted catapults launched rocks and flaming balls at the

Viking defenses on the east bank, while files of Welsh archers stood on the western shore and filled the air with shafts. Column after column of mounted riders headed for the ford, while over a thousand dismounted *fyrdmen* clambered aboard the ships designated as troop carriers.

The Danes, however, were no strangers to war, and few warriors in the world were braver. The big Northmen ran for the shore and manned their line of recently built defenses. The stones and fireballs launched from the Mercian side of the river could do little actual damage against the dirt and rock emplacements, but they at least added to the confusion. Occasionally, a ball would strike men in the open, and when this happened, there was little left except blood and mangled remains. The northern warriors kept low, held their shields over their heads, and waited impatiently for the enemy to come into range. Long before the mounted *fyrdmen* could force their horses out of the water, they would come within spear-casting range of the shore. For the Danes, that was the killing time. Stacks of spears awaited the foolish Saxons who were daring to try and enter Viking territory.

King Edward, surrounded by members of his Personal Guard and officers, stood on the riverbank and watched the West Saxon army preparing to invade Viking land. He anxiously scanned the horizon. Somewhere behind the Viking line should be Sigehelm and his *fyrd* of Kentish warriors, running hard to join the battle.

Phillip pointed out a smudge of smoke on the horizon, and Edward heaved a sigh of relief. The smoke could only be from the little Viking village to the east, which Sigehelm had promised to fire as a sign to the waiting Saxons. The king turned to his chief advisor.

"Phillip is right! I can see the column of smoke clearly now. Polonius, let us start the invasion!"

At Polonius' signal, the columns began their advance into the water, while the ships slipped into the river and headed for beachheads on either side of the waiting Danes. The Danes were gripping their throwing spears and choosing their targets when a brazen blare of war horns shocked them into turning their heads. Behind them came a horde of running warriors!

While the Vikings turned to face the new threat, the columns of West Saxon horsemen made the shore, and both to the north and south, ships disgorged more hordes of warriors. The Vikings suddenly realized that they were vastly outnumbered, were cut off from their horses, and their sturdy riverbank defenses were of little value when the enemy was behind them. Without panic, the warriors formed defensive circles and started withdrawing toward the inviting forest to the east.

The Saxons, Angles, Jutes, and Welshmen that made up the West Saxon army threw themselves at the retreating forces. They killed many, but the price was heavy. The Danes were masters at the shield-wall, where their large size, their bravery and their strength made them a tough foe.

At last, the Vikings who had not died in the savage fighting made it to the forest and ran. The open land along the riverbank was now littered with hundreds of dead or wounded Vikings. The Saxon army paused at the edge of the forest, and most turned back to finish off the wounded and loot the bodies.

King Edward rode across the battlefield and spoke to his uncle. "Ambrose, I will never get over seeing the carnage on a battlefield. Each time I see it, is sickens me again."

His uncle replied. "I hope that you never get over feeling that way, Edward. The king who is not distressed by the sacrifices made in his name on the field of battle is a poor king! Christ taught us that each soul is important, and life is precious. We must also remember, however, that the alternative is to see our young men and women wearing chains, with the rest callously butchered because they are considered of too little value to bother with. Sometimes you must spend lives for the greater good, but it should never be easy to do."

CHAPTER 27

AD 902: King Edward went after, as soon as he could gather his army, and overran all their land between the Foss and the Ouse quite to the fens northward. Then being desirous of returning thence, he issued an order through the whole army, that they should all go out at once. But the Kentish men remained behind, contrary to his order, though he had sent seven messengers to them.
.........The Anglo-Saxon Chronicles.

Edward showed a little of his fiery temper. "Where, in God's name, are my Kentish *fyrdmen*? I can not delay our departure any longer! Polonius, did I not ask you to send a messenger to recall Sigehelm?"

Polonius looked directly into the young king's eyes. "Aye, you did, King, and I have sent one a day for the last six days."

"Then where are my damned *fyrdmen*? Sigehelm commands a full third of my force, and your scouts tell me a whirlwind is on its way! We need to gather our men and ride for the border, or we are going to be trapped and overwhelmed. Is that not what you told me?"

"Aye, Sire. There are between three and five thousand very angry Viking warriors riding our way. Fortunately, they thought you would return the way you came, and most of the enemy army is concentrated to the south of us."

"You said six messengers?"

"One a day for six days, Sire."

"Could the Danes be intercepting our men?"

"Possible, King, but unlikely."

Edward stared at Polonius. Suddenly, the king smiled. "I am sorry, Scholar! I am not angry with you! Most of all, I am worried. Sigehelm commands almost five hundred men - men I am counting on if the Danes do manage to catch up and we are forced to fight."

Ambrose spoke. "Nephew, give me Polonius and Phillip, and I will find out what happened to Sigehelm and his men."

"Uncle, it is dangerous out there! We have riled up a lot of Vikings. You cannot just ride through hostile country with but two men at your side!"

"Canuteson can, Edward."

"Oh no! Uncle, you have played that trick over and over. They still sing ballads about you doing just that. You are too well known to pull it off in East Anglia, especially after the stunt you pulled not long ago, taking a fleet right up the river to Eohric's *tun*, and especially with a thin dark man and a giant at your side."

"Then give me an escort of thirty men, and we will ride hard under Wessex's banners."

"Ambrose, I do not want to lose my favorite uncle! The three of you are much too precious to risk in such a manner, and you do not even know where to find our lost *fyrdmen*."

"Nephew, the trail of destruction is plain to see. It will take few scouting skills to follow the path of havoc that the Kentish fyrdmen carved through the land. You need to get this force heading toward the border without any more delay. If we come across a sizable Viking force, then we will retreat in good order. You know we are your last chance to extract the Kentish *fyrd*. Sigehelm will not dare disobey a direct order from a prince of the royal house."

Edward sighed. "Uncle, I cannot approve. You must forgive a young and nervous king, but I truly believe that without you and Polonius whispering in my ear, I will lose this war."

Ambrose smiled. "I think you have already learned most of the lessons that we could impart to you. Let us go and find the rest of your army, before it is too late. You know Polonius will do his best to keep Phillip and me from doing anything foolish, and you will need the Kentish *fyrdmen* in your battle line if you are forced to fight."

Edward gave in with good grace and hugged Ambrose tightly. "Go with God, Uncle, and bring these two back to me!"

"I intend to bring you five hundred and two, Edward. Promise me something, however."

"Name it, Uncle."

"Do not wait for us, or you will get the entire army trapped."

"Very well, Ambrose, but I will hold you to your promise to bring these two back to my side. I think there are many more lessons for you three to teach me before we are done."

༞

The three men, followed by their escort, rode quickly through a land devastated by Sigehelm and his Kentish *fyrdmen*. Crops were trampled, animals, those not butchered to feed the Kentish army, lay dead in the fields, and most houses were nothing but charred wood and ash.

The land was eerily empty of any people. Ambrose felt several times that they were being watched, but any survivors hid themselves in the forests. It depressed the prince to see the extent of the damage, but he remembered his own land, which the Vikings had invaded at least six or seven times in his memory. It didn't make it more right, but he knew that the retaliatory raids were vital if they were going to eventually muzzle the fierce Viking beast.

Experience in the East with the conquering Rus had taught him that Vikings respected strength above all. According to their logic, a man who threw down his weapon and surrendered deserved to be made slave. Mercy was not a word in the Viking vocabulary. Eohric had to learn the price of constantly supporting the invaders of Wessex. Ambrose knew that the same demonstration would not teach Ethelwold a thing. The only cure for him was cold steel ruthlessly applied to his person. His hate was so great that only death could cure his resolve to conquer Wessex.

❧

The thirty men switched to their spare mounts and continued to move swiftly forward. Ambrose knew, unless a new band of Vikings had slipped past their many scouts, that there were no large armed bands in the area. There would be, no doubt, a lot of scattered and very angry armed men. The secret was to move fast enough that the refugees could not throw together a force large enough to threaten him and his escort. Thus they used spare horses and rode hard.

Polonius was the first to call out. "Look up ahead, Prince! Is it my imagination, or is that the walls of a fortified *tun*?"

Ambrose looked through the tiny hole made by bending his index finger inwards. The finger blocked the glare of light from the sun, and through the aperture he was able to see what Polonius had spotted with his sharp eyes.

"I do believe you are right, Scholar! The *tun* may be manned by Eohric's men. We might consider sending some scouts forward."

"Look again, Master. Is that not the banner of Kent flying from the tower?"

"As nephew Edward would say - 'By the many-colored coat of Joseph' - you are right again, my friend! It just may be that we have finally found the lost army."

❧

Thirty three men rode to the gate, which squealed open when Phillip called out to the sentry above it. **"Open the gate for Prince Ambrose, fool!"**

Ambrose led his little column through the gate, and immediately started looking around. There were household goods scattered indiscriminately everywhere on the ground, and most of the *fyrdmen* he could see were stinking drunk. Two *fyrdmen* right by the gate were holding down a naked woman, and a third was entering her.

The prince turned to Phillip. "Weapons-master, I think I now know why Sigehelm has failed to report! I want our escort to stay together - no drinking! Break a few heads if you have to - and destroy all the ale or mead you can find. I want the Kentish men in formation within an hour, and ready to ride by dawn!"

Phillip looked around angrily. "It will be done, Prince!"

Leaving Phillip and the men of the escort to start imposing military discipline, Ambrose and Polonius rode on, looking for the *ealdorman* who should be in command. Polonius pointed, and the two headed for the *tun's* Great Hall, where Sigehelm's personal banner flapped intermittently in the desultory breeze.

A sentry sitting on the ground by the main door got unsteadily to his feet at their approach. He slurred his words. "'alt! No admittance 'ere!"

Polonius shouted at the sentry. "Stand at attention when you stand before a prince of the royal house! Is *Ealdorman* Sigehelm within?"

"Aye . . . yes, sir, but 'e gave orders that 'e was not to be disturbed."

Phillip's voice boomed. "Out of the way, lout! You are a disgrace! Go get yourself cleaned up and then report back here! At once!"

The drunken sentry looked owlishly at the big man and the huge sword hanging down his back, and meekly stepped out of the way. When the sentry had moved, Ambrose and Polonius entered the hall. The light within was dim, but Ambrose could hear the sound of lovemaking from behind a leather curtain to his right. He thrust the curtain aside and stepped boldly into the *bower*. *Ealdorman* Sigehelm and a naked girl with the small conical breasts and pale nipples of a female new to adulthood looked up in surprise. The *ealdorman* spoke before he could see who had so rudely interrupted. "I said that I was not to be disturbed! . . . Is that really you, Prince Ambrose?"

"It could just as easily be an army of Vikings, Sigehelm. Your men are drunk and would be hard-pressed to beat off an attack of cackling geese! King Edward ordered you to return to his side almost a week ago, but you are still here! Shall I choose a new *ealdorman*, Sigehelm? You no longer seem to want the job!"

While the girl drew a blanket up to cover her nakedness, the *ealdorman* leapt to his feet. "Prince, I can explain!"

"There is nothing to explain, *Ealdorman*! You have almost a third of King Edward's army - men that he will need desperately if the Danes catch up with him - unfit for combat and miles from where they are supposed to be. Your king held up his retreat for six days waiting for you! Are you not aware that almost five thousand Viking warriors are killing their horses trying to catch up and kill us? To add to that, you have disobeyed six separate summonses from Edward!"

"I . . . I am sorry, Prince. My men fought like Trojans to take this *tun*. Many died in the storming. The least I could do is let them blow off a little steam. I told them they could take what they can carry, and couple with any of the women they could catch. It is the traditional right of the *fyrdmen*, Prince!"

"And did you tell your officers to destroy the supplies of ale and mead before you let your men break discipline, *Ealdorman*?"

"No, Prince, I thought they deserved it for their celebration."

"Well a squad of children could take this *tun* right now, *Ealdorman*! Your sentries are as drunk as the rest of your men!"

"Prince, I will go out right now and kick them into shape. We will be prepared to ride come morning!"

"At the moment, *Ealdorman*, I would not trust you to guard a latrine. You are as drunk as your men."

As he spoke, the smell of a fire reached their nostrils. Ambrose smiled. "It seems like someone is finally doing their job. I ordered Phillip to use any means necessary to restore order. Unless I miss my guess, we are smelling the destruction of the *tun's* supplies of ale and mead . . . Now get yourself dressed and give him some help! I will discuss later with King Edward just what to do about your disobedience and incompetence."

"Yes, Prince!"

Chapter 28

AD. 903: Whereupon the (Viking) army surrounded them, and there they fought . . . On the Danish side were slain Eohric their king, and Prince Ethelwold, who had enticed them to the war. And there was on either hand much slaughter made; but of the Danes there were more slain, though they remained masters of the field.

.........The Anglo-Saxon Chronicles.

Theomund, commander of the Kentish *fyrd*, spurred to his master's side. "*Ealdorman* Sigehelm, we are undone!"

The *ealdorman* looked visibly annoyed. "What are you prattling on about, man?"

"*Ealdorman*, the Danes have caught up with us!"

Sigehelm looked in all directions before replying. "I see nothing but trees!"

"No, *Ealdorman*, the advance scouts have just returned. The Danes have massed ahead of us, with over a thousand men. They have formed a shield-wall across the road and meadow, and they are between us and King Edward!"

At last the words sank in. "May all the saints show us mercy! You mean our line of retreat has been cut off?"

"Aye, *Ealdorman*, and we know that the main Viking army is moving up from the south, with yet more from the east. It is only a matter of time before we are surrounded."

The *ealdorman* turned to Prince Ambrose and his companions. "Do you or Lord Polonius have any suggestions, Prince?"

Ambrose spoke first. "We can't stay here, and there are

thousands of vengeance-seeking Danes behind us. That leaves only one direction left. We go forward! We will simply have to cut our way through their *skjaldborg*."

Theomund wiped his brow with a sweaty hand. "Mayhap, Prince, if we fortify and hold our present position, King Edward will move against the foe."

Ambrose replied. "Theomund, I specifically asked King Edward not to do that. The essence of this raid was to invade quickly, move fast, cause as much damage as possible in a short time, and get out before the full army could be brought against us. A fight against five thousand battle-trained Viking warriors would destroy the West Saxon *fyrd*. By losing our mobile force, we would be forced to fight a strictly defensive war, with little chance of hitting back. King Edward realizes the need to preserve his force of raiding horsemen, and he promised not to wait any longer. He already stayed for more days than he should have, waiting for a lost division of Kentish *fyrdmen* who were too drunk to follow orders."

Theomund looked very worried. "Then may God be merciful! We are trapped and outnumbered, deep in hostile territory. Is there anything at all that we can do, Prince?"

Ambrose turned to Polonius. "Scholar, do you have any ideas?"

"The odds are against us, my prince, but we can fight!"

Ambrose smiled. "I had not expected to hear that from you, Scholar!"

"As a famous trader of Alexandria used to say, it is *'kismet'*.

"Then you are saying it is our fate to dismount, form a shield-wall, and attack a force more than twice as large as ours?"

My prince, you must dig deep into your memory and remember the words of Sun Tzu! After all, it is he who said 'the clever combatant imposes his will on the enemy, but does not allow the enemy's will to be imposed on him'."

Ambrose looked exasperated. "Scholar, would you please translate that for a poor ignorant barbarian prince?"

Polonius smiled. "Prince, it means that we do not have to fight the way that the Vikings expect us to."

Ambrose sighed. "Then what, exactly, are you proposing?"

"You saw for yourself the might of the Khazar and Pecheneg lancers, Prince."

"They were magnificent, Polonius, but we have all of thirty men you trained as lancers, borrowed from King Edward's army. We have almost six hundred *fyrdmen* here."

"Prince, what problems do you foresee with a mounted attack?"

"First, my friend, we need six hundred lances. That seems to be a major and insurmountable problem. We have no spare metal, few smiths, no forges, and, most important, no time to remedy the situation."

"We are in the midst of a forest, Prince. How long does it take for each man to cut and strip one sapling?"

"We are going to attack with trees?"

"We are going to sharpen one end. With the power of a horse at full gallop behind it, such a lance can be driven right through a man if it hits in the right place. At the least, it can send the man flying and open a hole in a shield-wall."

"They will not last long, Polonius."

"How long does it take a galloping horse to charge through three lines of infantry? I do not expect them to last long. When they break, the riders throw them away and use their swords and axes. The main purpose of the lance is to help break up the tight Viking formation by virtue of its long reach."

"Scholar, you told me that a horse can not be made to ride at a solid wall without a great deal of training. A Viking *skjaldborg* will look very solid to a horse."

"You are right, Master. Our best chance is to ride as a mounted *Svinfylka*.'

Sigehelm looked confused. "*Svinfylka*? What is that, Prince?"

"You know it as a boar's snout. If we ride in a tight wedge formation, the horses in the center will try and turn, but will find their way blocked by the outer riders."

"But Prince, the horses on the edges will have the room to turn."

Polonius replied for Ambrose. "You are right. Those riders

can use their lances to keep the Vikings away until they can turn their mounts, but their horses will hold the rest in formation."

Sigehelm looked confused again. "And then, Polonius?"

"Then the outer riders turn, ride back, and try again. Some of them will be cut down, but they should have bought the horsemen in the center the pressure needed for hundreds of horses to break through. By the time they come around for a second try, we will have either punched a hole through the Danes, or we will be broken."

The *ealdorman* continued. "Lord Polonius, you told me once that the Rus Vikings stopped horsemen cold. Why will they not stop us?"

"The Rus Vikings used long lances and hidden pits to break the charge, but in spite of all that, their first rank broke under the avalanche of nomad horse flesh. The horsemen, however, lost their momentum. The second and third rank of Vikings then got to work with spears and axes. They stabbed the riders or hamstrung the horses. Once a horseman loses his momentum and tight formation, he becomes very vulnerable to determined infantry."

Ambrose, Phillip, Polonius and Sigehelm all looked at each other. The prince spoke.

"Polonius gives me hope. We either fight in the time-honored fashion, and the Danes, with their superior numbers, will hold in the center and envelop our ends, or we try a trick that they will not be expecting. Some of us will die, but there is a good chance that a majority of us can break through and make it safely to the Mercian border. Make no mistake. Our goal is no more than to escape the trap with as many men as we can. Are we agreed?"

Each nodded assent, and Sigehelm spoke. "I will go and inform my men to make lances immediately, Prince. Then I will explain the formation we will use . . . Prince, I had another thought."

"And what is that, *Ealdorman*?"

"Ethelwold and Eohric are proud men and will be overconfident. They may join the *skjaldborg*."

"It is possible, Sigehelm."

"Then we should aim the tip of the wedge directly at their banners."

Ambrose looked thoughtful. "They will have much of their Personal Guard there with them, Sigehelm."

The *ealdorman* shrugged. "Then a few more of us will not break clear, but if we can manage to kill the two kings, then the entire war is over!"

Theomund looked concerned. "*Ealdorman*, many of our *fyrdmen* will die if we target the leaders! Should we not target their weakest point?"

Ealdorman Sigehelm sighed. "We are warriors, Theomund, and we got ourselves into this mess. We will show the Viking bastards how the Jutes of Kent can fight! We cut our way through them, or we die."

Theomund looked unconvinced. "*Ealdorman*, I would humbly suggest we cut through the weakest point and ride for our lives!"

Sigehelm smiled. "There are worse ways to die, my friend! Every man we kill will be one more who will not be coming for our women and children. Tell the men to cut the lances. Go now, and be sure to tell the men we fight for our families, for Kent and for God!"

CHAPTER 29

Sigehelm Closes with the Viking Host

The first thing Ambrose heard as he and the vanguard of *fyrdmen* exited the forest was the thunder of swords and axes on shields. His eyes quickly confirmed the fact that the Danes had formed a long *skjaldborg* across the open ground and across the road to the west. Sigehelm's *fyrd* was clearly outnumbered, and the Danes were noisily waiting to avenge the rape of their women and the burning of their farms. He knew that there would be no mercy shown on this battleground. For the first time, the Danes of East Anglia had been attacked on their home ground by the West Saxons, and they were furious.

Sigehelm watched as three hundred of his men filed out of the forest, dismounted, and formed a screening shield-wall parallel to the Viking formation. They kept their horses close behind them, however. They would swiftly remount when Sigehelm ordered the advance. The *ealdorman* turned to Ambrose. "I see no white shield advancing, Prince. It appears that they do not wish to parley."

Ambrose nodded. "Keep riding, my friends. We must move to a position in front of the shield-wall . . . I am not surprised. I suspect that they are not very happy with us. We have devastated their land, stolen their treasures, and despoiled their women."

Sigehelm looked angry. "They have been doing all that to West Saxons since the days of the *Great Army*! It was time for a little pay-back."

"Well, *Ealdorman*, it looks like they intend to punish us for our deeds. They outnumber us, and somewhere behind us are thousands more, all closing on our location. We have been boxed in."

"This I know, my Prince, and I also know that it is my fault that you and your comrades are trapped here with me. My men will do what they can to expunge the stain on their honor."

"Order the rest of your men to exit the forest and move into the boar's head formation behind the shield-wall, Sigehelm. I will attempt to see if I can buy you some more time by parleying."

Sigehelm spoke. "They are mad as hell, Prince Ambrose. I do not think they want to talk to us, and we have very little to offer them."

"We are unlikely to gain much, *Ealdorman*, but it buys us time to form up the men. The worst thing that could happen right now is that they start an advance. If they close with us now, we will be fighting on their terms, and if we do that, we will lose!'

Ambrose turned to Polonius. 'Raise the royal standard, Scholar, and send a man with a white shield forward. The banner should get their attention."

The royal banner worked. Within moments after seeing it fly above the trapped Kentish warriors, four men, dressed in expensive armor and well mounted, rode slowly across the land between the two forces. Two wore crowns, and Ambrose recognized both his cousin and the Viking king of East Anglia.

Ambrose, Polonius and Sigehelm rode out to meet the approaching riders. When Ethelwold saw Ambrose and Polonius, he went red. "You again! Whenever there is trouble, you two seem to be in the midst of it. I should have known you were behind this latest outrage!"

"And good morning to you, too, Cousin. I see that you have managed to raise a new army. Did you tell King Eohric that you cowardly abandoned the last two armies you raised, fleeing to save your precious skin? You even left your loving bride, freshly torn from the convent, to our tender mercies in your haste to escape. You will be glad to know that I removed her chains personally."

Ethelwold spit out the words. "You go too far, Cousin! I knew I should have had you poisoned years ago!"

Ambrose smiled. "Funny, that is what Polonius said about

you soon after he met you, and I seem to remember that your last attempt to poison someone was yet another one of your bumbling failures. You are fortunate. The very king you tried to kill saved your worthless hide one more time by forbidding your execution. That is truly Christian mercy!"

"Well, we shall see who wins, today, bastard prince! I finally have you where I want you."

"Prophetic words, Viking lackey. They are disturbingly similar to the ones you uttered in the north - just before our thousand Welsh archers taught you yet another lesson in the meaning of the word 'failure'.

Ambrose turned to the Viking king. "King Eohric, I do not question your bravery, but I have to question your judgment. This man you follow has run several times now, once after swearing a sacred oath to stay and defend a *tun* with his very life. He has, in turn, abandoned the burial place of his father, his Saxon followers, his Viking subjects, and even his wife!"

Ethelwold was almost beside himself. "You slimy bastard, how dare you tell filthy lies about me!"

"If you are not happy with my words, Ethelwold, be a man! Draw that beautiful sword you wear at your side and meet me in *holmgang*. I am an old man, but I am prepared to meet you in single combat at any time. It is the tradition of the men you lead. I would be pleased to inflict on you yet another defeat to add to your long list. The good news, however, is that it would be your last defeat. I would cut your throat like a squealing pig."

While Ethelwold sputtered, Eohric spoke. "You and your king have done a terrible thing, Prince Ambrose. After we massacre your force today, we will be planning to visit Wessex again."

Ambrose spoke quietly. "You have reaped what you sowed, King. I warned you that we would retaliate if you were foolish enough to cross our border. In the past, we respected your boundaries. You crossed a line, however, Eohric. We offered you the hand of friendship, and, when your men raided our lands, again and again, we accepted your word that the culprits were young men who were acting without your blessing. We targeted them in your land, but we did not go after you. For the first time, however, you followed this fool and traitor here, and personally led your men into Mercia and Wessex. There are consequences for your actions, King! Go back and count the burned fields and the dead men. Listen to the screaming women. Ponder on why it happened. This was just a small raid. We are far from done with you yet!"

"Prince Ambrose, I told you before that in another time and place, we might have been friends. It saddens me that my men will send you to your Christian heaven this very day. What you have done - a Viking king cannot forgive."

Ambrose looked at his companion before replying. When Polonius nodded, he spoke. "Then I guess, King, that you and I have nothing more to say. I am willing to let my *Victory-Maker* speak for me."

Sigehelm chose the point of attack and pointed his bared sword at the small knoll, rare in this flat land, where the royal banners of both Ethelwold and Eohric flew. The two kings had not joined the battle line, but they were not far behind it. Sigehelm's *fyrdmen*, now each armed with their newly acquired long wooden lances, closed in until they were in a tight wedge formation, and then the Saxon horns screamed.

The three hundred warriors who had stood so resolutely in line scrambled out of the way and then mounted their own horses. Over three hundred men thundered forward as one, followed closely by three hundred more. The Danes were no cowards, and, seeing the advancing horses being whipped into a gallop, they linked shields and the second line moved forward to press on the backs of their comrades in an attempt to physically support the front line. The second and third lines threw their hand axes at the charging riders when they came in range, but those with spears held on to them. Spears were more effective than swords or axes against armored men mounted on horses.

The horses tried to turn from the seemingly impenetrable wall of shields that stretched before them, but they were so closely packed together that most could not. The tip of the wedge struck with incredible power. Hundreds of men and horses grunted and screamed. Horses were hamstrung and men were trampled. The newly cut lances gave the Kentish riders a long reach. Many of the lances were thrust aside or grabbed, but some, driven with all the weight and speed of a galloping horse, plunged into luckless Vikings or forced a break in the shield-wall. Within seconds the second and third lines of Danish warriors were broken at the point of contact. Suddenly, there were galloping horsemen behind the Viking *skjaldborg*. There were few things more frightening to warriors of any nationality. The Vikings would push and shove and hack all day as part of a shield-wall, but horsemen behind their formation was a thing of terror. Infantry could only hold against horsemen if they faced them in tight formation and had sufficient depth to their lines to absorb the shock of contact.

The Kentish *fyrd* had paid a stiff price for their passage. More than a hundred men and horses lay dead or wounded on the ground, but they had done the impossible. They had torn through a Viking *skjaldborg*!

The Saxon horns screamed again, however, and the riders, who had just broken through and were now free to ride for their lives, their freedom and their king, turned as one and rode at the noblemen and officers who stood on the little knoll.

The Personal Guard of two kings stood straight and closed their ranks. Not one warrior was seen to run, and both kings drew their gleaming blades. The avalanche of horses and men hit, and the remaining spears and lances of the hard-riding *fyrdmen* struck with the sound of thunder. Dozens of Danes died in a moment, and then the horsemen were amongst them! This time, the *fyrdmen* leapt from their horses and savagely attacked on foot.

The royal guards had been chosen for their battle prowess and their courage, and they fought both bravely and tenaciously. Ambrose and his thirty-three companions, dismounted, drove directly toward the royal banners. Almost half of the little group fell. Ambrose cursed as a trio of strong young Danes blocked his way. They were young, and strong, and good with their swords. He was forced back by their weaving blades. He tripped on a dead man, and the tallest of the three grinned and swung his sword high, starting a stroke that no helmet could possibly stop. The Viking paused in puzzlement, however, at the whirling blade that had struck his neck. When he tried to stanch the flow of blood, a sword almost as long as a man decapitated him and then sliced deep into his companion's arm. Ambrose skewered the third man with *Victory-Maker*, the exotic sword old Canute had picked up off the sands of Northern Africa and given to the young slave boy he adopted.

A big Saxon just in front of Ambrose screamed as a blade bit deep into his neck, and suddenly, Eohric and Ambrose were face to face. By mutual agreement, both paused to catch their breaths. Eohric smiled. "Have you come to escort me to Valhalla today, little prince?"

Ambrose replied. "Close. I have come to send you there, King."

Eohric sighed. "It is a good day to die, my friend, and, in any case, you have not won yet."

"You were a fool to follow Ethelwold, King!"

"I will admit to you here and now that you are probably right. My people are eager for more land, however, and a Viking king can fall if he does not keep his people reasonably content."

"A Viking king may fall today **because** he tried to appease malcontents."

Eohric started his blade whirling. "Then I can only hope that the Valkyries make me one of their chosen!"

His blade suddenly cut at Ambrose's neck. The prince threw up his shield, and stabbed with *Victory-Maker*. The thrust of his famous sword forced Eohric to step back. A piece of wood was gouged off Ambrose's shield, but he was otherwise unhurt.

Ambrose spoke. "You have great strength, King!"

"And you have surprising speed for an old man, Prince."

Suddenly, two men of Eohric's Personal Guard broke free and charged at Ambrose. The first lost his sword hand to a whistling blade, and the other received a dagger in the eye. Eohric paused for just a moment, and then started a slashing attack while he spoke.

"Your companions are as good in real life as they are in the ballads, Prince!"

Ambrose's arm was tiring from the battering it took. Again and again he needed to use his sword to deflect the powerful cuts Eohric threw at him. He spoke again.

"One of us will soon make a mistake and will die, Eohric."

Eohric shrugged. "The threads of the tapestry have already been woven by the *Norns*, Prince. I have no intention, however, of making it easy for you!"

With that, the Viking king threw himself at Ambrose. His blade swung in a mighty arc that struck Ambrose's left arm, numbing it and wounding him right through the chain-mail. Eohric smiled, but was surprised himself to find that *Victory-Maker's* exotic steel had been capable of cutting through his chain mail and penetrating deep into his intestines.

He grimaced with pain and spoke. "I fear your blow was shrewder than mine, little prince. I shall miss you."

"And I will pray that the Valkyries make you their first choice, Eohric."

That said, he withdrew his blade, and the Viking king sagged to his knees. Ambrose could see the blood seeping from the wound and knew that it was fatal, but a slow killer. With great effort, Eohric wrenched off his helmet, exposing his neck. He spoke one last time.

"Finish the job, you have started, Ambrose. I have seen many men die from gut wounds, and I have no wish to scream for hours before I succumb."

Victory-Maker slashed out and bit deep into the king's neck. Eohric fell in a gush of blood.

Within a sixty count, the Saxon horns blared the retreat. Almost two hundred men, Viking, Saxon, and Jute, had fallen in the brief but bitter battle. Ambrose looked around with puzzlement, but Phillip explained.

"Prince, the Vikings of the shield-wall were hammered, but they are recovering and re-forming. We have little time if anyone is going to escape!"

Sigehelm's men, along with Ambrose's remaining followers, broke off and ran for their horses. Six hundred men had made a crazy charge against massively superior numbers, and barely three hundred survived to mount up. The men turned their horses west and urged them forward. Behind them, they left hundreds of dead Vikings, and one dead king.

As they rode, Sigehelm caught up to Ambrose. "Prince, Theomund just spotted Ethelwold riding north with a small escort! It is our best chance."

Ambrose replied. "Ride for Mercia, Sigehelm! Your men are heroes and they deserve to make it home! We are riding for our lives."

"Then make sure my brave men make it, Prince! May God bless you!"

With that, the king turned his horse northward and called over his shoulder. "Personal Guardsmen of the *ealdorman*, follow me!"

As the Saxon horns blared for the last time, the *ealdorman* charged after the fleeing Northumbrian riders. He did not pause to look, but he could sense men beside him. He knew, without a doubt, that his entire Personal Guard - those who had survived the bitter battle, was charging alongside him. He yelled out.

"Men with lances to the front! Charge!"

The galloping horsemen struck the mass of fleeing Vikings, and many of the big men went down with spears or lances in their backs. This time, however, their impetus was successfully absorbed by the loose formation and the Kentish Personal Guardsmen started going down. Theomund, the brave warrior, made it to Ethelwold's side and plunged a spear deep into his side, but within seconds he was himself mortally wounded. Swords and axes came from all directions, and the entire Kentish band died in less than a minute. The last thing *Ealdorman* Sigehelm saw, as he was torn from his saddle, was the bulk of his remaining *fyrdmen* crossing a little stream and escaping west. In spite of the pain of a sword being thrust deep into his intestines, he smiled.

Ambrose slowed and started to turn his horse. "Polonius, Phillip, we must help the brave fool!"

Polonius replied. "Prince, he is down and all of his Guard are dead or seconds from it! Our job now is to help the rest of the *fyrd* to survive. We still have a long ride, and the Danes will sort themselves out all too quickly and be on our tail. They still outnumber us two to one and there is no guarantee that we can make it to the safety of the Mercian border!"

Ambrose looked back and saw no more fighting. Hundreds of Viking warriors were running to assist Ethelwold's chosen warriors. He prayed that Ethelwold had fallen. Sigehelm and his Guard had paid a terrible price for a chance to get the traitor.

CHAPTER 30

A Truce

Ambrose sat his horse on the riverbank just across the river from the marching fort that Edward had had constructed on the Mercian side of the river. He watched the battered Kentish force splash across through the shallow water of the ford. Most of the men were wounded in some fashion, and there were many Kentish warriors who could barely stay in their saddles. In all, there were far fewer *fyrdmen* than when the force rode boldly into East Anglia some weeks before. Far too many brave warriors had fallen in the battle at the Holme, yet these Jutish warriors had done the impossible. Outnumbered and trapped, they had broken through a *skjaldborg* of furious Danes, and then, after winning free, their plucky ealdorman and his Personal Guard of warriors had turned their horses and ridden at the two enemy kings. The Kentish fyrdmen had faced the cream of the enemy fighters, but they still managed to kill both kings before they broke off and the survivors made their escape. With their lives, they had bought both victory and the successful escape of the rest of their battered army.

Following Sigehelm's instructions, Ambrose had reluctantly led the survivors due east, heading for friendly territory as fast as they could move. Somewhere behind them, thousands more Danes were marching to join the Viking army of vengeance. Ambrose was upset at leaving hundred's of dead and badly wounded on the battlefield, but with the odds they had faced, he felt that he and the Kentish fyrdmen were lucky to escape with any survivors. He had sworn to make sure that Sigehelm's brave sacrifice was not in vain.

At last, as the final fyrdmen struggled across the river,

Ambrose flicked the reins gently to instruct his horse to follow. His two faithful shadows bracketed him, and together, the three friends rode through the shallow water to Mercia.

 ┌≈

Edward waited until Ambrose dismounted, then caught the prince in a great bear hug. "Uncle, I despaired for you! I sent dozens of scouts across the river to look for you, but they were driven back by many, many Danes."

"It was a great struggle, Sire, but the Kentish fyrd managed to break through the Dane's iron ring."

"Thank you, God! Uncle, I have prayed for you every day. I look across the river even now and expect thousands of the heathens to appear on the far bank. Shall I order an alert?"

"You can, Edward, but I doubt that the Vikings will follow immediately."

"But Uncle, why not? They must be furious that you escaped, and eager for revenge."

"They will first have to choose new leaders."

Edward's jaw dropped. "Uncle, what are you telling me?"

"Eohric died in battle."

"Are you sure he is dead?"

"After *Victory-Maker* penetrated deep into his gut, he exposed his neck to me and asked for the cut-of-mercy. He knew what he was facing and did not want to linger for days in screaming agony."

"And you did so?"

"Eohric was, by Viking standards, an honorable man. In other circumstances, we might have been friends. I was honored to be allowed to end his life cleanly."

"And Ethelwold? What happened to the traitor?"

"He is also dead. When we attacked the position the two kings held, Eohric fought heroically, while Ethelwold fled. Once Eohric fell, we broke off the attack and rode west, only to see Ethelwold fleeing. Sigehelm called his Personal Guard to him and went after him. The brave fools managed to kill Ethelwold before they were cut down by Ethelwold's Personal Guard."

"Then both enemy kings are dead. Praise God!"

Ambrose sighed. "You may claim a great victory today, Nephew, but it came at a considerable cost. The Kentish fyrd has been decimated."

"I consider that you surviving and bringing out any Kentish fyrdmen at all to be a great victory, uncle-of-mine. That you managed to kill two kings at the same time is nothing short of a miracle . . . Polonius, Phillip, you are hereby commanded to come over here and hug a grateful king!"

༺

Ambrose sat down beside his nephew the king, and both Phillip and Polonius joined them. Just across the river, a small group of Danes had arrived and were industriously building a defensive position of their own. Phillip watched for a time and then spoke. "King, shall I take a force and chase them off?"

Polonius pointed downriver. "Do you see that copse of trees, Weapons-master?"

"I am not blind yet, little man!"

"Then why did you not notice the many birds rising above the woods? There is something in the woods that frightened all those birds."

Phillip thought for moment. "Such as . . . a force of Viking warriors?"

Polonius smiled. "You will have to take a force across the river to find out, but I think there are several somebodies who are hoping that you are foolish enough to do just that."

"Because they have a large armed force hidden there?"

The scholar replied. "It is merely conjecture, oak-tree!"

Phillip nodded. "Nevertheless, I think we are safer if we stay on this side of the river. I could never trust a Byzantine to get it straight, but birds I always trust!"

Ambrose smiled at the bantering and turned to Edward.

"King, I have been wondering what you planned to do next, and then you called us to this meeting. I have the feeling I may soon get the answer to my question."

Edward smiled. "You are right, as ever, favorite-uncle-of-mine! I have been giving it a lot of thought."

"And what conclusions have you come to?"

"Once again I am in awe of my father's wisdom - though I know that he got more than a little help from you three!"

"I do not understand, Nephew."

"His burhs. The last invasion showed me clearly the value of the structures. The Danes were able to ravish the countryside, but the people, and their valuables, were safe behind stout walls - manned by permanent garrisons. No major tuns fell, and we closed the rivers to their fleets. Each major road, each ford . . . all were protected, and the Danes paid a price each time they tried to use them."

"I agree, Edward, his system of burhs was an excellent idea."

"Uncle, Mercia is twenty years behind Wessex in building fortifications, yet most of the fighting actually is here in Mercia. King Ethelred and queen Ethelflæd need time to catch up to Wessex.

I remember you telling me once that my father paid Danegeld to buy peace, because he wanted to send priests into Viking territory."

"That is true, Nephew. He was thinking long term. He knew it would be a generation or two before many Danes would convert to the True Faith, but he thought the northerners would become fine citizens eventually, once they found God and owned land. He even signed agreements with Guthrum that made Danes and Saxons equal before the law."

Edward looked thoughtful. "And he was right. More and more of the jarls are adopting Christianity, and, for the first time, we can threaten the Danes."

"What do you mean, Nephew?"

"Uncle, the Vikings used to travel our roads and rivers, and then just slip away when we finally gathered enough armed men to seriously threaten them. Now those same roads and rivers are blocked by fortifications and our permanent garrisons, and we have thousands of fyrdmen who can safely leave their families and home territory to fight where needed. It is now the Dane who faces famine if they call up their young men, and we can threaten their vills and tuns."

Ambrose nodded. "If you are saying that we now have the upper hand in our struggle, then I would have to agree with you, and yes, it is based on the ideas that Polonius and your father formulated years ago."

Edward looked at the three warriors, each in turn. "My friends, I think that the conquest of all the lost territories is possible, perhaps even in my lifetime. I think Mercia must be prepared, since it is most likely to be the battleground, and for that, Ethelred needs time. I will be damned if I will pay Danegeld, but, with both kings dead, we can probably negotiate a truce on favorable terms."

Polonius spoke. "Then you want a peace agreement, Sire?"

Edward smiled. "No, my friend. I want a truce, for a set number of years. Much land has lain fallow for too long, and our fyrds have been bled white. Trade was once our lifeblood, and it has suffered terribly.

Let us take a break from war, all the while preparing for the next phase. I have not lost sight of the goal - I just want time to properly prepare. The question is not **if** we are going to war - the question is **when**. Perhaps it is time to send peace emissaries to both Northumbria and East Anglia."

Phillip looked puzzled. "King, you have yet to lose a single battle. We have crushed every Viking advance into our territory. Both Viking kingdoms have been bled white, and are vulnerable. We are close to defeating them both. Are you sure that you want to call a truce at this point?"

Phillip, I have given it much thought. Polonius, what did you call that king who beat every Roman army but lost the war?"

"I think you are thinking of Pyrrhus, Sire, king of Epirus."

"That's the one! Wasn't he the one who, after a costly victory, said 'One more such victory will undo me.'?"

"That's the one, Sire."

"Well, I feel the same way. I think it is time to plant crops and repair all the damage, while we call up and train more young *fyrdmen.*"

Polonius spoke. "Then we are giving up on the conquest of the Viking lands, King?"

Edward smiled. "Not on your life! We will re-trench. After that, I think we should look at another approach to conquest."

Ambrose looked curious. "And what is that, Sire?"

"I have thought long on that. What would happen if, each year, we gather overwhelming forces from the southern *shires*, advance just a little into East Anglian or Northumbrian territory, and then build a strong defensive *burh* to hold the newly conquered territory?"

Polonius smiled. "Without a solid network of defensive positions, the Vikings would have trouble matching our buildups, especially if our northern friends raided south occasionally. I think our invasion of East Anglia showed the Danes their weaknesses. A few more *Long Rides,* or perhaps a few ship-born attacks up their rivers and deep into their territory would help to reinforce the lesson. If we can hit and hurt them in unexpected places, the Viking warriors will be reluctant to abandon their women and children - just as we once were - while we have the entire *fyrd* not assigned to garrison duty free to attack or defend anywhere we want!"

Edward nodded. "Exactly! We will do to them what they used to do to us!"

Ambrose raised his mug in salute. "Here's to the conquest of Viking Britain!"

Polonius smiled and raised his. "Amen!"

APPENDIX I

Glossary

Angelisc: The name the Angles, Saxons and Jutes had started calling themselves.

Archery Target: Edmund, king of East Anglia, was used as an archery target by Danish Vikings when they took over his kingdom.

Angleland: The land of the Angles, Saxons and Jutes. England.

Asgard: Where Viking warriors go if they fall bravely in battle.

Athelings: were 'princes of the blood'. The Saxon kings were chosen from the group by a Council, or *Witan*. The usual tradition was for the *Witan* to choose the eldest son, but this was not always adhered to.

Ayr: A coastal town on the west coast of Scotland, where Ambrose landed.

Black Arrow: One of King Alfred's small and fast courier boats.

Blood-eagle: When a person's ribs are broken and the lungs are pulled out through the back. The lungs will pulsate outside of the body until the man dies.

Bodkin: A long narrow arrowhead designed to penetrate armor.

Bones: Dice.

Bookland: Land given to the Church in perpetuity to support it.

Boss: a round, convex or conical piece of material at the center of a shield, generally made of metal.

Bower: A room off the Great Hall for Saxon notables.

Bretwalda: A ruler of Britain so powerful that all of the other kings recognize him as overlord.

Burh: A fortified settlement with a permanent garrison. When Alfred was through building these forts, no Saxon was more than twenty miles from the protection of one.

Caltrop: A sharp metal object made up of two or more sharp nails or spines arranged in such a manner that one of them always points upward.

Churl: A peasant. His property was guaranteed, but he had to farm and provide military service.

Coracle: was a bowl-shaped Irish boat that was made of interwoven laths covered with leather. They were clumsy but very light.

Danegeld: Is a payment to the Danes so that they would leave the land in peace. It was reportedly first paid in 865 by the *Ealdorman* of Kent.

Dreng: Young warriors who serve as the king's companions. If they serve well, they may be given land and elevated to the status of duguo.

Duguo: The proven warriors who have been allotted land by the king. They are expected to answer the king's summons at the head of their own household troops.

Ealdorman: A nobleman next in power to the royal princes. The Saxon kingdom of Wessex was divided into *shires*, and an ealdorman was in charge of each *Shire*. It was the ealdorman who called out the *Fyrd*, or local militia.

Dubh-gall: Dark foreigners, or Danes.

Finn-gall: A 'fair foreigner', or Norwegian. The Danes were called Dubh-galls, or 'dark-foreigners'.

Francia: is, in this case, roughly, the area of France, or, more accurately, Francia Occidentalis.

Frankland: The land of the Franks, Francia, or roughly the area of modern France.

Frisia: The people there were sea-faring traders who were located on the mainland coast just south of Viking territory. One of their main cities was Wyk Te Duurstede. Alfred had hired many of their sea-farers to help with his new navy.

Fyrd: Militias made up of thanes and churls. For every five hides of land, one fyrdman, mounted and armed, was obliged to answer the call-to-arms.

Great Army: The name given to the large Viking army that invaded England in 865 AD. Its leaders included Ivar the Boneless, Ubbi, and Halfdan.

Greek-Fire: A volatile substance that burns fiercely and could not easily be put out. It gave the Byzantine navy a considerable advantage in battle, and Polonius tried for years, unsuccessfully, to duplicate it.

Hersir: A minor Viking nobleman.

Hide: is a unit of measure. It generally denoted enough land to support a single family. In Alfred's day, every so many hides (generally 5) held meant that you had the obligation to send one armed and mounted warrior to join the *fyrd* when so instructed.

Holmgang: A duel that followed very specific rules.

Jarls: They were important Viking land-owners, who acted as both priests and judges.

Jorvik: Jorvik is actually the city of York. In this story, I use Northumbria and Jorvik interchangeably to represent the Northumbrian Vikings, whose capital is Jorvik.

Jutes: The Jutes were, with the Angles and the Saxons, the three major Germanic tribes to have conquered Roman Britain. The empire of Wessex was made up of people from all three of the original tribes.

Khazar: A powerful nomad tribe that was quite supportive of trade, and controlled the territory where the Dnieper River enters the Black Sea.

Kismet: is fate, destiny, or 'the will of Allah'.

Knarr: is a short, deep-keeled and beamy vessel that could carry up to 15 tons of cargo. Unlike most Viking vessels, it relied mainly on sails rather than oars.

Kiev: was a town just north of the open steppes on the Dnieper River. It was apparently seized by Dir and Askold of the Rus Vikings, sometime soon after 860 A.D.; after the death of three brothers who had ruled there.

Long-ship was a Viking sea-going vessel somewhat smaller than a dragon ship. It was up to a hundred feet in length, and carried up to 200 crewmen.

Long Ride or Long Gallop: A technique Ambrose and Polonius used to seize Carnarvon. With multiple mounts, the riders start a fast ride toward the target from far away. By changing horses and posting scouts in advance to ambush any couriers, they attempt to outride any news of their approach, thus achieving complete surprise.

Miklagard: 'Big City', the name the Vikings gave to the city of Constantinople.

Nights: The Anglo-Saxons counted time by nights instead of days.

Norns: The Norns spin the threads of fate at the foot of Yggdrasil, the tree of the world.

Norse: Norwegian

Odin: Was considered by the Vikings to be the chief god and ruler of the universe.

Pechenegs: A Turkish tribe of nomads that Ambrose, Phillip and Polonius helped fight when the nomads attacked Kiev.

Pig-Stickers: Polonius had been trying to teach the mounted Saxons the lance skills of the heavy cavalry of the Russian Steppes. He had helped the Varangians of Kiev and of the Dnieper River Valley fight off a massive invasion of these fierce warriors. Though the Vikings had emerged victorious, Polonius had learned to respect the steppe-warriors' skills. He had seen at first hand the shock value of their ferocious charge.

Primogeniture: The right of the first-born male child to succeed his father as king.

Quarrel: A crossbow bolt or short, heavy arrow.

Rus: A tribe of Vikings that lived in what is now Sweden. Their traders traveled all the way to the Black and Caspian Seas by boat, and were thought to have taken over Novgorod and Kiev around the time of this story.

Sax: A Saxon or Viking dagger.

Seven-night: For the Anglo-Saxons, each day began at sunset. Thus, a week was a 'seven-night.'

Shire: A portion of a kingdom ruled by an ealdorman.

Skjaldborg: Viking shield-wall formation of overlapping shields.

Sun-stone: The mineral Cordierite, which can show the direction of the sun on cloudy days.

Sun Tzu: Refers to the book - **The Art of War**, by Sun Tzu. This text was written some time between the fifth and the third century B.C.

Svinfylka: or 'boar's snout'. It was an arrow-shaped mass of warriors who would press forward and try to break an enemy shield-wall.

Thane: An Anglo-Saxon warrior who is granted land in exchange for yearly service in the king's army or *fyrd*.

Thrall: Male Viking slave.

Torque: A band of metal worn around the neck.

Tuns: Towns.

Valhalla: is the hall of Odin where the most heroic Viking warriors slain in battle drink and feast each night, until Doomsday, when the dead warriors would fight at the god's side.

Valkyries: were the divine maidens who took fallen Viking warriors to Asgard.

Varangian: I use it to mean the various Viking tribes that traveled the Russian rivers. The Rus was but one of the Varangian tribes, though it was they who provided leaders for Novgorod, Kiev, and several other towns.

Victory-Maker: was the name of the priceless foreign-made sword Canute had given his young thrall when Ambrose was still a captive in Denmark. It was originally taken as loot from Arabs on the North African coast.

Vill: Village.

Wergeld: Money paid as compensation for injury inflicted on another.

Witan: is the council made up of Saxon noblemen and Church elders. They had the final choice over the selection of each king.

APPENDIX II

CAST OF CHARACTERS

Aella: One of the rival claimants for the throne of Northumbria. The ensuing struggle weakened both rivals so much that the Danes were able to seize the country.

Alfred: The younger brother of Ambrose, Ethelbert, and Ethelred. He was an intensely curious man who wished to live the life of a scholar, but was chosen as king at the death of his brother, in 871 AD. A great general, he drove King Guthrum, leader of the Viking *Great Army*, out of Wessex, but was then almost taken captive in a surprise winter attack. Hiding first in Selwood Forest, and then at the island base of Athelney, he eventually started to strike back at the hated enemy. When his sworn men rallied to him in the spring, he was able to defeat King Guthrum. Somewhat surprisingly, he treated Guthrum generously and agreed to become his spiritual godfather.
In **Alfred the Great, King's Revenge**, Alfred was forced to march his army eastward to lift the Viking siege of Rochester, in Kent. After finding that fully half of the pirates were warriors sworn to King Guthrum, Alfred crossed the Thames and took London and part of Mercia.
In **Alfred the Great, Young Edward**, Alfred faced two invading Viking forces in the west while his son Edward and his son-in-law, Ethelred, took on invading army after invading army in the east and north.

Ambrose the Dane-Slayer: (Fictitious) A product of the king of Wessex and a beautiful slave woman with royal Celtic ancestors, he was raised as an *atheling*, an Anglo-Saxon prince of Wessex. Kidnapped by Viking slavers as a boy, he was taken to Denmark and then fled to Norway and Sweden. Pursued by the Danes, he joined Gunnar of the *Rus* Vikings, who sent him and his two companions, Phillip and Polonius, to trade on his behalf down the Russian rivers. Ambrose set up trading posts in Novgorod and then Kiev. Finally, he traveled to Constantinople as an emissary for the Kiev leaders. From there, he eventually returned to England to help his brothers fight against the Viking raiders.

He and his friends became a legend when they first joined the Danish *Great Army*, stole a princess from a Viking stronghold in Ireland, and spied on the Vikings from France. In this story, he helps his nephew gain the throne, and then keep it. Other names he used in various escapades were Hamar and Canuteson.

Andrew, Lord: (Fictitious) He is commander of the Scottish garrison, who met Ambrose when he and his friends arrived in Alba.

Anwell: (Fictitious) He was the ealdorman of Cornwall who had previously made an alliance with the Danes in return for nominal independence.

Askold: He, with his cousin, Dir, were the *Rus* Viking leaders who left Novgorod to settle in Kiev, a city they felt was ideally situated to control the Viking - Slav river trade. Under their leadership, the Dnieper River region came under *Varangian* control, and they participated in an attack on Constantinople itself. After the attack, in an attempt to end the hostilities, they appointed Ambrose and Polonius to negotiate with the Byzantine Emperor.

Asser (Bishop): A monk and then bishop who spent some time at King Alfred's court and was his biographer. He actually joined the court in 886 AD. and died around 908.

Canute: (Fictitious) Ambrose's Danish master, he treated the young Ambrose as an adopted son and arranged for Ambrose and his friends to be given refuge in Sweden when Phillip's life was threatened.

Cate (of Bridport): (Fictitious) The serving wench, who, under duress from *Ealdorman* Ethelwold, attempts to poison King Alfred.

Constantine II: was crowned king of Scotland in 900. In this story, he refuses to send his young warriors raiding into Northumbria unless Ambrose, Polonius, and Phillip come to meet with him.

Demetrious: (Admiral) (Fictitious) Was the Byzantine admiral sent by Grand Chamberlain Basil to catch and execute Ambrose, Polonius, and Phillip. He chased them from Alexandria, across North Africa, through Italy and into France.

Dir: See ASKOLD

Ealhswith: Wife of King Alfred.

Edred: Was the *ealdorman* of Devonshire, replacing Odda.

Eochaid: had been king of the united kingdom of the Picts and the Scots. He died in 900, and **Constantine** was crowned king.

Eohric: King of East Anglia, he met with Prince Ambrose and promised not to get involved in the power struggle in Wessex, but later joined Ethelwold when, as king of Viking Jorvik (Northumbria), Ethelwold seizes Essex and then plans an invasion of Wessex. Both leaders are killed fighting the Kentish *fyrd* at the Battle of the Holme.

Eric (Tall): (Fictitious) A fisherman and headman of a fishing village near Durdle Door in Dorset.

Ethelflæd: Daughter of Alfred the Great, she married Ethelred, king of Mercia, but sworn vassal to King Alfred and then Edward.

Ethelhelm: Ealdorman of Wiltshire.

Ethelhere (Fictitious): Is appointed Ealdorman for Dorset after Ethelwold.

Ethelnoth: Ealdorman of Somerset, he was a loyal friend to Alfred.

Ethelred: The Mercian king who seized control of Western Mercia and eventually married Alfred's daughter. Though a king in his own right, he accepted Alfred as his overlord. In this story, he sends his *fyrdmen* to the border to intimidate King Eohric of East Anglia.

Ethelwold: Alfred's nephew and *ealdorman* of Dorset. His father was Ethelred, older brother of Alfred. Ethelred had been king of Wessex from AD. 866 to 871. Ethelwold was resentful that Alfred was chosen by the *Witan* as king over him. When Alfred is on his deathbed, Ethelwold plots to be chosen as king by the West Saxon *Witan*. When Edward is picked, he storms back to Dorset, kidnaps and marries a nun, seizes two of Edward's royal estates, then states that he would live or die there.

When Edward appears with an army, however, Ethelwold
flees northward, to Jorvik. The Vikings there choose him
as their king, and within a year or two, he is leading an
army of Danes to Essex. The Vikings there submit, and
the next year, in alliance with Eohric of East Anglia, the
combined Viking armies invade Mercia and Wessex.
Edward the Elder strikes back, sending his *fyrdmen* deep
into East Anglia. On the way home, the Kentish wing of
his army was caught by a combined Danish force, and,
although the Danes keep the field, both Eohric and
Ethelwold are killed.

Garr: (Fictitious) The husband of Cate, he died at the siege of
Chester before the story began.

Giric: King of the Picts until 889 AD.

Godric: (Fictitious) The young warrior (*dreng*) who rode with
Ambrose years earlier. Now a *duguo*, he leads the troop of
men pursuing Cate's killers.

Godwulf: (Fictitious) Jarl and commander of the Viking
squadron that stops Ambrose's ships heading for Scotland.

Gretchen: (Fictitious) Was the daughter of Osmond, an
ealdorman in Mercia, and distant cousin to the royal
family of Wessex. Previous to this story, she first met
Ambrose at the Wessex court, and then nursed him back
to health when he was wounded during his earlier escape
from the Danes. They were betrothed, but Gretchen was
first kidnapped by Welsh, and then Viking brigands.
Ambrose traveled to Ireland to free her. After many
adventures, they were married.

Guthfrith: The Danish king in Northumberland in 893, he
pledged peace to Alfred but then sent a hundred ship

crews to attack in Devon, under the pirate leader called Sigefrith.

Guthrum: A Dane who was king of East Anglia, Essex, and part of Mercia, he died in 890. Earlier, he attacked Wessex, was bought off, and then attacked from Mercia at Christmas of 878. After almost defeating Alfred, he was forced to sign a treaty, and he returned to East Anglia. In 885, he broke his treaty with Wessex by allowing his men to go south and join some Vikings from France besieging the West Saxon city of Rochester. Alfred went north with his new fleet to punish the attackers and seized Viking ships at the mouth of the Stour River. In response, Guthrum attacked with every ship he could muster, defeating Alfred's fleet. A second treaty was signed after Alfred seized London and defeated Guthrum in battle. King Eohric replaced Guthrum in 890.

Haesten: The Viking pirate leader who invaded Kent in 892 as part of a coordinated attack on the kingdom of Wessex.

Hakim: (Fictitious) The merchant from Alexandria who escaped from slavery with Ambrose, Phillip and Polonius, and who escorted the three of them across North Africa after the Byzantines came after the prince and his friends.

Hamar: (Fictitious) Was the name Ambrose used previously when he pretended to be a Swedish trader in King Guthrum's camp some years before.

Hamesh: One of King Constantine's army commanders.

Hammar: (Fictitious) He was the *Rus* ship captain who took Ambrose on his journey to Kiev and Constantinople. He saved his life when the Grand Chamberlain Basil was after Ambrose in Constantinople. He gave Ambrose a precious *sun-stone*, the secret of Viking sea travel. In this story, he visits Ambrose in Wessex, and inadvertently brings him news of Ethelwold's coronation in Viking Jorvik.

Ivar the Fat: (Fictitious) Lieutenant of the Viking squadron commander, Godwulf.

Kenward: (Fictitious) A Thane under Edward who is chosen to carry the king's royal banner.

Knutr: A weak Viking king who took power in Jorvik on the death of King Guthfrith. Egbert of Bernecia was a rival for control. In 899, the Vikings of Jorvik accepted Ethelwold as their king after he fled Wessex.

Kuralla: (Fictitious) She was a Slav chieftain's daughter whose village defied Bothi, a *Rus hersir* settled near Novgorod. Bothi ordered her father tortured and killed, and she was about to be given to his warriors when Ambrose purchased her to save her life. Polonius married her before they returned with Ambrose to England.

Leng the Bold: (Fictitious) One of Ethelwold's trusted lieutenants, he had previously tried to stop Ambrose on his journey to visit his brother, Alfred. In this story, he is with Ethelwold at Winchester.

Mary-Eve (Sister): (Fictitious) The nun kidnapped from a convent by Ethelwold.

Odda: The elderly *ealdorman* of Devon, he had served four kings faithfully and killed Ubbi Ragnarsson when his army invaded Wessex. He died in 890 AD.

Osberht: A rival for the throne of Northumbria, he fought Aelle in a civil war. Both were weakened enough that the Danes were able to take control.

Osgar: (Fictitious) A scout who rode ahead to help clear the way for Edward's *Long Ride* to Benfleet in a previous story. In this story, he runs a horse farm south of Winchester.

Oswin: (Fictitious) The commander of the garrison at Wimborne Minister, he rides to Badbury Rings to surrender after being abandoned by Ethelwold.

Osred: (Fictitious) One of the sea thanes who sails with Alfred's southern fleet. In this story, he is captain of a ship of Ambrose's fleet on the southern coast. Later, he captains Ambrose's vessel on his trip to Scotland.

Phillip: (Fictitious) A giant of a man, he was the free-born guardian of Ambrose when the prince was a youth, and companion later. Often called the Weapons-master, he had trained several generations of West Saxon noblemen in the military arts. Wherever Ambrose went, there was Phillip. His great goal in life was to protect his prince. When he spied on the *Great Army* in 868, he called himself Edgar.

Plegmund, Archbishop: Was archbishop of Canterbury.

Polonius: (Fictitious) He was born to noble Byzantine parents and given an excellent education. When his family had financial reverses, he and his sisters were sold into slavery. He was taken to Lombardy, France, and, eventually, *Frisia*. There, he chanced to meet Ambrose and Phillip. Together, they embarked on a series of adventures that took them to Norway, Sweden, Novgorod, Kiev, and eventually Constantinople itself. An expert linguist and knife-thrower, he returned to England with

Ambrose, and, as Nicholas, helped Ambrose spy on the Danish *Great Army*. Soon thereafter, he helped steal Gretchen back from the Irish Vikings. He taught Alfred to read, and in this story he acts as the king's military advisor and spy-master.

Ramm: (Fictitious) King Alfred's chief interrogator at Winchester.

Seger: (Fictitious) A thane and faithful follower of *Ealdorman* Ethelwold. He rides to Alfred's court in order to force Cate into attempting to poison King Alfred.

Sigehelm: He was the *ealdorman* of Kent, who, in a previous story, sent his men into Rochester before the Vikings could attack. In this story, *Ealdorman* Sigehelm is killed at the battle of the Holme, in 902.

Sun Tzu: Author of **The Art of War**. This text was written some time between the fifth to the third century B.C.

Theomund: (Fictitious) Commander of *Ealdorman* Sigehelm's army. (Kent)

Ubbi Ragnarsson: He was the younger brother of Halfdan and Ivar the Boneless. Ubbi was killed by Odda's *fyrdmen* when he brought his army into Wessex in 878, in support of King Guthrum.

APPENDIX III

Timeline

The History of Wessex, of Russia, and of Ambrose and his Son and Friends in the Ninth and Tenth Century AD.

Historical facts are in plain text.
Fictional stories in this series and comments are in italics.
Parts specific to this story are in bold.

793: First recorded attack by (Norwegian) Vikings on England.

832-865 AD.: Danish Vikings attack East Anglia, Wessex, and Kent.

838: Cornwall surrenders to Wessex.

845: The king's mistress gives birth to AMBROSE.

849: Alfred the Great is born.

850: Vikings winter in Kent for the first time.

853: Alfred is sent to Rome where he is made a

Consul by the Pope.

855: Ethelwulf, king of Wessex, takes his son Alfred to Rome again.

856: Ivar the Boneless and Olaf the White take Dublin.

858: Ethelwulf dies. Ethelbald becomes king.

(Trader of Kiev)
860: *Ethelbert becomes king. Vikings sack Winchester before being driven out of Wessex.* Ambrose and Phillip are enslaved in a raid on the coast of Wessex.

861: *Pope Nicholas sends envoys to Constantinople to investigate Photius' ascension as patriarch.*

862: Rurik, a leader of Varangian Rus Vikings, is invited to rule at Novgorod.
Ambrose, Polonius and Phillip arrive in Sweden after escaping from Denmark. Pursued by their former captors, they hurriedly agree to go south with Rurik and his Rus tribesmen.

863: Dir and Askold, Rus jarls, take over the Slavic town of Kiev. Nb. There seems to be considerable debate about both this date and whether Dir and Askold actually really existed.
After setting up a trading post in Novgorod, the friends join Dir and Askold's force going

south to Kiev.

864: The Pechenegs, a savage steppes tribe, attacks Kiev. Only with Polonius' expert help, and the fanatical fighting bravery of the Vikings, do they survive. An attack on the Pechenegs at their most vulnerable point not only ends the siege, but forces the Pechenegs to pay to cross the Dnieper River.

(Emissary to Byzantium)
865: Kent is invaded by a Viking force and Danegeld is paid for the first time to stop the destruction. The Great Army (Danish Vikings) arrives in East Anglia from France.

Dir and Askold lead a combined Slav and Varangian force against Constantinople because of a perceived injustice. With both the Byzantine fleet and army away, they manage to do considerable damage, although they never seriously threaten the city. On the way home, a savage storm sinks many of the Viking and Slav ships. Meantime, Kuralla is kidnaped in Kiev. That there was an attack by Varangians, and a storm, within a few years of this date seems inconvertible. Since the Russian Primary Chronicles set the date somewhere between 863 to 867, I arbitrarily assigned it to 865.

866: Reign of Ethelred in Wessex. The Great Army seizes York. Ambrose and Polonius are sent by

Dir and Askold as official envoys to Constantinople. They return north to find word from Kuralla waiting for them. The friends rush north, free Kuralla, turn around, and travel again to Constantinople.

After attempts by Basil to involve them in a plot against the emperor, Ambrose, Kuralla, Polonius and Phillip sail for Wessex. Basil, aware they know altogether too much, sends agents after them.

(Southern Journey)

Basil is told by the Byzantine emperor, Michael III, to divorce his wife so he may marry Michael's mistress.

Bardas plans a sea campaign to retake Crete.
Michael has Basil kill Bardas.
Michael adopts Basil and makes him junior emperor.
Ambrose and his friends are captured and enslaved by Muslim pirates operating out of Crete. Polonius' skills allow them to break out of their prison, and they escape to the dubious safety of a Byzantine Fleet. When they realize one of Basil's agents recognizes them and intends to kill them, they flee to Egypt, where they join a caravan heading west.
The Byzantine admiral harries them across North Africa, but Ambrose and his friends do manage

to strike back and damage the Byzantine ships. Ambrose then finds a Muslim slaver to transport them to Calabria. Attacked and hunted, the friends finally cross the border from Calabria to Benevento. Ambrose feels that they are finally safe.

(Journey Home)
The friends start north. Ambrose and his friends pay a visit to Admiral Demetrious in Naples. They escape and make it back across the frontier just ahead of vengeful Byzantine soldiers.

Ambrose makes it to Rome, where he meets Pope Nicholas. He and his friends then head north for the mountain pass to France. They arrive after the pass is closed for the winter, and must spend the winter in Aosta.

867: Aelle, king of Northumbria, is killed trying to retake York.

Basil 'the Macedonian' kills his own sponsor, Michael III, emperor of Byzantium. (September) Ambrose and his friends survive an attack by assassins, and in the spring they head north into the mountains where they are captured and enslaved. After Kuralla rescues them, they reach France and relative safety. They reach Paris and meet the king. Then they head for Calais and a ship to England. The Vikings, however, are raiding along the coast. Finally, after many adventures, they reach Calais and Phillip finds a captain willing to risk the dangerous crossing.

867: Finally, Ambrose and his friends arrive in England, where Ambrose is welcomed back to the court. Ambrose meets a beautiful girl and falls in love.

(Warrior of the King)

868: The Great Army occupies Mercia. King Ethelred and his brother, Alfred, ride north to support Burgred of Mercia. The Vikings are besieged at Nottingham, but Burgred decides to pay Danegeld. The West Saxons go home.

Alfred marries a Mercian noblewoman - Ealhswith.

Ambrose and his companions return north and join the Great Army as spies. After finding out the Vikings are going north, they flee. Ambrose is wounded and nursed by his loved one. The Great Army pursues, and catches up. Strangely, the attack is called off.

Ahmad ibn Tulun, a Turk, is appointed by the Caliph to rule Egypt.

Pope Nicholas the Great dies.

(Gretchen; Future Princess)

Gretchen and her father head south for

Wessex and her marriage. She is kidnaped and taken to Wales.

In Wales, Vikings attack the group, and Gretchen is taken to the Viking stronghold of Wexford in Ireland. Ambrose visits Wexford, but is unable to free Gretchen.

869: The Great Army returns to York in the north for a year.

Ambrose attacks the Viking ship carrying his beloved north. They are finally re-united.

870: Danes kill King Edmund of East Anglia, then invade Wessex under the Danish leader Halfdan.

871: Alfred becomes king. After fighting nine battles, Alfred pays Danegeld to buy peace for five years.

873: Ivar the Boneless, 'king of Dublin and York', dies in Ireland. His brother, Halfdan Ragnarsson, becomes king in his place.

874: Edward, son of King Alfred and future king, is born.

(Alfred the Great; Viking Invasion)
875: Alfred takes out a small fleet and routs seven Viking ships. (Nb. For dramatic purposes, I arbitrarily moved this event to the following year, where I tied it in with Guthrum's

invasion.)

876: Danes under Guthrum break their word, slip past Alfred and seize Wareham.

877: Guthrum agrees to a truce, but slips away to Exeter, which the Danes fortify.
After a Viking fleet is dashed on the rocks in a storm, the Danes agree to withdraw.
Halfdan Ragnarsson is killed in Ireland fighting Norwegian Vikings.

878: Guthrum, a Danish chief, rides south across the Wessex border in winter.
Alfred at first hides in the forest of Selwood.
A second Viking army, led by Ubbi Ragnarsson and invading from Wales, is defeated in Devon.
As spring approaches, Alfred builds a military camp on the island of Athelney.

Battle of Edington: Alfred's forces meet the Vikings here in May. The Danes break and run to Chippenham.
The Saxons blockade the Danes within their fortress of Chippenham for 14 days.
At last Guthrum surrenders and agrees to be baptized.

879: Guthrum takes his retreating army to East Anglia, where the men eventually settle down.

882: Alfred fights a battle against four Danish ships.

883: Halfdan dies. Guthred is recognized as king of Jorvik.

884: Ethelflaed, daughter of Alfred, marries Ethelred of Mercia.

(Alfred the Great: King's Revenge)
885: A Danish army crosses to England and besieges Rochester. Alfred relieves the city before it falls.

885: Later that summer Alfred fights a naval battle at the mouth of the Stour River. He takes all 16 enemy warships.

Guthrum breaks his treaty. He gathers every Viking vessel and attacks Alfred's laden fleet. He wins.

Alfred calls up his entire force and marches on London. He takes it and garrisons the city.

886: Alfred signs another treaty with Guthrum, where he gets London and control over part of Mercia.

889: Edgar, son of Ambrose and Gretchen, is born.

891: Danes in France suffer two serious defeats.

(Alfred the Great; Young Edward)
892: Five thousand Danes land in Kent and seize an unfinished fort at Appledore. A second fleet

follows, led by Haesten, and lands at Milton Royal. Alfred arrives with his army, drives Haesten away, and then moves against the Danes at Appledore.

893: Haesten's fleet sails away, to Benfleet, and is eventually joined by the second, larger fleet. The Danes then raid deep into Hampshire and Berkshire. Edward, son of Alfred, inflicts a major defeat, and then chases the Danes across the Thames. After being forced to surrender, the Danes give hostages and depart. The Danes of Northumbria and East Anglia send two fleets to Dorset as a diversion. Alfred rushes to the west, while Edward marches on Benfleet. Edward wins a great victory.

The Danes gather all their forces and march along the Thames again. They are besieged, break out, gather fresh forces, and try again. Besieged at Chester, the Danes break out yet again and flee to Wales.

Late summer, 893: Edward, Ethelred, volunteers from the London garrison, along with reinforcements from the West Country, gather and march on Benfleet. The Viking army is away raiding, and the Saxons take the town.

All Danes now gather at Shoebury in Essex. They march west to the Severn River. They build a camp at Buttington, in Montgomeryshire. Though besieged, the Danes break out and make it back to Essex.

Early autumn 893: The Danes in Essex march without pausing along the old Roman Watling Road, into Cheshire, where they seize the tun of Chester. Besieged, the Vikings break out yet again, though they suffer heavy losses. They flee to Wales.

Spring 894: The Danes split up and flee back to Essex via different roads.

Winter 894: The Danes sail up the Lea River and build a fort.
London men attack, but are repulsed. Alfred arrives and guards the peasants who harvest the local crops. Alfred then moves his army to the mouth of the river, where he builds twin forts to blockade the Viking fleet. The Danes abandon their ships and ride north and west, to Bridgnorth in Shropshire.
Athelstan, future king and son of King Edward, is born.

895: In the spring the Vikings sneak back to Essex or move to Northumbria or East Anglia.
Guthfrith, king of Northumbria, dies on August 24.

896: *Sitric Ivarsson dies.*

(Edward the King)
899: King Alfred dies. Ethelwold seizes two royal estates and kidnaps a nun. Faced with an army under Edward, he flees northward. The Danes of Jorvik (Northumbria) accept him as king.

902: Ethelwold arrives in Essex with a Northumbrian fleet, and the Danes there submit to him.

The Norse are expelled from Dublin. Ingimund attacks Wales. Driven out, he settles on the Wirral Peninsula with the permission of Ethelflaed, since Ethelred is sick. (While the exact date is in doubt, the most likely year of this event was in 902.)

Elfweard, second son of King Edward, is born.

(Introduction to 'Ethelflaed, 'Lady of the Mercians')
903: Ethelwold convinces Eohric of East Anglia to join him, and together they raid Mercia and Wessex as far as Cricklade and Braydon before retreating. In retaliation, Edward gathers his fyrdmen and ravages the Viking lands as far north as the northern fens. He then orders a retreat, but the Kentish fyrdmen are slow to obey and the Danes catch up with them on December 13. Ethelwold and Eohric are killed on the Danish side, while Sigehelm, the

Ealdorman of Kent, falls on the other side. Both sides suffer serious losses. This is known as the Battle of the Holme.

(Ethelflaed, 'Lady of the Mercians')   (902 to 919)
905: The Norse under Ingimund demand land and the old fortress of Chester. When their demand is rejected, they revolt and besiege Chester. Ethelflaed provides extra fyrdmen and the garrison is able to hold the Norse off.
 Edgar is Kidnaped by Ingimund and Ambrose goes after his family in Hitchingford.

906: King Edward concludes a truce with East Anglia and Northumbria, and probably pays Danegeld.

907: Ethelflaed refortifies Chester.

909: Ethelflaed & Edward raid Danish East Anglia and bring back the body of St. Oswald.

910: The Saxons and Mercians defeat and kill joint Jorvik kings Eowils and Halfdan II at the Battle of Tetenhall. Ethelflaed builds the fortress at Bramsbury.

911: Ethelred dies.
Ethelflaed is chosen by the Witan as 'Lady of the Mercians'.
Edward annexes London and Oxfordshire.

912: Ethelflaed builds two more burhs along the
Welsh border - along the Severn River.
1. Bridgnorth - main crossing point to Wales.
2. Scargeat- location is unknown. Probably
upriver north and west from Bridgnorth.
Edward takes his army to Essex, builds a
fortress at Witham, and receives submission
from Essex.
Some of Edward's supporters moves to the burh
of Hertford and work on it.

913: Danish forces at Leicester look west and see
two new burhs: Tamworth and Stafford.
Danes march south to the village of Banbury,
joining forces with Danes from Northampton for
a coordinated attack. The Angles meet them in
battle and defeat the Vikings.

914: Ethelflaed fortifies the largest town south of
Danish Northampton - Buckingham.
She builds a fort on either side of the River
Ouse.
Danish armies of Northampton and Bedford
submit to Ethelflaed's army at Buckingham. Jarl
Thurcetel submits.
A Viking army arrives from Brittany, led by
Ohter and Hroald. They land in the Severn
estuary. They go inland, but the men of
Hereford & Gloucester meet them and put them
to flight.

The Vikings finally leave in the autumn.
A Danish Viking, Ragnald, seizes power in
Northumbria after Tetenhall, and defeats the
Scots in the First Battle of Corbridge in 914.

915: This allows Edward to establish a fort at
Bedford, directly across the Ouse from the
former Danish camp.

Ethelflaed now had a nearly straight line of
forts from Chester to Hertford.

There are two gaps. Ethelflaed closes the
Mersey gap with several more burhs.

914 - Eddesbury. Warwick.

915 - Runcorn.

916: Edward builds a fort at Maldon.
Ethelflaed sends her army into Wales. An abbot
had been killed. The army destroys a town and
captures a Welsh king's wife.

917: Ethelflaed signs a treaty with two Scottish
kings, both called Constantine, insuring their
alliance against Jorvik.

Ragnald is unwilling to face Ethelflaed. He
fights the Scots and Picts again at the Second
battle of Corbridge. He wins again but the
numbers of his army is cut in half.

Edward fights the Danes in the east - Towcester,
Bedford, Wigingamere, Tempsford. He kills
King Guthrum II at Tempsford and all resistance
in East Anglia collapses.

Ethelflaed's troops march into the Danish center at Derby and take it.

All Danish leaders now submit to Edward and accept him as their protector.

They are granted their estates and allowed to live according to their Danish customs.

918: Edward builds a burh at Stamford. The Danes there submit without a fight.

To the west, Ethelflaed marches into Leicester, where Danes surrender without bloodshed, probably led by Danes seeking support against the Norse threat from the west.

The last two Danish enclaves, Nottingham and Lincoln, fall to the West Saxons by the end of summer, but Ethelflaed dies on June 12, 918.

(Elfwynn, Traitor Queen)

The Mercian Witan gives the title of queen to the twenty year old daughter of Ethelflaed - Elfwynn. Ambrose and Polonius kidnap her during the winter. They return to rescue the boys of the Royal School in the spring of 919.

919: Edward calls Elfwynn to his court and officially annexes Mercia.

Edward moves his army to Gloucester and Betlic flees. Ambrose and Polonius chase him northward. They fight on the way, and Elfwynn finally kills Betlic.

Norse adventurer Ragnald storms York and

establishes a line of Norse kings.
During his reign he gives nominal allegiance to
Edward, who recognizes his new kingdom.

921: Edmund, son of King Edward, is born.

(Athelstan, First King of England)
924: There is a Mercian revolt in Chester. King
Edward is killed at Fardon-on-Dee. Mercia
supports Athelstan as king. Wessex supports
Elfweard, his half-brother. Elfweard suddenly
dies a few months after his father.

925: Athelstan is finally crowned as king. He is
crowned at Kingston-upon-Thames, by Ayhelm,
Archbishop of Canterbury. This is the first time
a Saxon king is crowned with a crown instead of
a helmet.

926: Athelstan arranges for his sister Edith to marry
Sihtric of York. They agree not to invade each
other's territory and not to support the other's
enemies.

927: Sihtric dies. Cousin Guthfrith leads a fleet
from Dublin to try and take the throne.
Athelstan captures York and receives the
submission of the Danes. (It is not known if he
fought Guthfrith). The Northumbrians are
outraged at this usurpation.

July, 927: at Eamont, King Constantine of Scotland (Alba), King Hywel Ddn of Deheubarth, Ealdred of Bamburgh and King Owain of Strathclyde accept Athelstan's overlordship, which leads to seven years of peace. Athelstan is now the first king of all the Anglo-Saxon people.

933: Prince Edwin drowns, possibly after a rebellion where someone called Alfred attempts to blind Athelstan.

934: Athelstan invades Scotland, though the reasons are unclear. Sometime thereafter, Constantine of Scotland marries his daughter to the Norse king of Dublin.

937: The Norse king of Dublin, Olaf Guthfrithson, joins with the Scots and Strathclyde Britons under Owain to invade England in the fall. Ambrose meets with the Scottish king. The opposing armies meet at the Battle of Brunanburh. Athelstan wins an overwhelming victory, though he also takes heavy losses. Ambrose and Polonius die protecting the king.

939: (October) Athelstan dies.

(Edmund, King of England)
939: Edmund is proclaimed king. Crowned in November.

939-940: King Olaf III Guthfrithson conquers
Northumbria and invades the Midlands.
Conquers as far south as Watling Street.
Olaf marches south from York to Northampton.
When that siege fails, he goes on to Tamworth,
which he takes by storm. King Edmund besieges
King Olaf and Archbishop Wulfstan at
Leicester, but they escape by night. Battle is
averted when Archbishops Oda and Wulfstan
reconcile the two kings and a truce is concluded.
Watling Street becomes the new boundary.

941: Olaf Guthfrithson raids Bernicia and dies
shortly thereafter. Olaf Sihtricson succeeds him
on the Northumbrian throne. He has his cousin
Ragnall as co-ruler.

942: Edmund defeats Idwal of Gwynedd.
Edmund reconquers the Midlands.

943: Edmund becomes godfather of King Olaf
Sihtricson of York.

944: Edmund reconquers Northumbria.
Edmund drives out of Northumbria both Olaf
Sihtricson and Ragnall Guthfrithson.
Congalach Cnogba, High King of Ireland, sacks
Dublin.

945: Edmund conquers Strathclyde, but cedes the

territory to King Malcolm I of Scotland in exchange for a treaty of mutual support. Blacaire of Dublin driven out by Olaf.

946: Edmund is killed in a brawl by an exiled thief named Leofa. Eadred, Edmund's brother, succeeds to the throne.

APPENDIX IV

The Kings of Wessex

EGBERT
802-839

ETHELWULF
 839 - 858

ETHELBALD   ETHELBERT   ETHELRED   (*Ambrose*)   ALFRED
 858 - 860   860 - 866   866 - 871   871 - 899

(Ethelwold)   EDWARD I
(Alfred chosen over him)   899 - 924

ELFWEARD
924 - 924

A THELSTAN
925 - 939

EDMUND
 939 - 946

APPENDIX V

APPENDIX VI

About the Author

After counseling teenagers and adults for more than forty years, Bruce Corbett retired to concentrate on his writing and photography. To date, he has written a collection of Science Fiction short stories and two Science Fiction novels. The project closest to his heart, however, is his series of well-researched historical novels based on a family of fictional heroes, set in the time of Alfred the Great, his children and grandchildren. **Alfred the Great; Edward the King**, is the first novel of the King Edward Sagas, and chronologically the tenth of the complete collection.

These novels are arguably the most comprehensive series of novels ever written based on the time of the Anglo-Saxon Chronicles. A complete description of the various novels, including samples, links and supplementary information, may be found on Bruce Corbett's web site:

www.brucecorbett.com

Bruce Corbett lives in Pincourt, Quebec, Canada. He is an avid landscape and wildlife photographer, and is generally found reading anything historic.

APPENDIX VII

Other Books Released by Bruce Corbett.

In chronological order

HISTORICAL
The Ambrose Sagas
1. Ambrose, Prince of Wessex; Trader of Kiev
2. Ambrose, Prince of Wessex; Emissary to Byzantium
3. Ambrose, Prince of Wessex; Southern Journey
4. Ambrose, Prince of Wessex; Journey Home
5. Ambrose, Prince of Wessex; Warrior of the King
6. Ambrose, Prince of Wessex; Gretchen, Future Princess

The King Alfred Sagas
1. Alfred the Great; Viking Invasion
2. Alfred the Great; King's Revenge
3. Alfred the Great; Young Edward

The King Edward Sagas
1. Alfred the Great; Edward the King
2. Queen Ethelflaed; 'Lady of the Mercians'   **2023 release**
3. Elfwynn, Traitor Queen of Mercia   **2023 release**

The First English Kings Series
1. Athelstan, First King of England   **2023 release**
2. Edmund, King of England.   **2023 release**
3. King Eadred of England   (under construction)

SCIENCE FICTION
Bruce Corbett's Speculative Short Stories
The Vuorran Pogrom   (coming soon)
The Goldmines of Alpha Centauri   (coming soon)

The above novels are available worldwide as e-books from your favorite online book sellers, and the paperbacks are available from Amazon and Drafts2Digital.

www.ingramcontent.com/pod-product-compliance
Lightning Source LLC
Chambersburg PA
CBHW070105030726
47506CB00002B/601